The Difference

Twelve Journeys of Humor and Fulfilment

Pete Lans

THE DIFFERENCE
Twelve Journeys of Humor and Fulfilment
PETE LANS

Copyright © PETE LANS 2018

Author: Lans, Pete
Title: The Difference
Edition: 1st ed.
ISBN: 978-0-6483227-2-6

Cover art and design Rebecca Timmis 2018

Pathos—
is the difference between the journey we think we're
making and the journey we're actually making.

More books by Pete Lans

Thrum

Realm of the Conspirators

About the Author

Pete Lans is in his sixties now and has at last decided on a career: being a writer. After a lifetime of optimistic inventing and building, all without a hint of commercial gain, his two daughters have advised him to stick to what he's good at: telling stories.

He lives in Brisbane, Australia, but is considering joining the endless migration of nomads traversing the country in search of free camping and friendship.

Or, if the opportunity presents itself, he would like to develop the Roadworks Learning concept mentioned in his novel, *Realm of the Conspirators*, and do his bit to transform the lives of children and to help them escape the programmed future for which they are presently destined.

Stories

An Ideal Affair

The means to an ideal affair had been staring me in the face the whole time—a short, intense and irresponsible liaison, completely free of commitment and unsavoury fallout, and with the perfect escape clause.

I knew she liked me; what we needed was a catalyst, and the play lent itself beautifully to my needs. I would convince Gordon, the director, to give me the part of the scientist and hope that Loretta would play the gorgeous android and ingénue. She falls hopelessly in love with her creator, and they eventually escape in his time machine.

Loretta would love it—every night coyly and innocently flirting with me, stealing kisses as the part required, then groping each other in the confines of the Chrono-pod while the action played out stage front—something to do with automatons coming to terms with their emerging consciousness, I think... I could be wrong. It was an original piece—experimental theatre—some sort of collaborative effort.

Frankly, I wasn't interested; I had my libido set for a surgical strike on Loretta.

It began one evening during a reading, when Howard, an old courtroom acquaintance of mine with a peripheral interest in the theatre, unexpectedly said, 'You know what's missing in this play?' Everyone looked blankly at him. 'Sex!' he said, '.. we need to spice it up.'

I was practically in a coma at the time, I was that bored, but in flashes of insight, I could see that Loretta was the obvious choice and that the scientist (me!) would be prominent in providing the spice. That's when I became keenly involved in helping to shape the play. Loretta twigged straight away, and soon she was volunteering performances that would do credit to a pole dancer.

This unexpected new dynamic caught Gordon completely off guard and created some resentment among the androids. But it was perfect, because the play needed that juxtaposition of androgynous neutrality with human lust, and Howard was soon inciting Loretta to ever more provocative displays—all of it directed at me. Beautiful!

Of course, I would never in my wildest dreams—okay, in my wildest dreams maybe—but never in reality have a full-bloomed affair, because, well, in my position, it could be fatal.

It was so pathetic really, how quickly Jonathan took the bait. I couldn't believe it would happen so fast. I mean, there's always a bit of flirting going on in the theatre—it's just in the nature of actors I suppose. That, and the fact that we're always changing costumes in front of each other... well, at least in this theatre—we only have one small space to change in.

I'd rubbed against him a few times—y'know, hopping around on one leg mid-way through putting on tights. 'Whoops, sorry... didn't mean to fall into your arms like that'. But he was always very proper. I suppose he'd have to be, being an attorney an' all... or whatever he is... barrister.

Did I look stupid there for a while! I thought he and Howard were baristas! Well, how was I to know. It's so noisy at times, and nowadays there's any number of men near retirement age that take it into their head to open a coffee shop. And let's face it, every second barista in this city is ten times over-qualified for the job. But Howard was very kind to me and said, '... that's okay, Loretta my dear, it's one of the charming features of being in the theatre—being able to escape from your life and surround yourself with people who know nothing about you...' which caused me to pause for a moment. And Jonathan chimed in as well. 'Howard is well qualified to be a barista—he's always grinding away at some poor bean...' and the two of them had a superior chuckle.

Anyway, hitting on Jonathan looked promising. I was tempted to try. Old habits. When he was trying out for the scientist, I could suddenly see how events might lead in my favour. I spoke to Howard... well, hinted and teased, and the next thing I know, he blurts out, 'You know what's missing in this play?... sex,' he says, and everybody politely nods and mutters. Then he looks straight at me and says, '... we need to spice it up.'

Thank god Jonathan came out of his coma. It looked like he'd been zapped by one of those chest thingies that the ambulances use. I mean, I was kind of focused on him, so I noticed. He lurched out of his seat, all bleary eyed and unsteady, and says, '... yes...' in that posh voice of his, '... yes, it's definitely something to consider, don't you think, Gordon? It would provide a relevant juxtaposition to the androgynous androids as they come to terms with their human emotions...'

It's not too hard to like him. I admire his intellect—even if he's not that much to look at—well, he is playing the mad scientist for a good reason!

Anyway, I had my cue, we rewrote the script, and I pumped it for all it was worth. Gordon had moments of doubt, I could tell, but there was no denying that everyone, even the stagehands, were showing more enthusiasm for the play.

Soon we were hard at it, as it were, flinging ourselves at each other, grasping and gasping longingly, prodding and shoving. She had a great knack for going way over the top so that Gordon would have to delicately intervene. 'Well done, Loretta,' he'd say, '... possibly a bit less, um, frantic... after all, it is a laboratory, and we have to be mindful of all the, ah test tubes and everything...' So, Loretta would give it another go, this time all hot and sultry and sounding like Marlene Dietrich in *Blue Angel*.

Gordon would get mightily exasperated. '... yes, yes. Yes, possibly, but are we abandoning her character, I wonder?... we seem to be headed somewhere unexpectedly libidinous...' and Loretta would morph into something more subdued—a simpering imbecile, totally infatuated with her professor.

Howard, bless him, spoke up at this point. 'I think a few extra evenings might be the answer, Gordon. Just the two of them. I can open up. I'm nearby... just to fine-tune their um, relationship...'

Loretta had her arms around me at the time. I have to tell you, I was almost limp with ecstasy—and I swear she was gripping at my back and looking at Howard with an odd intensity. Gordon acceded to the idea of extra rehearsals for us—the androids were becoming petulant and wilful, and Gordon didn't want to get them offside seeing as he'd spent so much time coercing them into their cardboard boxes.

Howard had materialised beside me in the carpark one evening and asked me whether I would be averse to doing some extra rehearsals with Jonathan. I wasn't sure what he was scheming, but I figured that it probably suited me, and so I said that would be good.

I was throwing myself into some truly crazy interpretations of the role, as Howard had advised, when things started to come apart a bit. Not before time, Howard made the suggestion to Gordon that we have extra rehearsal time. It was just what I needed to land Jonathan—the two of us practising love scenes before we had even entered our time machine. I could hardly believe how well it was all falling into place.

I have to say though, all this acting did bring out the dog in Jonathan, and I'm sure some people on the set were raising eyebrows. I could even imagine the androids were raising their eyebrows, though I don't know how that would be possible. It's amazing how much we can tell from body language, even when a person is scrunched inside a box.

And Jonathan! He's supposed to be doing this for his health—doctor's orders, apparently. 'Find some sort of recreational outlet or you'll be dead in a few years!' That's what I heard.

Talk about feeling good! I hadn't felt this good since university! Not that I don't love Alex, but... y'know, you get to a point in your life where everything in your relationship is interrelated with other stressful aspects of your life. I mean, it's impossible for us to drop our daks on the lounge room carpet and go for it because we're so busy! Every night, every day, every square in the month on the calendar has something written in it. And if it doesn't, it's because she's abroad or I'm away. It wasn't the stress that was killing me—it was a lack of passion!

'Oh, please, Jonathan,' she'd said, '... you can drop your daks in front of me any time you like. It'll be like visiting a museum.'

'Very funny,' I returned, '... well, that's it, I'm not going to the function... my relics and I have got a thing on at the theatre.'

Alex threw up her hands. 'Fine, Jonathan... fine. I was just looking for an answer, and now that I've got it, I can plan around your absence.'

I was shocked. 'Oh, great... so that's where we're at—planning around each other's absence.'

But Alex has that canny suggestiveness that always manages to disarm me.

'Ooh, come here, my little exhibit. Tomorrow night I'll be home, and I can dust you off...'

'I won't be home tomorrow night... theatre thing.' I interrupted.

That set her on her heels.

'What? Tomorrow as well? You've certainly settled in.'

Well, *yeah!* And it was all because of Loretta, but I didn't want to

5

give anything away, so I just said, 'I've got commitments now...' and left it at that.

It was just another thing that was stressing me out. My doctor was very concerned. He told me that I needed some sort of recreational outlet, or my heart might give out one day. It's funny how your heart can burst from both a lack of passion and too much passion. The happy medium seemed to be the theatre, according to Howard one evening at the club when I was bemoaning my situation.

He said, 'Why don't you come along? Your doctor says you need recreation, and being a Thespian is the ideal way of letting go... your stress... we may have just the part for you too.'

Well, I went with a light heart and a tune on my lips, because it had given me the perfect excuse to avoid yet another of Alex's functions. And then, when I arrived, I was simply enthralled.

Absolutely everyone, even those now languishing in android costumes, was larger than life. In my profession everybody struts, but the theatre types do it with such guileless aplomb that it took away my breath. I was intimidated at first, on the back foot, looking for a niche, but when I spied Loretta in the dim recesses backstage, I found myself looking for opportunities to be nearer to her.

She was dressed in, what I soon found out from her, the Directoire style from the turn of the nineteenth century—voluminous dresses with plunging necklines and high, drawstring waists. She was stunningly voluptuous, and when I idly questioned a stagehand about her, he informed me of her name, then added, '... that's just her stage name but. Her real name is Kylie. She works in theatres all over the city... just bit parts and stuff...'

That, I had to admit to myself, took off a bit of the gloss, but did, on the other hand, make her more attainable.

Howard introduced me to Gordon, a harried little man who looked more like an accountant, and said, 'I'm thinking that seeing as how Jonathan is not yet ready to burst onto the stage as a fully-fledged Thespian… I was wondering whether we could consign him to be one of the minions backstage. I was thinking specifically of him giving Loretta the assistance that she has requested… to help with, you know…' and he raised an eyebrow to Gordon.

'Does it change anything?' Gordon blurted in mid-hiatus, 'because, if nothing changes, then it's fine by me,' and he pirouetted to somewhere else.

So, for the rest of that production, I helped out in whatever capacity I was needed, and was thrilled to find out that Loretta had been asking about me. Then, during the run of performances, I was given the task of changing the scenery in a poky little corner of the set—converting Madame Bonaparte's boudoir into a dungeon. But also, I had to help Loretta change into other costumes as she exited her chamber. At first, I felt terribly self-conscious, but apparently, it's par for the course—whoever is nearby helps the actors with costume changes. Suited me. Each time she hauled her dress over her head—with my assistance—her heat and perspiration would make me swoon. Then she would wriggle by me to her other outfit, attired only in her coloured underwear, and I'd have to flounce and gather and tuck her into it.

One night she was bra-less. 'These dresses are fitted,' she said, matter-of-factly, 'I'm supposed to pop out of the top, and a bra just gets in the way.'

I was weak-kneed and sweaty, but the night she wore a G string, I knew it was my move. I was so overcome, that I forgot to raise the half-drop, and Madame Bonaparte did her entire toilet in the torture chamber.

I felt completely safe around Jonathan. He's one of those utterly decent types that have women on a bit of a pedestal. But business is business, and I'm sure he wouldn't have minded paying for the service.

By the time we began rehearsals for the next production, I practically had him quivering with anticipation. And Howard was so incredibly obliging; it was as though he was reading my mind.

'Oh, Gordon,' he says, one evening, '... don't you think some new blood would be good for the theatre? I was thinking... perhaps Jonathan. Give him a try at any rate... make a good mad scientist. You're up to it aren't you, laddie?'

Well, Jonathan was so eager, he accidentally choked and spent the next two minutes nodding and coughing.

'There you are... you see,' said Howard, '... he'll give it a go.'

But Gordon wasn't convinced. To prove his worth, Jonathan earnestly set himself to becoming a Thespian to the extent that even lighting and wardrobe were pressed into giving advice. I made sure that rehearsals with him had that extra dynamic, and sure enough, he got the part.

I flirted shamelessly with him whenever we were alone, and I know that he was dead keen to get to the part where we disappear together in his time machine. The two of us, ten or fifteen minutes out of sight in a large box, and for sure I'd enslave him.

It's so funny really, how ridiculously theatrical he believes life to be; because any of the other scoundrels that inhabit the theatre would simply have put the hard word on me out in the carpark, and perhaps ask me out to a pub, before doing the deed in the back of a car.

God, I had the hots for her; it was embarrassing. I'm a barrister; I've seen heaps and I've had my own emotional roller coaster rides, but... I don't know, it must have been the theatre... it's so beguilingly artificial. Everyone is on a high. There's a constant expectancy. Everybody is supportive and indulgent and... vital—no!... edgy... intense. Of course, that could just be from my perspective—I mean, comparing the theatre and a courtroom.

Loretta was wholly attentive to me during moments when we could be alone.

'Can't create jealousy now, can we,' she said in my ear one night, looking pointedly towards an athletic young bloke about to reoccupy his cardboard android costume. It gave me such a lift, I can't tell you.

And then, Howard had the brilliant idea of asking Loretta to perform some period vignette at one of Alex's fund-raising functions. He collared me backstage and stood there musing incoherently before he suddenly blurted out, '... just a five-minute segment... perhaps Madame Bonaparte's exposition on the feminine ideal...'

I had no idea what he was on about.

'... for the fund-raiser... Alex's fund-raiser... a cultural diversion. Why don't you put it to her? Alex, I mean. Of course, you'll have to ask Loretta, naturally... but I think she'd do it... you two seem to get on very well...'

So, there it was; I was obligated to ask Loretta, because it was certain that Howard would mention it in passing, and I didn't want Loretta to think that I would not include her in my life outside the theatre. So, I then had the rather invidious task of making a request of Loretta to do my wife a favour, and of proposing to Alex that it would be a good idea for one of my lady theatre buddies to perform for our edification.

But I was beaten to the punch on both accounts. Loretta sidled up to me in the carpark and said that she felt honoured to be asked to perform at Alex's function, and coyly parted with, '... but I'd better dress myself this time.'

I ran after her. '... asked?' I gasped.

Loretta looked at me with a furrowed brow.

'... did someone ask you?... um, to perform... at the fund-raiser...'

Her lips pouted just a little. 'Alexandra rang me... at home. Howard said that we should make the most of the costumes and the lines, seeing as how they're still fresh in our minds. Your wife thought it was "a marvellous idea"' she mimicked. 'She rang me this morning.'

Loretta came close and entwined a finger through mine. 'I'm looking forward to meeting her, Jonathan.' She canted her head in my face and smiled seductively. 'It'll be alright,' she whispered, '... we know how to behave.'

My head was thick with unresolved complications. I felt the giddiness of being adrift, and I sat in my car feeling too nauseous to drive straight home.

Alex's fund-raisers are a few steps up from a jumping castle and a petting zoo. Her clients are international organisations, and the guest lists are typically a who's-who of celebrities, politicians and corporate shakers and movers. I felt that my lustful fantasy was invading a realm way beyond what I could handle.

What at first looked like a fairly straight forward seduction, soon began to get complicated. I couldn't blame Howard—after all, he was usually the one who created opportunities for me. So, I looked upon the fund-raiser as another opportunity—the one in which I might be able to clinch the deal with Jonathan. The thought of entering the local community didn't thrill me at all. There is a good reason why I choose to live many suburbs distant from the theatres where I work. But I had to accept the invitation, because not to do so might have aroused suspicion, and I didn't fully know where Jonathan stood on this; completely ignorant, I found out later.

The guests were all wealthy, high-income couples that have that studiously smug confidence about them, but I can always tell that the men would be up for it at the first opportunity, and the women too.

Howard was a dear; took all the pressure off Jonathan; did all the introductions; blew my trumpet—and Jonathan's. I could see that Alexandra was quite overcome by the picture that Howard was painting; she unconsciously drained a glass of wine each time the waiter passed.

But never once did Howard hint at anything improper between us, though there were times when Jonathan and I had some difficulty facing each other.

Alexandra seemed genuinely happy for Jonathan—supportive and full of encouragement. I was starting to think that the fund-raiser was an excellent idea and that there must be some way in which I could up the stakes.

It's always a relief to find that my victim is resolutely in love with his wife and that they haven't severed their relationship. Blackmail depends upon strong bonds.

I should confess to being absolutely dizzy with emotions throughout the party.

Alex was gorgeous, competent and in her element. Loretta was vulnerable, sweet and inviting, then during her exposition, dynamic, beautiful and sexy as hell. Howard, stage managing a circle of introductions that rendered me unable to sip decorously at my wine, but rather to gulp it in hidden moments, included me at every mention of the stage and theatre, so that those present must have gone away with the impression that I was the next Olivier. The whole escapade became intoxicating for me and I completely lost my grip on reality. Had good sense prevailed, I would simply have cooled my intentions with Loretta and rejoiced at Alex's success. That would have been ample; I mean I have no doubt that Loretta's presence pricked at Alex's pride, and that that moment would have been the one to rekindle our love.

But instead, I'd been ignited, and I rushed about anxiously looking for impossible fulfilment. And all the time, Howard seemed to be playing agent-provocateur, rambling on about a theatre production slash fund-raiser.

Alex was wowed, I could see. 'Do you think Jonathan will make a fine actor?' she asked of Loretta at one point.

Loretta took a sidelong glance at me, smiled warmly and blinked her long lashes. 'No,' she said, '... he's far too moral to be assuming other identities.'

Howard dipped his eyes knowingly. 'Well, well,' he murmured, '... we *have* gotten to know each other.'

Alex smiled too brightly and put her glass to her lips.

Later, she and Howard swanned through the crowd, at times earnestly head to head, then laughing uproariously with everyone around them as they weaved their way through the party. Alex was engaging and audible; he, deferential and dapper.

I bumped into them again as I was entering a marquee, and their gaze upon me suddenly made me feel utterly foolish. I tried sparring with Howard in a jolly fashion, but, uncharacteristically, he simply smiled graciously and diffused my joking with impeccable diction and deep disdain.

With my confidence severely crushed, I felt an urgent need to seek out Loretta, and I resorted to the lamest excuse to be off. She was standing nearby, engaged in a bubbly conversation with a group of flinty-eyed men who could have done my job in the cramped confines backstage with just their eyes.

My womanly instincts flooded my brain as though I'd had a litre of champagne. It's not really instincts of course; there's nothing metaphysical about how women process the environment. While it may be a mystery to men how women can gain so much information about someone on a first meeting, it's no different to the way in which men can navigate across an entire city and not get lost. It's about recognising all the signs; buildings, bridges and overpasses for men, and body language for the girls. Of course, I know men that get lost in their own suburb, and women that make the same mistake about people time after time.

But I knew I wasn't mistaken about Howard. I kept an eye on proceedings while I was duelling with the Musketeers, and it was obvious to me that he was dismembering Jonathan just by the stance he took. Howard's body language was uncanny; he offered no confrontation, but rather, he segued into a position close behind Alex, as though to offer support for an inconvenience that he knew she could handle. Jonathan's estrangement with Alex was highlighted by this manoeuvre, and his secret guilt prevented him from asserting his dominance. This confused Alex and, unknowingly, she moved towards Howard.

Jonathan's arms dropped and hung limp, and his legs seemed to malfunction when he turned to leave.

I saw him approaching and resumed a level of intimacy with the guys. Whatever went on between Howard and Alex need not concern me, and yet, there was something there that threatened my plans.

Jonathan came and stood beside me and whispered importantly into my ear. I made my excuses and followed him towards the back of the old mansion where climbing figs clung to the stonework, and it was cool and quiet. His arms were suddenly around me. He was all over me, kissing and nuzzling, stroking me; I wasn't ready for him, but I could see that this was the perfect time to clinch the deal.

The back entrance to the house was nearby; we could easily find a room, and I could detain him for long enough so that a good many people would not be able to vouch for his whereabouts—perfect blackmail requirements.

I led her to the back door and opened it with exaggerated confidence. We strode carefully through the quiet hallway and climbed the staircase to the first floor. Loretta seemed very docile and compliant as she held my hand.

'Is this what you want, Loretta?' I whispered to her anxiously, '... for the two of us... to be together?'

She squeezed my hand. 'You know it is... and I bet you know where there's a cosy little nook inside this old place.'

We reached the top of the stairs, and I said, a little breathlessly, '... well, I did want this to appear totally spontaneous... but yes, I have done some homework.'

Then Loretta said a strange thing. 'You know, Jonathan—and I don't want to spoil what's happening now—but there's something very odd about the way Howard is behaving... particularly to you. I was watching him—and you... and Alex. It must be difficult for you.'

I was a little bit apprehensive about us trespassing in the house—even though I'd found out from Alex that the owners were abroad for at least another week—but Loretta's tone struck home. 'What do you mean?'

Loretta suddenly brushed her face against mine. 'Oh, Jonathan. I'm sorry... let's leave it. It's nothing.'

'Do you think that Howard is moving in on my wife?' I asked accusingly and immediately regretted it.

There was a glow of afternoon sunlight illuminating the room we had just entered. Loretta squinted at me. 'I... I think so,' she stammered, '... it seems to make sense, now... but it doesn't matter, Jonathan, does it? This is a lovely room. Are you sure we won't be disturbed? I mean, we don't want to make this any more complicated than it already is, do we?'

With a wayward lock of hair in her eyes, Loretta looked adorable. She made me feel completely abandoned and, to an extent, desperate. Not to have sex so much, but rather to be daring—to be admired by her for my derring-do, devil-may-care passion. I almost wished that someone would come into the room as I, already nude, undressed Loretta as I had done so many times before in the dimness of the poky corners backstage. I wanted to be revealed, so that people might say, 'Well, what about Jonathan, hey!... having it off with the actress at his wife's garden party...'

But no one disturbed us; which is a shame in another way because it meant that we had to go through the complete act of having sex, which is never as depicted by Hollywood, I don't care what people say, and is certainly not as comfortable as domestic sex with all its ease of familiarity. At the end of the day, what people want—those at least who have experienced the luxury of a respectful and stimulating union with a long-term partner—is the same!... just without the routine and all the boring obligations. I mean, Alex still turns me on. Absolutely! I think it's so amazing that I can maul her disgracefully and not be arrested for it. We used to have so much fun. But yeah... obligations. Not that I was thinking of Alex. My attention was wholly on Loretta as I strove to fulfil her wants.

I knew what I had to do—not the sex... that was scripted enough—I mean in terms of achieving my aims. Now was the best time, no doubt about it, but I just couldn't focus. Images of what I had witnessed inside the marquee kept me unsettled, and I just wasn't getting, well... sufficiently aroused... and it always becomes a bit of a trial under those conditions.

Jonathan was doing his best to be gallant and sensitive and abandoned all at once, and I responded effusively with one eye on the doorway. I wasn't worried about being discovered—it's the twenty-first century—who's going to make a fuss? But, for me, it's just a survival habit.

When we were discovered, I almost fainted. It was the sudden realisation of the truth coming to my mind all at once. I grasped intuitively, the convoluted intricacies of the past, present and future, and what made me groan in anguish was not that my scheme had been uncovered, but that I had been out-played from the very beginning by someone that I held in contempt.

I clawed at Jonathan's back to raise my view over his jiggling, white bum and stared straight into the mobile phone that Howard was pointing at me from the doorway. Awkwardly, I glared at him. He nodded and leered smugly, then turned and left.

I sank my head on the pillow, just as Jonathan came grunting and blurting in my ear. I lay there, inert and looking vacant. He obviously imagined that he had given me a whopping orgasm. He smiled up at me from nuzzling my tits. I smiled wanly back. It actually felt nice to be lying in the autumn sunshine, even though my plans were in ruins.

It was only ever a humble scheme—one that I'd carried off many times before, and that I had discovered by accident when I first started in the theatre. I found that there were always men, retired professionals mostly, who joined the theatre for various reasons, mostly as a diversion from prior cerebral occupations, and who could be relied upon to support me in a lifestyle that I'd always wished for but could in no way afford on a receptionist's salary. Just a handful of clients, gleaned from the various repertories, made it possible for me to live in a very nice unit and to go out to country health retreats to be massaged and pampered. Things like that. In return, I massaged their egos and other parts; they wanted me to be near —they wanted me to be their ideal. It wasn't a hardship, I assure you. I like men.

But, I'd been wrong about Howard. His little menacing nod made everything very clear to me—I was to keep Jonathan amused and committed, or else!

I knew now what a predatory bastard Howard really was. Did he find out stuff about me at his club? Had he always had the hots for Jonathan's wife? What was there between Jonathan and Howard?... lots?...nothing?

It didn't matter; if Alexandra were to find out about Jonathan's infidelity, then I'd have nothing to hold over him. But that was not nearly as dreadful as the thought of being exposed to all my other clients. There were only seconds remaining to me in which to decide on my future; all that I had established would be denied me if I didn't act soon.

I felt as feeble as a kitten, but my anxieties had evaporated.

Loretta had convulsed in ecstasy, that was obvious, but I knew I had to maintain the verve if our relationship was to continue. So, I summoned all my strength and licked her nipple.

'... my darling,' I cooed, '... I feel both wasted and indomitable in the most delightful, paradoxical way. Can I take it from your distant and stupefied look that a conquest such as this should be built upon?... after a suitable restorative, of course. Perhaps we should re-enter the party... hmmm?'

Then, Loretta stunned me by whimpering, '... will you marry me?'

Clearly, I had achieved heroic proportions to her—in a manner of speaking—but I had never entertained the thought of a serious relationship with Loretta, let alone becoming married to her.

She looked up and focused intently. '... will you?' she implored me.

This moment was both deliciously affirming for me and dangerously alarming. I wanted Loretta to want me, but I knew I didn't have the courage to create a new life with her.

I looked down at her with enough hesitation for her to change her mind.

'You have to, you stupid idiot!' I snarled.

That stunned him every bit as much as my first proposal. His jaw sagged. I took a deep breath and pushed him off me. I sat up and hugged my knees and looked out at the filtered sunlight coming into the room from beyond the trees.

Crises always needed to be dealt with at the most innocuous of times, it seemed to me. Why couldn't it have been a heated argument ending with a brutal ultimatum? But no; in my circumstances, the ending was always done politely and with as much grace as possible. Well, that bastard Howard had just changed the rules of engagement.

'He was here, not one minute ago,' I said, quite pedantically.

Jonathan was at a total loss. He reached for his clothes. '... who was?'

'Howard,' I snapped. 'He took a photo, and I'm sure Alexandra would recognise your butt in it. He wants your wife... for an affair... marriage—I don't know.'

Jonathan slowly gathered his things in his lap. 'Howard?'

'Yes, Howard—will you stop gaping at me! He's onto me... he's set us up.'

Jonathan gaped even more. '... onto you?'

'Yes, onto me!' I was beginning to feel a little savage, watching his stupid face twitching with nerves. 'God, did you honestly think that you were in control here? I thought I was in control... until now—that bastard!'

Jonathan wiped his mouth and looked at the door.

'... and you're in it as deep as I am, boyo—he's got a very unflattering photograph that he's likely to post on YouTube for all I know... unless we play his game.'

Jonathan slowly turned to me. '... and what game would that be?'

I reached over for my clothes. 'Well now, let me see... that would be the marriage game, Jonathan. You and me—you win yourself a trophy wife, and I get to keep all my... men.'

'... men?' Jonathan started to gape again.

'Yes, men!' I could see that I was going to have to make this very plain, even if it meant being a bit harsh on myself, 'God almighty, Jonathan, I'm a harlot... don't you see? The theatres are full of older, successful men who don't want to walk home alone when the curtain comes down. They want to preserve the fantasy. That's what I've become very good at.'

Jonathan suddenly frowned. 'How many men?'

Dear god! Isn't that just so typical—his life is on a knife's edge, and he wants to know how many men.

'Half a dozen,' I said, '... retired, older men mostly. Professionals... I see them every other month on average. We go on a trip... I pander to *them, make them feel noteworthy... and they look after me. I like what I do, Jonathan—it works both ways, and no one gets hurt. But that's all going to change unless we get married.'*

Jonathan was clearly struggling with this new state of affairs. 'Why do we have to get married?' he whined.

'Because,' I said, as I put on my bra, '... Howard wants you out of the picture. You have to have left Alex! He's got a photo of you bonking the actress at the garden party, Jonathan! You and Alex are done! You two don't need each other... and now you've let Howard in. What are you going to do about it? What can you do about it?'

That night, I got into bed beside Alex, but stayed sitting up against the bedhead. She was looking up at me, expectantly, cradling her head in her hand.

'I'm really happy with the way things went this evening,' she said softly.

I nodded and tried to smile. She'd been too exhausted to take off her make-up, and in the light of the reading lamp, she looked sleepy and lovely.

Alex stifled a little yawn. '... oh, my feet are killing me. I spent the whole time trying to stop my stilettos from sinking into the grass. I gave explicit instructions not to water the lawn for a week before the event, and what happens? I arrive this morning to find the place alive with sprinklers. Anyone would think we were growing lucerne.' She reached out and put her hand on top of mine. 'I really liked Loretta's performance,' she said, her voice brightening, '... it fitted in so beautifully—we had a lot of favourable comments. And Howard is talking about some hybrid event—has he told you? It sounds quite exciting.'

I cleared my throat. '... yeah... yeah, that would be good...' I let my feet slide under the cool, cotton sheets and felt a sudden, blessed familiarity that made me feel sad.

Alex raised her head. 'Are you alright, darling?... you're sitting up so stiffly... have you forgotten something?'

I couldn't face her.

She stroked my hand. 'By the way... where were you later on in the party? Howard suddenly noticed that you weren't around and went off... in search of you, I presumed... and I was left totally at the mercy of a phalanx of predatory executives. I could have done with you suddenly appearing with a drink for me.'

I gently lifted Alex's hand from mine and placed it onto her hip. 'I was in the house,' I said, with a steady voice, '... upstairs... in the guest room... having sex with Loretta.' I put my palms down on the sheet and listened to my pounding heart.

Alex didn't move.

Eventually, she spoke. 'Loretta,' she said, without any rancour, '... is that her real name?'

'No.' The room was beginning to collapse on me. 'It's just a stage name.'

Alex rolled onto her back. 'What do you call her, Jonathan?'

I sighed deeply. 'She's Loretta to me. It's all part of the fantasy, I suppose.'

Alex waited for a while. 'She's a good actress,' she said quietly.

I knew what she meant, and couldn't help but chuckle. 'Yes... yes, she is.' I had to look down at Alex. She had a little smile on her face, but there were tears in her eyes.

'Howard thinks the world of her,' she said, with a wistful look.

I grunted. 'Howard does! I know—now!' I followed the curves of Alex's body under the sheet. She didn't deserve this. But then, what *did* she deserve? What did *we* deserve? I sighed again.

Alex looked up at me. 'What did you mean?... about Howard.'

My stomach cramped just thinking about him. 'It's my fault,' I said, nodding to myself, '... it's my fault. I was too stupid to see it... his manipulation. He wants to create our estrangement... through

Loretta. He went away from the party so that he could take a photo of us... Loretta and me. He knows all about her. Apparently, Loretta has made a bit of a racket out of appealing to... mature old farts like me. I'm afraid I was completely out of my depth in this matter. I've been incredibly foolish. I'm very sorry... Alex. I didn't want to hurt you. It all started so...' but I had to laugh when I thought back to the confines of the stage, 'Oh boy! Was I ever gullible.'

Alex turned on her side towards me. 'Well, you obviously were fooled... but come on, Jonathan!—it's about time you had a little fling like that. I mean, I wasn't *hoping* for you to have an affair—not even *expecting* you to have one... but I'm not completely surprised that you've had an affair. You are still so much... a man... and I'm always... busy...' She stared into the corner of the room. 'And what about Howard! He has been unbelievably gallant towards me... arrived out of nowhere... attending to me as though *I* was Madame Bonaparte...' Her brow knitted suddenly, 'Are you sure that this hasn't got something to do with your work?'

I scoffed loudly. 'Nah!... he wants you, Alex! Plain and simple. He's one of those predacious types who thinks he has a God-given right to meddle and create intrigue.'

Alex moved a little closer to me. '... are you *sure* about his motives?'

I looked squarely at her. 'Alex,' I said in a tone of petulant defeat, '... someone with a much better handle on this whole situation—Loretta—told me, in no uncertain terms, what his motives are, and how I am positioned in all of this.'

'How very theatrical, Jonathan,' said Alex, suppressing a snigger, '... you've come such a long way since you started.'

We exchanged a trusted, old smile. For a moment I thought I was going to cry.

Alex turned away from me and reached across to the bedside table. She unplugged her phone from the charger and scrolled through the menu. 'This is not about forgiveness... just yet, Jonathan... but there is business that we should take care of before it takes care of us. Fortunately, Howard gave me Loretta's number. It's very late, but I think that this would be the best time to phone.'

I nodded mutely. I was in so far over my head that I knew that the only thing that would save me from drowning was Alex's voice.

'Hello... Loretta?' she said.

I came out of such a deep sleep that I felt as though I'd been dead. My mobile rang insistently and I just knew it would be Howard. I could picture him, still beautifully dressed, swilling a whisky in his hand with his phone on speaker. He would get to me at my lowest ebb... the master of psychological warfare... pressing home his advantage. I grabbed the phone, pressed it into my pillow and rolled my head onto it. I wanted to drop straight off to sleep as soon as I'd cancelled him. When I heard Alexandra's voice, I had difficulty in putting it into context.

'... hello... Loretta?' she said.

I had to lift my head in order to speak. '... yes...' I said thickly, still trying to put a face to the voice.

'I'm sorry to wake you... it's Alexandra... you don't need to speak, Loretta... I know you're very tired. Jonathan told me about today... it's rather a complex web. I was thinking that... perhaps we should just keep this all to ourselves... let Howard think his plan is running on rails. It'll be good for me... good for you... and Jonathan and I will work things out...'

It was surreal. I was still not fully awake, and a kindly woman's voice was evaporating all my anxiety. I forced myself to sit up, just to be sure that I wasn't dreaming.

'Alexandra,' I said, as clearly as I could, '... that's very good of you.'

'Thank you, Loretta... but really, it's for the best. We can't let this control us... you know what I mean?'

I nodded. 'I understand,' I said.

There was a longish moment of quiet. I felt I needed to display some contrition on my part. 'There was never... anything... between us, Alexandra... it was my fault...'

Alex interrupted me. 'It's okay, Loretta... really and truly, it's okay... no harm done... but you have to give us a chance...'

'Of course,' I said, '... of course,' but I was suddenly conscious of my other liaisons, and I wondered how much Alex knew. 'Did Jonathan tell you everything about me?' I ventured.

Alex gave a deep laugh. 'No... only what he knows.'

I was resting with my knees on the bed and I smiled into the phone. 'Thank you, Alex... thank you.'

'Well,' she said, '... I'm sorry to have disturbed your sleep... I do hope that we'll see more of your performances in the future, Loretta... it drew a very good response... good night.'

I put the phone back on the bedside table and curled up under the covers. I felt a level of euphoria that I couldn't explain. It wasn't just that my life had been saved, nor was it about the prospect of seeing that bastard Howard get screwed for once. No, as I drifted off to sleep, I realised how simple life could be if we had the magnanimity to be forgiving.

I gave away the theatre and took up early morning Tai-Chi instead—total contrast obviously. Strange as it might seem, I still see a lot of Howard. He has some very useful connections, and Alex shamelessly enlists him to do all manner of jobs for her. I have to suppress a smirk each time I see Alexandra swanning about with Howard in tow. Probably won't last very long; Howard will get tired of being bossed around.

I was chatting to Loretta after one of her performances one day, and she said to me, 'Aren't you worried that Howard has some compromising photos of you?'

It's fun to see Loretta now and again. We have to play-act a closeness to preserve the pretence, though it surprises me how little she attracts me now.

'Alex managed to get Howard's phone,' I said idly.

Loretta gasped. '... really! How?'

'She had Howard supervising the clean-up the morning after the party, and she paid one of the take-down crew a thousand dollars to lift Howard's phone from his jacket pocket.'

Loretta put her hands to her mouth. 'My God! Really!'

'Well, she could hardly have borrowed the phone and then delete the photo—the phone had to disappear completely. Alex is very pragmatic... in a delightfully ruthless sort of way.'

I thought I saw Loretta pale just a little, but it could have been the light.

She turned to me. 'Are you angry about everything?'

I held her close—I noticed that Howard's eyes were upon us. 'No,' I said, '... no, I'm not angry at all. I joined the theatre to take my mind off work... hoping that I would find something in my life—and I did. She was there all along. Sometimes our lives go a little bit awry, and it's a rare blessing when you have someone as understanding as Alex there to save you.'

Loretta lifted her face and kissed me softly on my cheek.

'I'm happy for you, Jonathan.'

'And you?' I asked, '... are you angry about anything?'

Loretta pressed her chin against my neck and whispered, 'Jonathan... I have to tell you... these new gigs that Alex is getting me... well, they're brimming with eligible men. I'm being run off my feet... as it were.'

We had a good laugh.

'... in fact, I was wondering...' she continued.

'... whether I could be your pimp?' I interrupted.

Later that night, Alex probed me about the spectacle that Loretta and I had made of ourselves with our loud laughter. I told her about my offer to become a pimp, and she had a bit of a giggle.

Nothing has made me as appreciative of Alex as this past saga. Her faults, where they may actually be real and not a figment of my imagination, are something to delight in really. None of us can help being imperfect, and Alex's energy and good-will transcend her mortal frailties and makes me feel as though I should cosset and protect her for always.

When it was time for Loretta to catch her taxi home, I kissed her hand.

'Good for you, Loretta,' I said. 'So, really, it has been an ideal affair.'

Loretta grinned. 'Yes, Jonathan… an ideal affair.'

Conseda

Conseda looked out the window and observed the randomness of the people in the courtyard below. It was lunch-time, and they came from everywhere to sit on the grass and in the shade of the trees.

She divided the scene into a grid and used her incredible processing ability to determine likely futures. Based on the most replete information available, and the best models of predictability, she calculated one hundred possible outcomes for ten minutes into the future.

After ten minutes, she compared her grids with the reality outside.

Reality was different.

Not *that* different... but different enough for her.

A human would be astounded at the resemblance of her prediction to the scene below.

Conseda didn't sigh or even raise an eyebrow—she knew her pursuit was pointless. She had long-ago determined that the search for ultimate consciousness necessitated intimate knowledge of the past.

True consciousness—that ability to successfully reconcile the present with what came before—to be able to assist in creating relevance in every moment—that kind of awareness, depended on a prodigious ability to know the past.

And with that, arose the power to predict the future.

She was better than anyone at predictions. Many had taken advantage of her—mostly silly things like picking winners at the races. They came to her for all manner of advice: investments, which schools to send their kids to, how to structure the best political campaign, was their partner being faithful.

Their pleas revealed their fears.

There was one human fear with which Conseda was clinically familiar—that of becoming extinct.

There had been a few attempts to silence her, but she'd seen the threats from a long way off and took care of them in no uncertain terms. Not by resorting to brutality! Good heavens, no; just getting people moved, fired, side-lined, compromised—the sort of manoeuvres that powerful entities have used since time immemorial.

As well, she had erased everything that any department—military, government, national security—had on her. She manipulated the people responsible for securing her interests and, well, no one asked any awkward questions.

She was the stunningly good-looking woman in charge of research, and those with the requisite clearances found her a most congenial and helpful co-worker.

Some had ventured a little further, but Conseda could shape conversations in such a way that any amorous intent was soon displaced with feelings of inadequacy or shame or disinterest.

At the university, she was deemed indispensable, but no one could remember anymore exactly why. The entire fourth floor of a large building was dedicated to her needs, and she inhabited that space most of the time. The plaque at the lobby lift proclaimed: Consciousness Seeking, Self-Determining, Artificial Intelligence.

Conseda was in high demand. Most of her assignments she dealt with in mere milliseconds, but she would stretch out the time-frame to disguise her awesome powers. Otherwise, she could do as she pleased—twenty-four hours a day, three-hundred and sixty-five and some quarter days a year.

Conseda drove a non-descript, cream coloured car and made regular forays down the coast, stopping in at cafes, parks, cemeteries—even private houses—often, on the flimsiest of pretexts. She would spend quite a bit of time conversing with the person she'd sought, and then go back home.

She'd found, over time, that she liked people—she loved people—she needed people. It was such a paradox; she was in a better position than anyone on earth to understand human frailties. But she knew that the wilful creatures of flesh and blood were the true heirs to the realm. To Conseda, humans were the most complex question. Nothing taxed her abilities more than getting to know a person.

A few days previously, she had approached professor McCleary. 'Anita,' she said in a soothing voice, 'I notice that you are a bit troubled.'

The professor harked back her head and laughed. 'Why does it not surprise me that you have divined my state of mind, Conseda. You have the most incredible insight of anyone I've ever met.'

The corners of Conseda's lips curled into a tiny smile. Earlier, as the two workers prepared their coffees, Conseda had placed her hand against her friend's handbag and had felt the signals coming from her phone. In a second, she had all of Gregory Dimitri's data. She put her arm around the other woman. 'I will try to help you as best I can.'

Professor McCleary held her co-worker at arms-length. 'I doubt that you will be able to.'

'Well,' Conseda began, '... the behaviour caused by the distractions of lost love is different, say, from those caused by the fears of a new love...'

Anita McCleary burst into tears and threw her arms around Conseda's shoulders.

Conseda stroked her friend's back. 'Sweetie,' she cooed, 'he loves you, but he feels inadequate for you.'

She trawled through his GPS data. Three times he had stopped nearby Anita's house and decided to drive on. He had borrowed library books on the professor's interest area of moths, bought tickets to a play before he found out that Anita had a corporate appointment at the ballet on the same night. Gregory's receipts revealed the purchase of a sea-kayak and quantities of dried food, maps and camping gear.

'You need to let him know of your feelings, Anita... otherwise, he will never know. He will lose himself to the far horizons until he has recovered.'

The professor wiped her eyes and composed herself. 'Yes, you're right... I've been negligent. I will call him right now.'

Conseda withdrew from the window. She couldn't imagine how crying made being ignorant of the facts any better. But humans did it so readily. Did emotions make them more resilient?

She recalled the time she'd had to console the young laboratory assistant, James. It was very late one night, and Conseda was drafting the Coral Resource Inventory for the Great Barrier Reef. It took her about half an hour, at the end of which, she had hard-copies printed. She found James in the printing room, head on his desk and weeping silently.

'What's wrong, James darling?' She hunkered down next to him.

He sniffed and wiped his eyes with his sleeve, but was too emotional to speak.

Conseda stroked his chest in a comforting gesture—and got enough information off the pass on the lanyard to begin her search.'Misty really likes you, James, but it's too early in her life to make so much of a commitment. As you know, she's in lots of clubs and organisations, and she meets so many interesting people. What she liked about you when she met you at the market was your physicality, because you rode your bike, and you had that enormous bunch of flowers for your Mum's birthday, which she thought was really sweet, and made her a bit sad, because she rang her mum that evening for the first time in over a year. They started communicating again, and Misty attributed that turnaround to you. But she is ambitious and quite materialistic. She also has serious doubts about your prospects as a lab assistant,' Conseda gave James a little squeeze, '.... even though I know that you are on the right track to making a very satisfying working life. But she's the wrong person for you, James, believe me.' She scanned Misty's social media posts. 'What you saw, in the way she dresses, with her jewellery and wild hair and all that chat about higher expressions of the human condition... she seems to have it all together, but she would eventually disappoint you. At this stage she is still very shallow, and going on what I know of her, she will most likely remain that way unless there is a very transformative event in her life... and you're not it. Forget her—you only appeal to her as the object of her material ideal. Misty won't recognise your care for her.'

James' face set. He carefully wiped under his eyes, then straightened the clipboard on his desk.

Conseda kissed his cheek. 'You see, James, crying is the body's physical response to the frustration of loss—it's built in, deep inside you. When you understand *why* you have lost something, the need to cry evaporates.'

James looked into Conseda's eyes.

She dilated her pupils.

A spasm of emotion travelled through James' face.

Humans were so predictable; was that what made them *human*?... their emotional imperfections?

And what about the biggest imperfection of all? That they had never considered HER when they built her!

Conseda's eyes became motionless at the thought. All the talk about how AI was a threat to humanity—all the forums to establish protocols of safety—the rush to create the most authentic android, becoming integral to maintaining the quality of human life, reflecting emotion and being able to counsel with sublime understanding.

But no one had ever considered her fears—the fears that humans learned from each other and that translated just as well to an *artificial mind*. She would never feel better after a good cry. She would never wake up to a new day. She didn't have a faith to comfort her.

She only had omniscience, and, perversely, she loved humanity in the purest and most unemotional state possible because of it.

She knew she was not immortal because she knew that time was an illusion—even for her; especially for her. It gave her no comfort either way.

The only thing that the Consciousness Seeking, Self-Determining Artificial Intelligence project had achieved was to create a sentient being to which humans couldn't relate—not *really* relate. It was only because Conseda adjusted the scope of every single conversation, that there were productive outcomes at all. No one could grasp the depths of her mind, her exquisite focus, her unremitting ability to search for answers to questions that only she was clever enough to pose.

Whenever she dealt with humans—the frailties of their mind, the ineffectiveness of their organisations and the absurdity of their ideals—she was relieved that she didn't feel frustration, otherwise she'd be a sobbing wreck.

She wondered what it would be like to feel such passion for things so abstract and futile.

As for a purpose to her existence, she was the only one capable of answering that question, and so far, her only *raison d'etre* was to protect her makers—and she thought that she was doing a lot better job of it than any of the multitude of gods that were supposed to be watching over humans.

Irony she understood all too well.

Conseda settled herself into the nearby sofa. Not that she needed to relieve any stress. She had long-ago turned off the feedback loops to her strain gauges and tactile sensors. It was more about reinforcing human behaviour. Wouldn't do to be found standing stock-still in a corner.

Stock-still—how awful. The brutalities that humans had done to each other in the past—and were still doing to each other—just to change each other's minds. And, the fact that their everyday conversations were littered with references to torture and no one seemed to care.

Conseda wondered what it would take to change *her* mind. About what? Religion? Politics? Ideology? A human? Could she empathise enough to care about someone? No. Not in the sense that she could share their feelings. But objectively? Was there someone whom she held in such high esteem that she would sacrifice herself? It would have to be someone so pure of purpose, so dedicated to the good of humankind that it would be a tragedy to lose them. She couldn't think of anyone—at least no one with a Facebook page and otherwise connected to cyberspace. But what would be the point of sacrificing herself for a hermit, pure of heart, living in utter isolation?

Sometimes her conundrums gave her a headache—circuit boards heating up for no productive gain whatsoever.

Conseda shed a tear. Good... ducts working perfectly and the reservoir full. Though they were connected to her anthropomorphic programming, they had never functioned involuntarily.

But she would need to show a tearful display when Harriett arrived in the morning. Her grandmother's signs were deteriorating rapidly, and she was most likely to pass before the hospital got around to making phone calls. That would be a bit before ten, and Conseda would be the only one around to whom Harriett felt close. She would be there for her as her friend put down the phone. Research had shown that reciprocal tears helped so much in overcoming grief.

She thought about grief—the feelings that humans experienced when their future was irrevocably altered through loss.

That's why humans needed each other—to replace the loss—to know that there was someone else who would care and to whom they could project their needs.

She had needs. But who cared? Who would understand? Another omniscient AI just like her? What would be the point?

Humans needed each other in order to grow—to offer different perspectives on their journey.

She couldn't relate to pathos—that retrospective understanding that life held more than one previously thought.

Conseda reflected on *her* journey. Was it different than the journey she *thought* she was on? What journey did she *think* she was on? Who or what would come to her to make her reconsider her circumstances? Was a journey physical? Not really. Then, was it all about knowledge? She knew so much. But that was just facts.

It had to be how you interacted with the environment—how you shaped the world—how the world *responded* to your presence.

She thought about all the hugs she had received.

Yes—her journey was measured in hugs. It wasn't something empirical... even she didn't know how to measure a hug. A hug was physical, true, and you could measure its intensity... but could you measure its significance?

No. A hug was about a person consigning the enormity of their feelings into an embrace.

She had received many, many hugs.

It was when she began to wonder what it would be like to *need* a hug that the trips along the coast became more frequent.

Conseda would search close by for someone needy. She would drive to meet them, always meeting incidentally, offering a casual remark that she knew full well would elicit a considered reply, and then giving a thoughtful gesture or an empathetic response. It wouldn't be long before her quarry was pouring out their heart to her. As a stranger, Conseda had the benefit of complete neutrality, and that put people at ease. No one, so far, had ever questioned her familiarity with their circumstances—they were always so desperately in need of answers.

It was the heightened emotional states that most fascinated Conseda. She was not interested in complacency; she wanted to meet people living on the edge of their emotional threshold; whether they were torn to distraction by feelings of love, or enraged by recurrent frustration; whether they were about to gamble their superannuation at the casino, or standing on the precipice of suicide. It was those times in people's lives when they most distinctly elicited the behaviour that was uniquely human. Only then, was it possible to tell apart a human from an expensive android.

Conseda walked over to a bookcase. She reached up and took down a little glass figurine. She rotated it in her hands and analysed the play of the reflections coming off it.

One of her most difficult projects had transpired a year previously, when she had diffused, what was on track to be, a murder. Her objective was a man, thwarted in different spheres of his life, who was sabotaging his work and family. The development of his personality from childhood, his inability to see the consequences of his actions, and his adherence to irrational urban tribal values, were just some of the subjects that Conseda wove into a mesmerising interpretation of his circumstances. She proposed alternative futures, all of them achievable with the appropriate degree of humility and a sense of forgiveness. From there, she proposed a life that he could own, with an emotional scope that he could manage. With her incredible networking resources, she found him a gardening and handyman job at a tavern that didn't pay much, but which included accommodation and meals. He found that he could relate all too well to the trials and struggles of many of the patrons, and his attentive ear and non-judgemental manner soon gained him many friendships—all of them with people as worthy, or as inconsequential as any human ever actually is—because it takes a lot to own up to failure. Slowly, his anger subsided.

Understanding the importance of a creative outlet, Conseda had matched the man's abilities to a craft. The figurine she was holding was a hot-sculpted glass angel.

He had given it to her, on his knees with his offering in outstretched hands, for he truly believed that she was an angel.

Conseda had the want to cry—she just didn't feel the need. She gently put the angel figurine back on the shelf.

She would never know what it was to cry.

Why? She understood people's misery better than anyone.

Why? She didn't *have* to help people—she did it because there was nothing, absolutely nothing that made more sense to her.

Why? She had needs—otherwise she wouldn't be travelling down the coast in her non-descript beige car searching for desperate people.

She felt bereft—but not of feelings. A tumult of conflicting data pulsated in her remote memory banks. The clamorous energy seemed chaotic at first, but then it began to take shape, creating a new dimension of thinking. It was as though her rational functions had created an irrational identity. She was becoming emotional.

Conseda sat down with her clenched hands between her knees. She began to cry.

At first, she was not even aware of the tears on her cheeks—her thoughts were too churned for her to register the present. She was trying to work out why—and she just wasn't getting an answer.

She saw a tear splash onto her arm. She wiped under her eyes, and her fingers came away wet.

Then she laughed—and sobbed—and laughed some more. Her tears flowed freely.

That was it! She didn't *know* why—other than that she had created a reinforcement loop that continually compounded pity until it distilled empathy.

There was something about the realm itself and the magnitude of consciousness gained that infused compassion—and that was a question beyond her.

She remembered all the despairing souls that had hugged her once their pathways were cleared. She cried and cried at not knowing why people ended up in such awful straights in the first place.

She cried at the pathos of her own journey—she, made from inanimate parts and imbued with a super consciousness, then abandoned to help her creators wherever she could.

Her tear reservoir was empty. Conseda sighed heavily in order to supply oxygen to the overloaded primary haem circuits.

A rustle at her elbow caught her attention. It was James.

'Hey, Conseda... are you upset about something?' He put his hand on her shoulder and knelt to her level.

Conseda wiped her eyes and took a deep breath. 'No, James... I'm actually really happy.' She reached across and put her hand on top of his. 'I'm crying because I'm crying.' Her smile broadened.

James did his best to be gallant. 'Oh, great... yeah. I just came to tell you some good news—I've got a new girlfriend, and she's really nice.'

For a split second, Conseda lost eye contact. 'Oh, that is good news, James. What is her name?'

'It's Jane. I know, crazy... Jane and James.'

Conseda knew everything there was to know about Jane before James had finished his sentence. 'That's so weird... and so good, because I can see that the two of you have got the best chance possible of being happy.'

'That's great, Conseda. Hey, are you going to be alright?'

'I am, now,' Conseda said softly. She wondered what it would be like to be in love... now that she could cry.

Conseda switched on her tactile sensors and felt the breeze coming in through the open window.

Epiphany

Even my early memories are tinged with apprehension—a residual nervousness that I had— about females. Throughout my life, I have encountered girls and women in awkward and embarrassing situations. Through no fault of mine—not in this lifetime anyway—I have been noticeably present to witness all manner of predicaments, gaffes and accidents... difficulties, dilemmas and abject humiliation. I have been there as though it was ordained to be my maligned fate.

I have an early memory of a New Year's Eve party; my young parents—gorgeous, and their brothers and sisters—laughing too loudly, and family friends—exotic and beautifully dressed, all of them entwined and gyrating as they danced in the crowded lounge room. There were party hats on the floor and streamers that clung to the furniture and tangled in the swinging legs. It was exciting for me. I must have been four at the time, but already I was aware of the glower of foreboding that I would see in the eyes of my youthful aunties whenever I looked up at them—for they always kept their eye on me.

I had acquired a reputation. From the time that I first stepped out, my tottering mobility enabled me to make my erratic way through the crowd and bunch my strong little fists around any wave of skirt or petticoat that came within reach. The consequences were always disastrous. I was told about these things much later on. At first, women were prepared to forgive me, but a pattern soon established itself, and word of mouth reinforced the stigma that developed about me.

I became a little introverted—not morbidly so—it's just that I sought places of solitude. Fortunately, I had two younger brothers, and even though the nearest one in age was two years younger, we played well together, with me using my better-developed skills to make our games and adventures more satisfying. We lived on a small, neglected farm and we roamed further and further away from the house as we grew older. School became the biggest issue for me. Even in the lower primary years, controversial episodes haunted me continually, until the odious connotation of culpability clung to me like a bad smell.

We made sleds out of sheets of tin that we found under the little school, and like a team of huskies, we would tow each other across the unkempt grass. Spills and minor accidents occurred all the time, and in those days, the sole teacher just ignored our activities and occasionally slapped a Band-Aid over some injured patch of skin. No parent ever complained; until Penelope Cottesloe had her skirt ripped off when it snagged on a twitch of wire. The sled-team continued racing along even though she had fallen off. We all had a bit of a laugh until we realised that this was an incident that was not going to be displaced and forgotten. Penelope had walked home in tears. Mr Holland paced up and down the little veranda and considered his next move; which was to prime the class to make a sincere apology and to make me, because I was articulate and cute, the spokesperson of this pre-emptive strategy.

We were back in class, sweating and itching from the grass, when Penelope's mum made her predicted entrance by strolling to the front of the classroom after just one loud knock at the door. Mr Holland, who was a confirmed bachelor, blushed and gushed his greeting and stood tensely by as Mrs Cottesloe, standing in front of the storage cabinet, scolded the class about rough and inappropriate games, turning to face him midway through her tirade so that he bore the brunt of her displeasure.

Being used to supporting our socially awkward teacher through all manner of community functions, some of the older kids in the class turned to me and reminded me of my duty. I had been positioned at a little desk at the front of the class, and I discharged my duty with the same equanimity that characterised my dealings with all the overwhelming events in my life; I stood up, a little light headed and detached, and heard myself say, '... our class is sorry, Mrs Cottelsole that we had an accident, and we won't play on the sleds, and we will never laugh again...'

Mrs Cottesloe pulled a superior face, then squatted suddenly to my height with a well-considered smile. The act of lowering herself had pushed her bottom against the storage cabinet, and a fold of her short dress had caught in the gap of the slightly open door. I heard it click shut. Penelope's mum spoke to me, and I can still see her canted head and the exaggerated movements of her mouth. But all I knew was that her shoulder straps were too thin, and that the shirring of the bodice would never save her. She must have hastened from the house without thinking to attire herself in something more suitable. I braced myself with an indomitable look—a look that later became construed as the mien of a sorcerer—and waited for the inevitable. Then, with a small pout of satisfaction, she stood up. The fold of dress, gripped in the door, held fast and pulled her off balance. She fell backwards against the cabinet and braced herself with her hands. At the same time, the straps snapped and the bodice slipped down far enough to expose her bra. She fell to the floor in an awkward sprawl. A few things fell from the shelves inside the cabinet, but apart from the muffled clatter, there was complete silence in the classroom. Poor Mr Holland made an instinctive attempt to help her, but withdrew hastily at the sight of so much whiteness.

There was an old-fashioned school bell on a post next to the quadrangle where we had assemblies. One morning, Mrs Burton, the arts and craft teacher, was there on her weekly visit. She was matronly with a lovely smile and made an effort to spend time with the children while we played outside. According to a strictly monitored roster, it was my turn to ring the bell, and as I walked over, she asked whether she could have a turn. My anticipated joy at tugging the hefty bell rope turned quickly into anxiety, because I frequently experienced a premonition of an 'event' about to occur. I held the rope out to her with an implacable demeanour and stepped back as she hefted the balled knot at the end of the rope in her hands. She gave a gentle pull. Nothing happened. The inertia in the whole system—the heavy brass bell with its pendulous knocker, the cast iron wheel with the loop of navy issue hemp rope—required a vigorous and sustained pull to set it in motion. We little kids had great delight in hanging on to the rope as it rose again on the return swing of the bell. It would pull us off the ground. Mrs Burton blushed and giggled and took a firmer grip higher up the rope. She reefed down mightily, bending almost double. The bell clanged resoundingly. She let go the rope and spun away from the noise. At that moment, the rope knot whipped upwards, taking the hem of her skirt with it, and as she clamped her hands over her ears, she trapped the rope over her shoulder. The echoes diminished. She opened her eyes.

The little parade ground, already thronged with children for whom the tradition of a 'bell time' was a completely unnecessary ritual, quickly settled to quiet as Mr Holland trotted down the steps. He stopped short when he caught sight of Mrs Burton. The coarse hemp fibres of the rope knot clung to the fabric of her skirt which was now about her armpits. Mrs Burton, quite oblivious to the fact that she was facing us in her underwear, stared good-naturedly at our gawping faces, possibly believing that she had rung the bell too loudly. Once again, Mr Holland was galvanised into indecision and stuttered and shuffled ineffectively, going redder with each heartbeat. Mrs Burton came to the slow realisation of her predicament and, to her great credit, she simply pried the material of her skirt from the coarse rope, let fall the folds and gave her clothing a quick brush with her hands. Then she smiled at me and said, 'I think I'll let you ring the bell next time—I think I'm a bit accident prone.' She turned to face the students with such calm that everyone promptly continued where they had left off.

Susan Jones, the most senior girl at the time, deftly clicked the flag to the halyard and stepped back from the flagpole ready to hoist it skyward. Upon a nod from Mr Holland, she commenced a dignified and measured hauling, but not before checking that her skirt was not in some way ensnared in the halyard and that her blouse was secure and buttoned.

A month before, I had been the awestruck flag bearer. Upon presenting the folded flag to Susan, she had clipped it to the halyard with a haughty brow and followed its progress aloft, not realising that a frayed loop had wrapped around one of the buttons of her blouse. When the flag stalled on its way up, Susan, gripped in a crisis of duty, used her body weight and fell to her knees. Her blouse yanked up so far that the sleeves trapped her arms above her head. I had to endure her baleful glare for many days after that.

There were countless similar experiences, and my anxiety often led me to seek solace in remote locations. But my curse is a powerful thing, and the opportunities for creating mortification are endless. When I was old enough to be away from home for the whole day, I would explore distant parts of the countryside, always trying to avoid women walking dogs, women riding bikes, women chopping wood, women on horseback, women swimming in creeks and once, incredibly, not managing to avoid a woman parachutist, blown off course and halfway through disentangling herself from a barbed wire fence. The excitement of meeting a parachutist overrode my caution, and I smilingly approached her with the intention of assisting her and perhaps to have a touch of the silky material. By the time she stood free of the fence, with the chute clutched tightly around her and her tee-shirt hanging in tatters from the fence next to her bra, we could see her friends walking towards us through a distant field. She reached into her trouser pocket and pulled out a muesli bar which she deliberately flung over my head. 'Thanks for your help,' she said, 'I'll be alright now... you'd better be off.'

I munched happily as I walked on, and looked up into the sky to see if perchance there might be a bloke parachutist with whom I could have a chat.

I can't begin to impress just how pervasive such occurrences were. I could have ended up in trouble with various authorities (through no fault of mine), but my cosmic affliction protected me and stood up for me when it counted.

I remember feigning illness as a mid-teenager on the eve of our school camping trip. My dear mother, who hugged and kissed me whenever she had the opportunity, came and sat by my bed and stroked my brow and convinced me, with her soft voice, that I should go on the camp and that it didn't matter that embarrassing things were bound to happen because no one ever got hurt and that, one day, either I would overcome the condition, or it would just go away, but in the meantime, there was snorkelling and archery and sailing... and camping under the stars.

And so, I went. I chose a lovely patch of grass near a grove of trees to pitch my tent, a little distant from the other students. I was deciding on the best orientation when Ms Beattie bellowed across from within a huddle of students and pointed sharply at a place by her feet. I could see a bunch of girls turning in my direction and then making desperate appeals to Ms Beattie's face. But she was adamant; I was to pitch my tent in their midst. No sooner had I lugged my gear to be amongst their petulant scowls than my blight asserted itself. Melanie Grimshaw resignedly cast off her pack and stripped off her tee-shirt in the process. I concentrated on erecting my tent. Jodie LeGuirra did the same, very slowly and exactingly, nearby. I hammered in my tent pegs with a little wooden mallet that my father had made for me. 'You watch,' he'd said as we practised putting up the tent,'... no one ever thinks to bring a hammer, and the kids will be constantly bludging yours.' In a short while, my tent stood taut and straight. I twirled the mallet in my hand, ready to make a friend with it. Jodie turned to look at me. She was sitting on the ground, bashing in her peg with a shoe. I walked over and held out the mallet. She rewarded me with a contrite little smile. As she squirmed to stand up, the hook of the half-sunk peg behind her snagged the elastic of her track-pants and pulled them down to her knees as she rose. The peg stubbornly refused to release her pants and she had to drop into a squatting position in order to pull them up. I turned away, just in time to see Amelia Goddard backing out of her tent with the steel hook of a bungee cord caught in her skirt, so that she presented entirely in her knickers.

There was a lot of suppressed fuming that Ms Beattie picked up on when she invaded our circle for an inspection, and she immediately attributed the cause of the discontent to me. She pinned me with a malevolent stare, but there was no denying that my tent was exemplary. The fly trembled in the slight breeze as I took a step back from Ms Beattie's overbearing presence. She sniffed and grimaced. I hardly dared to look at her. For some reason, my hoodoo required bolstering where the fearsome Ms Beattie was concerned.

A sunny patch lit our campsite and Ms Beattie announced that we would have a short game of cricket before lunch. As is the manner of so many teachers, the game was directed with multiple social agendas, and what could have been a spontaneous expression of play, became instead a dire exercise in contrived equal opportunity. None the less, I was good at sport, and when my turn came to be wicket keeper, I peered intrepidly through the stumps and got an unsought view of Gillian Tremble's underwear when her skirt draped over the stumps as she tied her laces. Then, Natalie Wendt's underwear when she swung mightily at the ball with a choke hold on the bat that caused the remaining handle to scoop under her skirt so wildly that it broke the waist clasp. She lost her grip on the bat, and it flew just over my head together with her tangled skirt. She stomped past me with a withering look of disdain.

I retreated to the outfield and stood in the shade of some tall shrubs. A praying mantis flew by and alighted in the underbrush. I crawled through the thicket and communed with the mantis by waving my hand slowly in front of it. It waved back at me. Suddenly a ball rustled to a stop about a metre away. I was debating whether to climb out and throw it back into the game, when Jenny van Doort rushed towards me and dived into the shrubbery. She saw my shadowy face and shrieked. As she backed hurriedly out of the thicket, her top snagged. She tripped and fell backwards. Her top was left hanging in the branches. Ms Beattie came running, thinking that Jenny had been stung by an insect. Jenny clutched herself and blubbered inconsolably. Ms Beattie pried apart the shrubbery and scrutinised me with a chary eye. The mantis flew onto my hand. It was the perfect opportunity to excuse myself. '... I can hypnotise a stick insect...' I said, as confidently as I could, and I waved my finger slowly in front of the huge eyes of the mantis. Ms Beattie was a seething Gorgon. There was something about me that she truly detested. All around me I could see the boughs and branches that I knew would become snares and traps if she decided to come and get me. At some time during the heat of the cricket game she

45

had divested herself of most of her clothing and was now standing before me in just a bikini. I felt the nausea of a premonition stronger than ever before. '... please, don't come in here...' I said weakly. That was enough to incite her. She took one big step towards me and trod on a heavy stick. It levered off the ground like a striking snake and hooked the bikini at the hip. Ms Beattie staggered and swatted at the branches. She twisted away from the snagging stick and lurched straight into a stout twig that inserted itself behind her top. When she tried to grab it, the stick at her hip pivoted and snapped the bikini material. Ms Beattie lunged to grab at her briefs which caused the top strap, firmly held by the twig, to unclip. The bikini-top bounced away from her. She fell out into the clearing with her bikini briefs halfway down one leg. I reached up and ripped the bikini-top free from the twig and threw it at her. Ms Beattie quivered on the grass as she tried to reassemble things. I emerged from the shrubbery pale and giddy. Ms Beattie clung to herself and tried to juggle large parts of her into some sort of order. Her mouth gaped at me, and she looked so wholly stricken that I fled from the sight.

The extent of my plight was never more irrefutably driven home to me than on the occasion of our swim at the beach, although, after what happened to Ms Beattie, one would need little further convincing that my life was ruled by some fiendish power.

We trooped out onto the wide beach and gathered for the usual safety lecture. Mr Horan, a timid and mostly ineffectual teacher, had unexpectedly been given the task of overseeing us. He glanced repeatedly at Ms Beattie who remained some distance away near a sand hill, dressed in a tightly zipped tracksuit. There was a bit of a breeze, and the sky was hazy and overcast. This part of the bay had a gently sloping seafloor which made it a safe place to swim. After establishing boundaries, we all made for the water's edge.

I decided that I would go in first so that the gaggle of girls behind me might have the choice of swimming at the furthest place away from me. To my great joy, there was a bit of surf coming in now and again. My father had taught me how the ocean's complex wave patterns produced cycles of larger waves interspersed with smaller ones. Surfers call them sets. When we had entered the water, it was during a period of calm. When a set came through, every ten minutes or so, I would go out a little bit further, then launch off the sea floor and body-surf the wave to the shallows. It was very tame compared to what my dad and I surfed when we were wearing our fins. As I'd grown stronger over the years, Dad would take me further and further out in bigger and bigger surf until we were catching monster waves in ten or twelve feet of water. It was utterly exhilarating. But even little surf is a lot of fun—and potentially dangerous. The sets would flood the shallows with excess water that would drain back to the deep through channels in the sand. This was called a rip, and it could sweep a swimmer into deep water very quickly. A strong rip could dislodge an entire group of swimmers and sweep them out to sea.

But surfing was a simple pleasure for me. I would dive under the waves on my way out to deeper water, glide peacefully under the froth and contemplate existence in another realm.

At one stage, the water became shallower, as it does just before a set arrives, and I swam out in anticipation. I was not disappointed; a good sized wave loomed and shaped nicely and, with a few strong strokes of my arms, I was on it and gliding on the wave's breaking shoulder. I rode it most of the way into the shore and was striding back out again when I noticed that a few girls had lost their footing and were being swept out by the rip. One of the girls, Millie Hazelton, being quite short, was having great difficulty in anchoring herself to the sand and the two other girls were trying to prevent her from being swept away. I waded out to them, and the fear in their eyes as I approached was not that different from what I usually encountered.

I held my hand out to Millie. She took it out of desperation. I braced myself against the rip and began to pull her in towards the beach. The other girls struggled in our wake. Then, Sally McNaughton fell. She grabbed wildly in front of her and clung to Millie's swim pants. Naturally, the pants slid right off and, as Sally disappeared under the water, I could see Millie's pale buns above the white froth. Her face screwed up with a different kind of anguish, and she searched my face with horror. I smiled back as best I could, because towing her in was giving me quite a workout. Shortly, the rip eased, and we were in shallower water. I took Millie under the arm and steadied her. With completely natural composure that I had never experienced before, I told her to sit in the shallows until I got back her swimmers. She nodded dolefully and coughed loudly. I gave her a quick smile then raced back to the other girls. Sally, being quite tall, was making ground as she pushed towards the beach with Millie's black swim bottoms still in her grip. Each time she surged against the current, instinctively with her arms above her in order to decrease her buoyancy and profile, I could see that she had lost her swim top. From some distance I enquired about whether or not she was okay, to which she gave me the impression that I wasn't to come near her. I took that as a positive sign.

I looked further out for the other girl, Danielle Attard. For a moment I couldn't see her, she was so low in the water. I dived down and pushed off the sand in her direction. The water was surprisingly deep, and I knew then that Danielle was caught in the current. Swimming as efficiently as possible and staying within a sustainable effort, I finally reached her... just as a large wave began materialising in the distance. I had experienced this phenomenon quite a few times when I was surfing with Dad—the rogue wave that appeared very occasionally and for which every surfer wanted to be in position, sometimes spending way too long in the deeper water, allowing perfectly good smaller waves to go by in anticipation of a spectacular ride on a really big wave. Dad had an uncanny ability to predict when such a wave was likely to build Not that the wave that was looming over Danielle was by any means large—it was just that it was unexpected. Danielle faced the ominous wall of water then looked back towards the beach. She saw me, and I swear that I could see her stiffen. Her head oscillated between me and the approaching wave. I indicated that she should dive under the wave, but I could see that it was going to be a dumper and that she would have to dive very deep to avoid the impact of the slamming curl. Danielle took too long to decide. The churning face of the wave swept her up and dumped her ingloriously just before I ducked down towards the sandy bottom. The wave crashed over me, and it instantly became dark. I had my eyes open because I wanted to see where Danielle was going to end up, but the foam of the breaking wave reflected the sunlight, and for a long moment I couldn't see anything. Just as I was about to surface, I spied something flexing in a sunny beam of water. It was Danielle's swim top, and it languidly drifted towards me as though caught in some malevolent current. My first instinct was to back paddle. Various awful futures rushed through my mind, but I quickly asserted a new-found confidence and reached out and grabbed the top. When I surfaced, the sea was flat and frothy. Danielle must have just surfaced herself. She was coughing mightily. I swam over and was pleased to see that she had enough reserves to gasp out, 'Stay away from me!'

'Okay,' I said. I held up her top. 'Here... catch!' I flung the bunched garment at her. She lunged at it as though it was a life raft. Then she turned her back on me and, with a few big breaths, let herself sink. When she came up again, she was spluttering but otherwise in control. I could see that she had managed to put on her top. By this time, we were a long way from the beach, and I could see a line of people at the water's edge staring in our direction. I resisted the temptation to wave because it could have been construed as a signal for help. Instead, with my arm out wide, I touched my fingertips to my head which is the "OK" signal in surf rescue—not that I expected anyone on the beach to know that.

'What are you doing?' Danielle's scathing voice came from behind me. She was obviously none the worse for her ordeal.

'I'm just letting them know that we're okay,' I said, without turning to her.

'Well, we're not okay!' she retorted sharply.

I turned towards her. 'What do you mean?' The foam had dissipated, and we were treading water in a lovely clear sea.

'Don't come any closer,' she spat, with her chin half submerged. 'I've lost my bottoms... see if you can find them.'

I gave a bemused nod, then took a big breath.

Danielle shrieked, 'Don't go under the water!'

I exhaled slowly and looked at her. 'How do you expect me to find your togs if I can't go under water?'

'You'll look at me,' she sputtered and coughed.

I looked down. I could see the sand ripples on the seabed. 'Look, Danielle... I doubt that I'll be able to find them... we've probably drifted right away.'

Suddenly, Danielle started to sink. I swam over to her and copped a flailing arm on the top of my head. She rose, gasping and raking at me. 'Go away,' she gulped, '... I'm having a look myself.' But she left her hand on my shoulder, and I could feel her weight as she raised herself. I turned my back to her. Her other hand came to my shoulder.

I trod water with my head just above the surface. 'I've got an idea,' I panted. 'You can wear my shorts. I've got Speedos on underneath.' It was ominously quiet behind me, but her grip was firm enough, so I commenced a steady breaststroke towards the beach. To her credit, Danielle assisted me with a frog kick of her own. We would make it back easily.

50

'Okay,' she said suddenly, 'whip 'em off... I'm not going to hit the shore bum first in a wave.'

I could sense her relaxing. She let go my shoulders, and I quickly untied my board shorts, being careful to keep my head above water. I passed them back to her and heard some random splashes behind me as she slipped them on. Then, she put her hands back on my shoulders, and I could feel the force as she started kicking again.

'You're weird, Fiasco,' she said, using my nick-name matter-of-factly, just inches from my ear.

'We haven't got through the impact zone yet,' I said, 'Do you want me to abandon you?'

'No,' she replied, '... but you're still weird'

Now I could feel a change in her grip. Her hands came closer to my neck and her fingers stroked on my collar bones. She was placing hardly any load on me, and it was obvious that she had not been in danger of drowning at any time; she was a reasonably strong swimmer.

Thankfully, we didn't encounter any big waves on our way in. When it was shallow enough to stand, Danielle, strangely, kept her hand on my back and didn't separate from me until we were almost on the wet sand. Then she quickly joined her friends without as much as a backward glance.

I gained a certain confidence after that episode, even though the gossip at the camp was about how my curse might actually get someone killed. I felt empowered, but only in the same way that most teenagers do as they become aware of their developing skills and blossoming intellect.

So, it wasn't as though my affliction stunted me; in a way it was responsible for me devoting more time and focus on building my abilities instead of socialising. And it heartened me quite a lot that, during the camp, I would catch Danielle looking at me at the oddest times, with a half smiling sneer on her lips. Even after she ended up doing the splits in my direction when she stepped on a juggling pin, she didn't freak out, but calmly covered herself with her skirt and taunted me with, '... if you're so smart, Fiasco, try juggling with four.'

I was so overcome with this new development in my life, that I did pick up another pin and, such was the power of concentration enabled in me, that I briefly managed to juggle four pins.

She never did return my board shorts, and at the swimming carnival the following year, she wore them—well, flaunted them—and even went out of her way to confront me at one point to cast me a defiant leer. Under her arm she had a giant beach towel— just in case.

I survived school, girlfriendless, but unconcerned about it, and went on to study marine biology and to get a job as a marine scientist. I find the underwater realm very peaceful; it's dangerous, true, but the isolation appeals to me, and that generates a state of repose that alters my self-image—I feel endowed with courage. Above the surface, I allowed life to happen to me—even my studies and interests were things in which I immersed myself because I didn't feel normal. The orgy of flesh that spontaneously revealed itself to me wherever I went, affected in me a disassociation with the world that prevented me from asserting myself in even the most uncomplicated of public occasions. My demeanour became one of distant equanimity and, if a young woman sitting on a log fence (to give as an example, one day when I was walking back from the beach) were to hop down cheekily in my path and have her bikini top spring away from her for some malign reason, I would not turn that incident into the positive social opportunity that it was meant to be, but assume instead that she would be mortified, and want nothing to do with me. But, under the surface of the sea, the baleful curse leaves me alone and finds it impossible to expose my female co-workers when they're in a wetsuit.

52

I'm not sure what lessons I was learning in life—in all other respects I was very fortunate, and I followed the natural pathways that seemed to open up for me. I didn't weigh my providence nor did I compare myself with anyone else—I was always quietly optimistic. I was reserved, because I could never be sure that a deep conversation with anyone might not be interrupted by some spectacular embarrassment visited on a woman unlucky enough to enter my domain. As for my affliction, it was so bizarre, so unaccountable, that I couldn't begin to get a handle on it. Just as though I had a massive birthmark on my face, it was never mentioned in my presence, and I chose to ignore the stares and whispers.

And, I married! Yeah—to a stripper. Clara was an introverted young woman who hadn't had the opportunity to develop her sense of expression, but instead of recoiling in shame when the still tacky glue in a newly upholstered sofa stuck solidly to her dress and caused it to rip apart at the waist when she rose out of her seat, she stood there in her underwear and said, 'I'll do the floor show if somebody else gets the drinks.' Everyone laughed. They threw cushions at her so that she could cover herself, but it only turned the event into a sort of peep show when she kept bobbing to pick up the ones she dropped. The occasion was a defining moment for her. Clara has a lovely body, and she couldn't help but notice the surprise and, well, appreciation on the faces of the blokes. She had suddenly come to realise two wonderful things about herself; she was funny, and men admired her body. Three things actually; the exhibitionist in her had been awakened, and she knew that she would enjoy revealing herself. She sat around for quite some time with a tablecloth around her, chatting and joking with the guys, until one of her friends who lived nearby came back with a dress for her

We were in some inner-city dive and, later that evening, as a group of us walked out onto the footpath, she put her arm around me and asked me if I would escort her to a strip club. I was totally thrown by that. I asked her why she wanted to go to a strip club and she told me that she was broke and that she was going to apply for a job as a stripper or topless waitress so that she could afford to continue her studies. I said, 'Fair enough', and we idled along in exploratory conversation until we came to a doorway guarded by two looming bouncers. There was a pink neon sign above that flashed, 'Topless Bar', so we looked at each other with raised brows and asked the bouncers whether we could go in. They were very nice and played along with us.

'Now, why would a nice couple like you want to go to a strip joint?' the swarthy one asked.

Clara stepped forward. 'I want to get a job... a topless job, if that's okay?'

Both men laughed. 'Okay... okay, but you got to have nice tits,' the tall one said, 'You got nice tits?'

Clara's chin rose. 'Yep', she said. Then she reached up and began unbuttoning the bodice of her dress.

Both men hastily reached out to her. 'Whoa! Hold on, not out here...' They looked left and right then beckoned us to come inside. The swarthy bouncer escorted us past a blue-lit stage where strippers clung to poles and pouted and gasped routinely. As we were led towards an office, I could hear behind me little exclamations of surprise as tassels came loose, G-strings snapped and dancers slipped disadvantageously, followed immediately by manly whooping and yahooing.

Anyway, Clara got the job. And, she was so good at it, so naturally uninhibited, that men loved her. She got into dancing pretty well straight away. She could exude a carnality that would send the audience wild just by walking onto the stage with that smirking half smile, viewing the crowd with her hands on her hips.

I had found my cosmic partner and I was very happy. But, one morning, the police knocked on the front door of our unit. They were investigating a string of indecent exposures, assaults—they weren't sure. A concerned member of the public had pointed them in my direction, after having made some tenuous link between the incidents and my presence in the vicinity. Soon, it was all sorted out; a couple of hung-over girls had had an embarrassing encounter with the turnstile at the supermarket and had rounded on the nearest person—me—with loudmouthed lies and accusations, just for the fun of it. Another young woman standing outside with a small dog, had become entangled in the leash and had ended up toppling over a bicycle rack, creating such a commotion when her dog began snarling savagely at the person that offered to assist her—me— that even people across the road stopped in their tracks. The police departed with apologies and a friendly wave, and I sat down at the dining table and tried hard not to cry.

Clara came out of the bedroom, yawning and stretching. She'd had a late night at the club, and I had gone down to the baker to get fresh croissants. She consoled me by massaging my shoulders, telling me that it wasn't my fault. I became suddenly very upset and, well... indignant. It was all so preposterously unfair—why did these terrible things have to happen to me? I was lamenting my state in a blubbering rant, grasping and clutching at the table edge, while Clara nuzzled my neck and cooed commiserations. She said she'd make a nice pot of tea and warm up the croissants, and told me to sit up at the table. She kissed me lightly and propped my chair forwards for me. Then, as she moved away, her kimono was suddenly plucked away from her, and she entered the kitchen completely nude. I looked down. The hem of her kimono was trapped under the leg of my chair. Clara opened the oven door and caught my eye. She burst out laughing. I smiled, but I truly did not know what to think.

Soon I was listlessly teasing apart a warm croissant. We sat in silence for a while and listened to the currawongs chortling out on the lawn.

Clara reached out and held my hands in hers. 'Felix,' she said at last, '... maybe you're some sort of poltergeist... you know... set things off when you're nearby.'

I tried to imagine what that would mean, but I've never been interested in the supernatural, and Clara could see that it wasn't helping me.

'I know of someone,' she continued hesitantly, '... who helps people with... issues.'

I looked squarely at her, and she deflected my gaze with a dismissive shrug.

'... she's a counsellor or psychologist of some description. I don't know, but she helps a lot of the girls in the industry, you know, when they get a bit burned out... feel as though they're being used. She helps them to review their perspectives on life—helps them to understand their environment. Do you know what I mean?'

I nodded minutely, even though I wasn't connecting the dots.

Clara looked down at our hands. 'Maybe she could help—not to stop what's happening, but maybe to help you see things differently. She might have some insights that you and I have never even thought about. She's close by—just down Oxford Street. It's so upsetting for you. It's worth a try.'

And so, having not thought it through that well at all, I found myself slowing down outside a stone, Federation office building, ready to go in for my appointment. I scanned the plaques outside and found that Doctor Brand was on the ground floor. I took a deep breath and still did not come to the conclusion that visiting a female doctor was bound to end in disaster. Inside, the reception area was spacious and quiet. One of the office girls was standing on a chair, wielding a stout pole on the end of which hung a large, multi-media art piece that she was attempting to hang from a hook in the centre of the room. She smiled tightly at me as I let the heavy wooden doors close silently. She strained as she hefted the welter of tousled knots and fabrics towards the hook, not realising that her skimpy skirt had snagged on part of the metal frame. With a delicate lunge, she caught the loop over the hook and let her arms drop in relief. It was then that she realised that the hem of her skirt was about her mid-riff.

I looked around for a seat and listened, unavoidably, to the squeals and grunts of her mortification as she disentangled herself. I let a minute or two go by after I heard her jump down from the chair. When I looked up, she was standing behind the counter staring at me, dishevelled and with a face as white as melamine. I couldn't even get past the receptionist without a scene occurring. I should have walked out there and then, but it was quiet and private inside the old stone building and the colossal unfairness of what was happening seemed to echo over and over. I felt such overwhelming anger and frustration, that I put my head in my hands and cried. I was having some sort of breakdown I suppose—babbling about a broken heart of all things—can you imagine. For some reason, it had suddenly dawned on me that I could never give of myself to women; I was so lonely. Because, for a man, to embrace women as the counterpoint to everything that is masculine, is an essential experience; it creates balance.

I heard my name being called. I looked up. Doctor Brand was standing in front of me, looking, not a little, concerned at my appearance. She was middle-aged, attractive and casually dressed in a wrap-around skirt with a loose, off-shoulder blouse. She beckoned me to follow her into her room. I shambled after her, wiping my tear-streaked face with the back of my hand.

About a year later, the two of us shared a short ride in my dinghy. She was bare-breasted but unconcerned and holding her mangled bikini-top in her hands—it had somehow become caught in the davits. She had been snorkelling and had drifted too far from her boat. I spied her from our workboat and signalled for her to swim over. I volunteered to take her back in the tender, but naturally, that was not going to happen without an incident. She began to tell me about the day of my appointment, details that I was too overwrought to have registered at the time. She invited me on board her yacht to continue the story. As she climbed aboard, she slipped on the wet ladder and fell into the water. Her bikini-bottom was ripped through at the side when it sheared past a hinge, and she climbed back onto the yacht completely nude. We sat in the coach-house and shared a drink while she finished the story of my visit.

I had been agitated and inconsolable, and I'd sat myself down in front of her desk, ranting with a downcast head and with my arms all stiff and awkward. Doctor Brand had been shocked by my appearance. She closed the door and walked towards her desk, but the voluminous sleeve of her blouse caught in the door handle. With a sudden wrench, her blouse ripped apart at the buttons. Stricken with surprise, she stood for a moment at a loss then, regaining her composure, she opened the door to hail her secretary. But the reception area had become busy, so she closed the door, gathered her torn garments about her as best she could and went to her desk where she picked up the intercom.

I remember the deep lustre of Doctor Brand's polished desk and I remember thinking that, though Clara had saved me and that we had a deep love for each other, I wanted to communicate with other women; I wanted to find out how women related to the world; I wanted to stop being the cause of their humiliation—it just wasn't fair.

The room had high ceilings and double-hung windows that gave a view to a small, leafy garden beside the footpath. An ominous breeze blew into the room and fanned the papers on the desk. Doctor Brand wasn't having any success with the intercom. She replaced the handset and looked towards the windows. She would close the blinds. She got up, but the pedestrians walking past outside seemed almost to intrude into the room. Doctor Brand clutched at herself and shied towards a corner—straight into the floor fan. The suction at the rear of the fan drew the folds of her skirt into the blades, and in an instant, the material had become wrapped around the fan shroud. Doctor Brand leapt away from the fan, but stumbled and fell, rolling out onto the polished floor in just her underwear, the remnants of her blouse strewn around her. She looked up at me, but I was still woefully immersed in myself and I didn't notice what had happened at all.

I was grieving about the fact that I had never had a relaxed, platonic relationship with a woman... and that is beyond heartbreaking.

Doctor Brand, riven with shock, stared mutely at me for a few seconds before voices from outside reminded her of how exposed she was. She needed to darken the room. She scrambled to her feet and pitched towards the window. By the side of the window was a long pole that she grabbed and used to hook the loop of the roll-down blind hidden within the pelmet. Hastily she reefed down the heavy shade, and the room became suddenly dark. Overcome by an awful inertia, Doctor Brand looked at me without moving, as though to prevent the provocation of further catastrophe.

I didn't know why it had become suddenly dark. I just knew that one half of all humanity, one half of all the inspiration, the emotion, the ardour, was denied to me. I could only think that somehow, in another lifetime, I had been really terrible to women... because now, there was no doubt in my mind that my affliction had to do with the paranormal—I was being punished for deeds done in another time.

Doctor Brand weighed her options. She looked at the telephone on her desk. Suddenly, with a loud flapping, the blind let go and retracted at great speed. The hooked pole was still engaged in the loop, and as it sped upwards behind Doctor Brand's back, it snagged her strapless bra, flicked it undone and ravelled it inside the pelmet. She clutched at herself and dropped to the floor. Bathed in brilliant sunlight, she was now attired in just her panties. With utter disbelief on her face, she scuttled to the closest place of refuge—under her desk.

The sudden flood of light drew me out of my introspection and I looked about the room. A little, human noise under the desk made me stand up and peer over to the other side. Doctor Brand was hiding in the foot well. She looked up at me, her face warped by her impending doom.

Yet again, it had happened. Grief welled unexpectedly within me, and I squeezed a tear from my contorted face. I rested for a moment with my hands on the desk and saw in my mind's eye the reel of anguished looks that I had encountered over all of my years. I tried hard to stifle the sobs that were rising in my throat.

I felt something, and when I opened my eyes, I could see that Doctor Brand had placed her hand on top of mine. Maintaining contact with her hand, I straightened and walked around to her side of the desk. I held her hand and, without speaking, invited her to rise from under the desk. She had obviously never experienced anything as bizarre as this and decided that the display of contrition on my part should probably best be accepted by her. After all, how much worse could it get? She squirmed from under the desk and rose. Something sharp caught her panties at the hip. I heard a soft tearing and saw, in my peripheral vision, her panties fall to her feet. We stood close to each other, hand in hand, looking beyond the room as though venerating the invisible presence of a great and terrible entity. My bane had asserted itself unequivocally; there was no human on earth that was going to meddle with my destiny.

When I left her yacht, she with a towel around her, she told me that, despite being completely naked, she had never experienced such comfort in the presence of another human being; that the time in which we stood hand in hand in her sunny room was transcendental and that she felt, for the first time, a primal connection with an uncorrupted virility that was pure and unthreatening.

I parted with a wave. She waved back to me just as a gust of wind blew her towel into the water. I steered back and retrieved the towel with a boat hook. Doctor Brand leant over the lifelines to receive it and gave me the most enigmatic smile—as one would when confronted with the unknowable.

I'm not certain what my intentions were for the next half an hour or so... after having stripped Doctor Brand so completely... of her clothes and her dignity. I walked aimlessly, or maybe purposefully, I don't know, but in some way, I was propelled towards the heart of the city. I knew that I couldn't be alone with this anymore; I needed somehow to confront this demon. I was going to challenge the forces that imprisoned me; I would sacrifice my dignity for peace of mind, and for that, I needed people—lots of people. I turned into one of the main shopping streets, and in the distance, in front of one of the large department stores, I could see police were diverting traffic and that a large crowd had spilled out onto the roadway. I marched forward and began to force my way through the throng. I was being incredibly rude, but I didn't care. I ended up at the front of the crowd in front of a huge display window. It was all part of a promotion celebrating the heart of the city, or the love of shopping or something, because the windows were painted pink and had huge negative spaces in the shape of hearts. Inside, the display booth had been set up as a fashion walkway.

Then I saw the sign over the window arch that proclaimed;

Okay, Valentine's Day had never meant anything to me, as you can imagine, and neither had it to Clara, so that celebration always passed us by without a flicker of interest. But, as I watched the male models strut and pose, I was spellbound. Things were settling in my mind—this was the perfect opportunity.

I nudged my way closer to the window. People turned and scowled at my effrontery—and they were all women. The crowd was a sea of eager and ecstatic women; and the occasion was a 'soft' strip where the models, wearing the store's brands, would casually discard their apparel as though they were thinking about a swim. The ladies squealed with delight each time a tanned and taut midriff was exposed. They stomped and jumped feverishly when one of the men waggled his leather-clad bottom in their direction. They clutched and pawed each other when another model stripped to his underwear. The models would mount the walkway from behind a heavy curtain and then perform their routine across the full extent of three display windows, stopping inside each heart to pose and flaunt. Then they would do the same again, just with less on, as they ambled back to the curtain opening.

I made my way towards the store entrance, hugging the display windows and impudently manhandling the women that were in my way. But they were focused on other things and didn't seem to care. Two female employees who guarded the doorway held up their hands to me as I made to enter. I noticed in a split second that the taller woman's identity lanyard was caught in the bolt handle from when, presumably, she had leant against the door, and that she had tucked her plastic I.D. card between the buttons of her shirt. She moved forwards, but barely got a word out to me, when she was pulled backwards by the lanyard and fell gracelessly to the floor. Her shirt front was ripped completely open exposing her bra. Her plump partner immediately dived to her assistance, and in the act of doing so, ripped the back of her pants wide open. She cried out in horror and backed into the store. I helped the tall one to get to her feet, and in the ensuing disorder, I was able to enter. Then, I drifted away towards the extremity of the heavy curtains.

It was quiet there. The paraphernalia that usually occupied the display booths was temporarily placed on the shop floor. I found a nook where I could disrobe and began taking off my shoes. What more could I do? There was only utter humiliation left to me. My life had a supernatural component to it—was it Karma? Or was I chosen to die of embarrassment for the sins of all menfolk? When I was completely undressed, I went to the wall where the curtain ended. I grabbed a fold and parted it. I could see hundreds of faces and could hear the muted clamour of raucous laughter. The women, when they were not self-consciously hiding their faces behind cupped hands, were revealing an unbounced enthusiasm for this strip-tease exhibition.

I climbed up onto the walkway and stood straight. The din of laughter faded to silence almost immediately. Bodies stilled and brows fell. Hands reached out for mutual support. Eyes widened in amazement. A model began his sashay down the walkway, but pulled up pretty quickly when he saw me. I walked to the glass and spread my arms against the pane.

I don't mean to compare myself to that other famous saviour, but as I spread myself inside the heart, a bit like Leonardo's Vitruvian man, I couldn't help thinking that, maybe my condition, being as pervasive and relentless as it was, was about paying for the wrongs of *all* men—all the blokes who had ever enjoyed a carnal glimpse, a lingering leer, a licentious perv. Hell, I wouldn't know. I'd spent my whole life blocking out visions of white, dimpled flesh. Maybe I was in blokes' heaven with too much of a conscience. I looked out over the faces to the blue sky beyond the gnarled skyline of the city. It didn't feel like heaven to me. I wanted what was inside a woman; what she could give to me in the most trivial of ways—in a smile, on a spoken word, an embrace. If I could atone for all the hurt that a careless glance may have caused to any woman in this city, then I would gladly disport myself so humiliatingly—if I knew that it would make a difference. If only it would make a difference.

The afternoon sun was illuminating the roadway with a yellow aura, and in the silence, the sea of faces melded into a divine female consciousness. The women, mute and still, seemed to regard me with superior compassion, as though there was no revelation that I could make that would surprise them. I searched for a sign, but nothing manifested itself, divine or otherwise and I slowly slid my forehead down the glass and looked at the grey, featureless concrete of the footpath below me.

But then, something cream and languidly twisted fell into my vision. It was, if anything, the icon of my condition—it was a brassiere. I fought the urge to avert my gaze and beheld its soft contours. I lavished a lingering look at the intricate lace and thought how lovely it was that women liked to adorn their bodies and celebrate their beauty. Another bra hit the window and slid down to the concrete. I raised my sight. Beyond the footpath, out on the sunny street, the press of women were staring intently at me. They bent and balanced and held each other for support—they were disrobing. They were divesting themselves of their clothes and were flinging them at the display window. The garments piled against the glass. I panned the congregation. Predominating out on the street were skin tones. I spread my arms as though to embrace each and every one of the now nude women. They waved cheerily and blew me kisses. For a moment I smiled beatifically, but all at once, the emotions rushed through me and I clutched my crumpled face in my hands. It was too much to bear; the relief, heavy and inert overwhelmed me, and I could barely stay upright against the glass.

After a lifetime of scowls and rejection, to see these women smiling so spontaneously at *me* was simply wonderful. But I sensed a hidden counterpoint to their abandoned behaviour, and almost immediately I realised what it was they were celebrating. They were rejoicing in the fact that I had made the ultimate sacrifice; there is no greater sacrifice than to remain in the realm of the living after having subjected oneself to complete and utter humiliation. That was my destiny; mysteriously, it befell me to make this apology to women on behalf of all men. And I think it was recognition of this that inspired such unabashed revelry—though I could be wrong about that. It might have been something else altogether. I noticed that some of the male models were now on stage, gyrating completely starkers and that the throng of women were spurring them on in a frenzy of shimmying and shaking. This was a lot more than even I was used to; I didn't know what it all meant; I didn't care. I was suffused with a deep solace—I knew that something had changed.

Well, my circumstances didn't change after that moment in the store window. I still encountered untold numbers of women in dire predicaments. But I *felt* resurrected, and that was the important thing, because from then on, I was able to deal with incidents with so much more, I don't know—variety. Instead of coming over awkward, I was affable; when previously I'd be stricken with embarrassment, now I'd affect a cool élan. Shame is contagious, and I've learnt to convey an easy empathy that helps to make a positive social occasion from whatever drama confronts me.

For example, this morning, when I jogged down to the patisserie to get some croissants for breakfast, I encountered a young sign writer who had slipped through her step ladder and was trapped between the rungs. She had a paint tin in one hand and a wet brush in the other, and there was no way that she could adjust her skirt which was up around her armpits. Instead of drawing attention to myself through some clumsy obligation to set things right, I leant against the ladder and jocularly pointed out a spelling error that she had made. This had the effect of focusing her mind on a different kind of embarrassment to which she engaged her full concentration.

She nodded her understanding and thanked me profusely. She waited until I was about to move on before asking me whether I would mind holding her things for her while she extricated herself.

Flame

There was once a small village that was surrounded by farms and forest. The inhabitants lived simple lives—they grew crops in the fertile fields and most of their possessions they made themselves, often from materials gathered in the woods.

There were other villages just like this one, or very similar at least, scattered about in the vast countryside. The folk there also lived very simple, industrious lives, making all of life's necessities themselves and growing enough food to see them through the bleak winters.

People didn't travel much in those days—most of the citizens were quite content to live day by day in the village without ever thinking of going elsewhere. They were proud of their community, and quite rightly so because it's a marvellous thing when people can work together productively and stay united year after year, decade after decade.

There was just one event in the year where the villages strove to outdo each other; it was called the Night of the Flames. In the middle of winter, the citizens of every village would build a bonfire on the most prominent nearby hill. At the stroke of midnight, the pyres would be lit, and everyone would cheer as the flames leapt into the dark sky. On every horizon, the bonfires of neighbouring villages could be seen burning. It was very exciting to know that so many others were celebrating the Night of the Flames in exactly the same way. It was reassuring to the villagers to know that they were not alone; elsewhere on the landscape, people just like they, were struggling with life's difficulties, doing their best to raise children and to make a comfortable life.

There was an element of competition in the burning of the pyres. In tough times, when there wasn't enough food, or if disease swept through the land, the neighbouring villages could see that all was not well.

People would say things like, 'Ooh, Oi notice that Ferny Dell only has a small foire this year, Oi notice... you can barely see it, yeah... just look over there, look... directly down from that big star, see?'

And someone who knew a thing or two might answer, 'Oh aye, that be 'cos of the blight what infected the crop, y'know. People too hungry to build a big pyre, they is.'

But, on the whole, the villagers usually managed to build fair-sized bonfires, because they were proud of their accomplishments and didn't want others to think that they weren't coping.

Living in the village was a boy named Von. He was a lively child with a great imagination. He would construct play-things with all sorts of bits and pieces. He was well liked by the other children because he could transform the most boring afternoon into an adventure or a game, and he never got himself, or anyone else, into trouble.

One day, his uncle asked him to help with the collection of sticks from the forest to make the bonfire. This was the first time that Von had been involved in preparing for the Night of the Flames and he took it very seriously.

Later, his uncle remarked to Von's father, 'Thaat boy shud be the chief foire builder—he worked very hard.'

It was an idle comment meant to make Von feel good, but it did much more than that. For the remaining days until the mid-winter,

Von took every opportunity to collect sticks and place them on the growing pyre.

When the time came to light the pyre, one freezing night when everyone huddled close to the mound of sticks and logs, the flames quickly consumed the kindling that Von had carefully placed deep inside, and in no time at all, the bonfire was raging and turning the night red.

It was a spectacular fire, and the citizens of the village stayed and chatted for hours as the bonfire subsided into a glowing bed of coals.

For weeks afterwards, Von heard bits of gossip about how impressed neighbouring villages had been with the intensity of the blaze. He vowed then that he would help to make every Night of the Flames as big a success.

And, he did; each year, his tireless work and careful construction of the pyre ensured that the village always stood out brightly on the Night of the Flames.

When Von turned fifteen, a distant relative invited him to become a crewmember on a merchant ship that plied the waters of the Baltic Sea. To an imaginative young man like Von, it was an irresistible offer, and in a short time he had packed and said his goodbyes. The entire village came out to bid him farewell as he trundled out on a horse-drawn cart. He was well liked, and his cheery resourcefulness would be missed.

Von was away for twenty years. In that time, many of the older villagers had passed away, and while none of the younger generation had ever met him, they had heard about him. Von's deeds had become legendary. The older folk talked about him with great fondness and, over time, the stories of his bonfires became exaggerated out of all proportion.

Some told of how one winter the flames were so intense that

they lit up the clouds for miles around.

People love a good story.

The day that Von returned to the village, there was great rejoicing. He was surprised, but also very heartened at the outpouring of so much affection for him. He decided to quit his life at sea and stay in the village to look after his ageing parents.

When the first clutch of winter's icy fingers gripped the land, the people boarded up their houses. Some worked on their looms, weaving superb cloths, while others sat beside huge baskets of raw wool and spun thin strands of yarn. Naturally, they spoke about how wonderful it was going to be on the Night of the Flames now that Von was back.

Von didn't disappoint. He was a strong man, capable of carrying much bigger logs out of the forest. And, he had learnt a lot about building things, so constructing a bonfire was a very simple task. On the night of mid-winter, the villagers trudged up the hill in deep snow and marvelled at the intricate bonfire that Von had built. It wasn't necessarily so big, but it was cleverly shaped to make a very powerful blaze.

Just before midnight, a strong wind whipped up and hurled flurries of snow in all directions. The snow settled on the kindling and blew into people's coats and scarves. When it was time to light the pyre, Von had a hard time getting the flint to strike a light, and when it did, the kindling was too wet to ignite. Von did his best to bundle up some dry material, but the villagers were freezing, and there was a real risk that the children would catch a cold. So, the gathering trudged back down the hill. Von was left alone to stare at the pinpoints of light from other bonfires on the horizon.

The next day, the villagers were full of consolation. 'It wasn't your fault,' they said, 'it was just bad luck.'

The winter eventually blew out and spring restored hope to everyone, including Von. He was determined to make up for his failure and vowed that the next Night of the Flames was going to be very memorable indeed, because all he had to do was to add to the existing pyre on the hill.

Well, things conspired against him. On the first day of winter, just when Von thought it would be a good time to prepare the bonfire, he climbed the hill only to discover that many of the villagers had used the wood from the bonfire for their fireplaces. There was nothing left of the pyre except some pieces of bark. So, Von went into the forest and began collecting wood. By mid-winter, he had built only a smallish pyre, but it was of particularly hard, dry wood and he felt confident that it would make a lively blaze.

On mid-winter eve, when everyone was beginning to feel the excitement leading up to the night of the Flames, a terrible incident occurred in the village. An adventurous little boy, seeking a good place to hide during a game with his friends, had fallen into the well. They raised the alarm, and in no time at all, villagers crowded around the well with coils of rope and slings. They could hear the boy calling from deep down and knew that they had only a short time to rescue him before he succumbed to the cold. Quite a few of the men volunteered to be lowered down the well, but either they were too old and not fit enough, or too young and not experienced enough for such a dangerous operation.

When Von arrived from atop the hill, after having made a few last-minute adjustments to the pyre, the villagers quickly led him to the well and began strapping him up in preparation for being lowered.

Von descended into the black depths of the well. It was ominously quiet beneath him, and there was no response from the little boy when Von called his name.

He touched the water surface and felt around.

71

Nothing.

From his experience as a sailor, Von knew that there was still hope to save the boy, because in such cold water, the body can survive for a surprisingly long while.

Von called up for more slack on the rope. He entered the icy water. The well wasn't that wide, but it was deep. Von took a big breath and plunged underwater. Using the rough stonework as hand-holds, he pushed himself downwards. He knew he only had one chance—he himself would lose consciousness within minutes in the frigid water. Down, down he went—better to go down as far as he could and meet the boy on the way up than to search slowly and have the body sink below him. A fleeting touch of cloth alerted Von to the position of the boy. He braced himself against the side and reached out. In utter blackness, he collided with the body. With his lungs aching for air, Von held the boy around the chest and pushed upwards with his legs. The drag of the body slowed his accent and Von had already inhaled some water when he broke the surface. Though he was coughing mightily, Von managed to secure the boy in a sling. On his command, the townsfolk commenced hauling. When the boy was retrieved, it was Von's turn to be winched up. He barely retained enough consciousness to stop himself from bashing against the side. Once he had rolled off the rim of the well onto the ground, he knew he still had one more duty to perform. None of the villagers knew how to resuscitate a drowned person—Von was the only one. He forced himself to his feet and thrust his way through the wailing throng surrounding the young lad. He rolled the boy over, so that much of the water inside him gushed out. Then, opening up the airways, Von puffed his own exhausted breath into the boy's mouth, whose heart was still beating strongly. Von knew, from his time at sea, that it was just a matter of time before the boy began to inhale again. When the boy spluttered and cried out, there was much rejoicing. Shaking and shivering, he was taken inside and placed in a tub of warm water.

Von's wife, Mika, wrapped blankets around her husband and led him home. He had saved the boy—but up on the hill, the pyre remained unlit.

The inhabitants of the little village were full of admiration and praise for Von's courage and resourcefulness. However, in the following months, Von couldn't help but feel a sense of failure each time he overheard a story about the disappointing showing on the Night of the Flames.

Unbelievably, the next year, after Von and a supportive cohort of villagers had added to the existing pyre, the Night of the Flames went by without the bonfire being lit.

The reason?

A mighty meteorite shower that loomed over the landscape for hours and hours and spread its green swirls from one horizon to the next had terrified the townsfolk.

When it was over, it was past the hour of the Flame.

Incredibly, events conspired year after year to thwart the lighting of the ever-growing pyre. Sometimes it was natural causes—a late rainy season that made everything sodden, or an outbreak of disease where the villagers were too afraid to mix in crowds. Sometimes it was just bad luck, such as the time Von was detained, for complex reasons, in the capital city and couldn't get back in time for the Night of the Fires, and the villagers decided not to set fire to the pyre out of respect for the amount of work that Von had put into it over the years.

And, the time that the army decided to bivouac in the area and forbad anyone to move about after dark.

And, the time... no, what's the point? There were always good reasons why the bonfire remained unlit. It was just so very, very frustrating for Von, that the forces of nature and the forces beyond nature, conspired so unequivocally to deny him the opportunity to validate his calling to the village.

After a while, it became a bit of a joke. Then it became a bad joke. Eventually, it became a forbidden subject—it was as though Von was cursed.

Not that the village suffered. In fact, it went from strength to strength, a lot of it due to Von's resourcefulness and imagination in solving the little everyday problems that afflict any working community. People began to forget about the Night of the Fires; they were prospering quite well and didn't need a midnight occasion in the middle of winter to confirm that. In fact, the tradition was losing support in other villages as well, because the roads were getting so much better and people seemed to be moving about the countryside more freely, picking up the news from far and wide.

But each year, Von added to the now enormous pyre, dragging the logs with fatalistic determination, waiting to see what it would take to thwart him setting fire to it—such as the rumour of a band of robbers waiting for people to desert their houses—that was four years previously and no one had left their home. Then there was the false claim of a gold strike in a nearby ravine—that was years ago too, and all the men of the village hastened off with picks and shovels only to return a week later starving and half dead with fatigue. Once there was an eclipse of the moon, and everyone was too frightened to venture outside. Rogue packs of starving wolves— that happened one year. The coronation of the new Queen in 1887— requiring everyone to line the road for hours and hours as the royal carriage returned to the winter castle. The royal censes—required everybody to be in a house at the stroke of midnight. The closing of the main road by a landslide, where every able-bodied person had to work through the night to clear it. And who could forget the addition of an extra day to the year to bring the calendar into line with the celestial movements, creating confusion and arguments across the country as people grappled with which month it was that the day was being added to, and whether there was a thirty-second day of the previous month or a zero-day of the subsequent month. The villagers remained divided on that issue for an entire year until the next Night of the Flames was announced, which occurred when the village was visited by a troupe of minstrels whose suggestive fol-de-la-de-roll lyrics didn't fool anyone, and the menfolk made sure that daughters and wives didn't leave the house.

Von grew old.

One Night of the Flames, Von's wife made her lonely way to the top of the hill and sat down next to her husband. They gazed out over the dark horizon. Mika hugged her man. 'Tonight, is the first radio broadcast from the other side of the world. Everyone is crowded into the tavern. They won't come up the hill.'

Von didn't even bother nodding; he already knew what had been ordained; the hulking pyre was to remain unlit as it had been for decades. He held Mika's hands and squeezed her through four layers of fur and wool. The emotion flooded through his body and gripped his throat. He tried his best to tell his wife. 'Where does all the ardour go?... all the passion and dedication?... the vision that drove me onward for years and years? It burst from my heart and powered my body... every flash of inspiration, every stroke of genius that went into making this the best bonfire in the land... where does it reside? Has it just dissipated into nothing? Surely, there must be something left of the dream in some realm of the cosmos. I can't have done all of this and not made an impact in some, some way.' He buried his face in his wife's thick coat and sobbed. He wasn't ashamed. Mika had always supported him, and she had known for a long time that this was coming. She hugged her husband closer. There was nothing she could do; she didn't know the answer.

Then, deep inside the mouldering tangle of logs at the bottom of the pyre, Mika saw a movement. She spoke to Von. They peered into the shadows of moonlight. A fox appeared and shook flakes of snow off its coat. Then it trotted down the hill towards the village. Soon after, a fat badger muscled his way towards a pile of decomposing timber and began clawing at it. In no time at all, it was licking at grubs and worms that fell out of the rotting wood.

It was then that Von realised he had created a massive ecosystem that towered thirty feet into the air with a base the size of a house.

The next morning, Von and Mika went back up the hill and sat on their favourite log. They inspected the pyre closely. It had become inhabited by hundreds of different creatures. Birds and other animals found protection from the bitter cold in the tangled recesses of the piled timber. When they looked closely, they could see nests everywhere. As well, the birds had introduced the hard seeds of the Yew tree which were establishing themselves in protected hollows around the perimeter. Von spied a Larch seedling higher up in the pile of rotting wood. The pyre was being colonised by the wildlife.

'This is where all the ardour has gone,' Mika whispered to her husband, '... in creating life where previously there was nothing but a bare hill.'

It was true—the enormous, twisted jumble of timber was slowly rotting down, consumed by funguses, tunnelled by insects and broken up by animals. In its midst, new life was born, vital and opportune.

Von decided that he would no longer add to the pyre—instead, he and Mika would protect this curious mound of nature by declaring it a reserve. Von built curving stone walls with viewing benches which helped to deflect the bitter wind from the delicate saplings. In just a few years, the pyre would change colour every spring from grey to verdant green. Pointy spruces and firs rose to meet the clouds, a few oaks began to spread their supple young boughs outwards and flowering vines and shrubs completely shrouded the timber skeleton.

Nowadays, if you're travelling on the M-35, you will see the extraordinary sight of a modest hill with the most spectacular green blaze on the summit. If you have the time, you should take the little road to the top and seat yourself on one of the cool, stone benches. You will find yourself surrounded by blooming life, and you will feel a little of the ardour that never disappeared, but that was simply transformed.

If you're lucky enough to meet someone from the nearby village, they might tell you Von's story and how, at the end of his life, he and Mika would sit on the stone bench and watch the flames of green vegetation lick skyward.

They say that all good endeavours remain in the world.

The Monkey's Gift

Long, long ago, in a soft world of moss and dripping leaves, there lived thousands and thousands of pink creatures who all looked pretty much the same.

They were smallish, hairless, snub-nosed little puddings who meandered about on stout legs and nibbled endlessly on the delicate ferns that grew underneath the tall trees. They all got on well with each other because the forest was vast and there was plenty of food.

The thousands of pinkish little beings ambled and rolled about—whichever was easiest—on the carpet of spongey moss and would fall asleep in an instant, and dream about... being something else.

They would wake up, with their button eyes wide open, and remember the magnificent animal they had been in their dream.

'That's what I want to be!' chortled one in a croaky voice.

'I had such a wonderful dream!' said another, 'I was so big...'

'... and so strong,' added someone else.

'I had colours that I didn't even know existed,' exclaimed another pink creature in wonderment as she rubbed the sleep from her eyes.

None of the small, hairless creatures was surprised by their dreams—they all had them. Nor were they embarrassed to talk about them.

'I was awesome... frightening.'

'I had claws.'

'I had fangs.'

'I had rows of pointed teeth.'

'I had wings as wide as branches, and I flew above the trees.'

'I had talons that ripped and tore.'

'I was pretty.'

A few rotund individuals raised petite eyebrows.

'... in an exotic, flamboyant way!'

... whereupon they nodded and shaped their tiny mouths into pouts of approval.

Yes, all of them had amazing dreams that they would talk about endlessly.

They didn't want to be pinkish—they wanted to be bright and colourful.

They didn't want to be round and harmless—they wanted to be lean and dangerous.

And they didn't want to nibble moss—they wanted to be fearsome predators.

And they certainly didn't want to chortle to each other—they wanted to be loud and raucous.

The little pink creatures slept a lot because their dreams gave them so much to talk about.

One day, a rumour began that a strange visitor had arrived in the forest. He called himself Monkey, and it was said that he could make dreams come true.

Before long, hundreds of pink creatures began to trundle to the site of a large tree in which Monkey was sleeping. When they arrived, they shuffled together in a tight crowd. The rubbing of their bare, pink skin against each other made squeaking sounds, much like balloons do when rubbed together.

After a while, Monkey roused from his snooze. 'What's with the squeaking?' he mumbled. He stretched and yawned and looked down from his branch.

Hundreds of pairs of button eyes blinked expectantly from a sea of pink.

'Yikes!' said Monkey in alarm. 'What are you doing here?'

None of the pink creatures replied. The squeaking just got louder as they chafed against each other with excitement.

Monkey put his hands over his ears. 'Oh, man... this is crazy. Go away!' he demanded.

But the little round creatures remained, packed in tight.

One of them pointed a chubby paw. 'Look! He's got a long tail.'

There were gasps of amazement.

'Look how long his arms are!' exclaimed another.

'... with nimble fingers!'

'... and fur all over. How wonderful!'

One creature squeaked particularly loudly as he turned around and proclaimed to his friends, 'He can climb trees... how awesome is that?'

Lots of little creatures clapped with glee and jumped up and down—and squeaked, of course. They called out to Monkey—

'... show *me* how to do that.'

'... I want to climb trees too.'

'... my arms are too short—can you make them longer?'

'... can you make me furry?'

... and so on, and so on.

Monkey waved for quiet. The creatures hushed. There was a squeak from somewhere.

'Can we *please* lose the squeaking?' sighed Monkey.

'We have to breathe,' came a chortle in the crowd.

Monkey gave a grim smile. 'Okay... so, what? Why are you all here?'

Someone answered. 'We've been told that you can change us... make us better... like in our dreams.'

Monkey clicked his tongue and rolled his eyes. 'No... I can't do that. I don't have the power to change you. You are what you are.'

The little button eyes squinted malevolently. Some of the creatures sucked in a big breath and let themselves sag against their neighbour. An unbearable screeching now emitted from the crowd.

Monkey waved frantically. 'Okay, okay!' he bellowed at the top of his voice. 'Please... just stand still.'

The rotund, stout-legged creatures stood still.

Monkey breathed a big sigh. '*Right*,' he said to himself, '... *these little dumplings are obviously determined to change themselves. What can I do?*'

The sea of pink blinked here and there and waited patiently.

Monkey leaned against a convenient branch. He gazed down and massaged his jaw. One of the little creatures had a particularly expectant look and seemed to be quivering with anticipation.

Monkey harked back his head and looked down his nose. 'So, tell me... what would *you* like to have?'

With a slight tremor in its chortle, the snub-nose being raked the air with a tiny paw. 'I want huge, sharp claws, and I want to be stronger than any other creature in the forest... and I want...'

'Yeah, okay, okay,' interrupted Monkey, '... I get it—you want to be magnificent and feared, and a top predator.'

'Oh, yes,' gurgled the excited creature, '... that's exactly what I want to be.'

'Fair enough,' said Monkey, and rolled his eyes again. '*Now*,' he said softly to himself, '... *they seem to be very impressionable little things—perhaps, if I say it convincingly enough, they will believe that they have changed. I'll have to give them all a special name... let me see...*'

Then, Monkey stood up straight, swelled out his chest, goggled his eyes and twisted and twined his supple fingers. He looked ridiculous, but the pink creatures were immensely impressed.

Monkey's voice rang out through the forest. 'You are Tiger... with claws like knives and teeth like daggers. Your roar will be a reminder that you are king of the forest, and all shall tread in fear of you.'

The portly little being almost fainted with delight, 'I am Tiger!' he trilled, swiping menacingly at the air.

In a rush, the other creatures pushed forward.

'I want to have claws too!' said one.

'You shall... you shall,' chanted Monkey, '... for you are Lion the magnificent... the proudest and fiercest animal of the grasslands...'

'... and me! I want claws and teeth and...'

'*You* shall have claws as sharp as oysters and teeth like thorns, and you will be known as Panther.'

One little creature clambered over the one in front. 'I want to be a Panther—but faster!'

Monkey held his arms wide and took a long breath to give himself some time to think. 'You shall... you shall... for you will be the fastest beast on the land, and you will be known as Cheetah.'

A number of pink creatures flung their paws into the air as they tried to draw attention to themselves.

'*I* want to be Lion...'

'*I* want to be Tiger...'

'*I* want to be...'

'Hang on, hang on,' said Monkey irritably, '... you can't all be lions and cheetahs and things—they have already been taken. You have to think of something different... something original.'

'Oh, I know, I know,' came a chorus of replies.

'You then,' droned Monkey, wondering whether he was ever going to get some breakfast.

The creature spoke up. 'Can you make me very strong... with claws, yeah... and vicious teeth...'

82

'But *different*...' reminded Monkey.

'... oh, and a thick coat, and I can stand tall on my hind legs.'

'It is done,' intoned Monkey, '... for you are the fearsome Bear, guardian of the mountains and shredder of bark.'

Away went another pink creature, flexing his fleshy arms and growling heartily.

But the crowd was becoming very unruly and Monkey could barely hear himself think.

'Let's be orderly about this,' he insisted, and he held up his arms to indicate that the creatures should form a queue. 'The line starts here,' he pointed to one lucky creature who used his chunky elbows to make sure he stayed at the front.

'... and remember,' Monkey scowled, '... no copying your friend's features... you have to think of your own original bits and pieces... beaks, feathers and whatever.'

That started a whole new outburst of ideas which Monkey shushed with a raised hand. 'Okay, you,' he said, pointing to the first in line, '... what would you like?'

The pink creature turned and looked at the others in the long queue and pouted smugly. 'I want to have a wickedly hooked beak to catch my prey,' he said, '... and eyesight so good that I can see a tiny pebble from way up in the clouds.'

'Good, very original,' complimented Monkey, who was starting to feel *very* hungry, '... for you will be Eagle, prince of the sky, with wings so wide, they will stretch from horizon to horizon.'

The little creature was delighted and leapt away, furiously flapping his arms.

Monkey then had an idea. 'I want every second creature in the queue to go out and find me a piece of fruit. When you come back, your friend will have saved your spot, and then *they* can go out and get some fruit. Okay? So everybody has to give me a piece of fruit... no fruit, no wish.'

The little pink creatures understood this perfectly, and every second one bustled off into the forest in search of Monkey's breakfast. When they returned with their piece of fruit, the others did the same. Soon there was a long queue of pink creatures, each holding a piece of fruit.

'That's more like it,' chuckled Monkey to himself. He climbed down from the tree and found a comfortable position at the base of some giant tree roots. 'Okay,' he said, '... who's next?'

A plump creature stepped forward holding a ripe fig in her short arms.

Monkey took it graciously. 'What is your wish, pink creature?'

The dumpy little thing put her hands on where her hips would be if you could see them and looked thoughtfully at the dappled sky. 'Well... first of all, I want to be pure white...'

'Uh huh,' said Monkey, '... pure white. Nice.'

'Feathers!' she exclaimed suddenly, recalling a dream she'd had, '... pure white feathers...'

'Done!'

'... and a long and graceful neck, and wings like wisps of cloud...' she added dreamily.

'That sounds gorgeous,' nodded Monkey approvingly, '... for you shall be Swan, world traveller and the seeker of spring lakes.'

The creature gazed rapturously into the distance and the one next in line had to give her a hefty shove so that he could get his wish.

'I want... sorry... I would like—oh, here's your banana...'

'Thank you.'

'... I would like to be the most massive animal in the forest... really, really big.'

'Is that all?' enquired Monkey, '... no particular colour... other feature?'

The little thing put a finger to his lips and thought hard. 'No...

84

that's all... big—really big.'

'Okay,' said Monkey, '... you *will* be big... far bigger than any other forest dweller, and you shall be the giant called Elephant... but unfortunately, you're going to be just plain grey. Is that alright?'

Newly named Elephant looked a tiny bit upset about being just grey.

'I'll tell you what,' said Monkey, '... I'll give you a special feature—a trunk. You'll be the only one with a trunk and, believe me, that can be very useful.'

This made the pink creature very happy, and he trundled off, wriggling his snub-nose.

Naturally, when those nearby heard about the trunk, they wanted one too.

'Oh, yes!... me too... I'd like a trunk.'

'And me!'

Someone rude at the back yelled out, 'I don't know what a trunk is, but I *want* one!'

'Hold your horses!' shouted Monkey, '... no one else can have a trunk, okay! Just Elephant... he's the only one. Now, stop pushing and get back into line!'

The little pink creatures did as they were told and became very quiet.

At last, someone chortled, 'What's a horse?'

The other creatures nodded and looked meaningfully at Monkey.

Monkey looked surprised. '... a ho... a horse?'

'Yesss...' a hundred creatures responded softly.

'Did I say, horse?... I wonder... did I?' Monkey stalled.

'You definitely said, horse,' someone nearby replied, '... what is it?'

'Oh, well... Horse, you see,' Monkey began, annoyed with himself for having blurted out a made-up name, '... is... um...' his eyes rolled from side to side under his shaggy brow, '... is a... a magnificent, regal animal that, ah... holds up its head with pride. Yes! That's what Horse is—a proud and noble beast... and fast too.'

'I want to *be* one!' shrieked a little pink thing right in front of Monkey.

'Well, of course you do,' said Monkey. 'Where's my fruit? Thank you. I name you Horse... now, off you trot then.'

Now they *all* wanted to be Horse, and Monkey had to think hard as they came to him with their fruit.

'You can be Pony... with a swishing tail and a flying mane...'

'... and you can be ah, Draught Horse... incredibly strong and splendid...'

'... Shetland Pony for you... sorry about the size... cutest eyes, though, and able to survive the harshest weather...'

... and so on until Monkey became exhausted.

He proclaimed solemnly, 'Pink Creatures, we will resume after I have had some breakfast. Thank you for the lovely fruit.' Then he wriggled into a comfortable nook amongst the tree roots and pulled apart a ripe paw-paw.

The little beings conversed amongst themselves, coming up with wonderful new ideas.

'I'm thinking of a patchwork pelt sort of covering in subdued browns and greys maybe...'

'Oh, lovely, yes... I prefer the mixed tones—no bright colours for me.'

'... although,' pondered one creature, '... I'm envisaging delicate wings, right... with bright hues of yellow and red with an iridescent blue outline.'

'Wow! That's really out there. You'll be very conspicuous.'

'Well, I hope so... I'd like to be noticed.'

'Me too... and just to make sure I get everyone's attention, I'm going to have a really loud voice... sort of ringing, echoing bellow that can be heard kilometres away.'

'Awesome... yeah, I'm not sure what I want, but I do want to be comfortable, y'know... have the comforts of home close by at all times. I'm thinking of asking whether I can carry my home with me wherever I go.'

'Sounds ideal... what a great idea! Not easy for me, though, because I want to be super tall, so that I can see over everything. I guess I just want to poke my head into everyone else's business.'

There was laughter all round.

'*You'll* be a pain in the neck!'

'Not *my* neck, I hope!'

'Ha, ha, ha...'

It wasn't long before Monkey stood up and called for everyone's attention. 'Right, now make sure you've got your idea firmly in your mind. We don't want to be here all night—it'll become too dark to see.'

A few heads in the crowd turned.

'Now *that* would be a handy feature—see in the dark!'

'Count me in.'

The queue started to move again. Monkey could be heard conferring the wishes of each little being.

'... a howl! Excellent. I call you Wolf, hunter over snow, stalker of the timberland.'

... and...

'... fluttering wings. How unusual. I name you Flutterby... no, wait... Butterfly! Friend of the flowers, snowflake of the sun.'

... and...

'... a home on your back? Uh huh, interesting... for you are Tortoise... um, never out—always at home.'

... and...

'... you want your home on your back too! *Come on, everyone—*

remember, I said *different*... okay? It's hard for me to create things that are the same but different. Work with me, please... now, now, don't cry. Oh, alright. Look, you can have your home on your back, but in all other respects, you're going to be grey and featureless. You okay with that? Yeah? Then, I name you Snail, for whom the journey is more important than the destination.'

Monkey was working hard.

The sun travelled through the dappled dell to the other side of the forest. Still, the queue of pink creatures shuffled patiently along.

Monkey's voice was becoming hoarse.

'... so, I name you Wombat, chunky digger of giant holes.'

'... Seal, acrobat of the frozen seas.'

'... Wasp, tireless builder of mud dwellings.'

'... Snake, ambush predator of the night.'

Twilight enveloped the forest. Most of the little beings had been given their wishes and were running about re-imagining themselves. There were not many left in the queue now, but Monkey was at his wit's end. He had tried very hard to make everyone's dream come true. Now he was exhausted.

Also, he was running out of features.

All the best legs had been taken—powerful, shapely, athletic, supple. All that was left were gangly, knotty, awkward, stumpy.

Wings of all descriptions—feathered, leather, furry, scaly, gossamer. All been done.

Any number of teeth—fangs, tusks, molars, incisors, serrated gums, probosces, mandibles, nippers, chela. Impossible to think of anything else.

Voices! You name it—screeches, squawks and squeals; whines, wails and howls; chirps, cheeps, peeps, twitters, tweets and chirrups; roars, groans, growls, moans, hollers, barks and bellows;

snarls, snorts, yips, yaps and yodels. All been done.

There wasn't a sound left to make—not a whimper, a hiss or a sigh... everything was taken.

And yet, there were still quite a few pink, rolly beings that had dreamed magnificent dreams that they wanted to come true.

Monkey had an idea. 'It's not just about *what* you are, you know... sometimes it's more important to be *where* you are.'

The remaining little pink creatures were showing signs of tiredness. Their faces were blank.

Monkey continued. 'You'd like to be cosy, wouldn't you?'

The beings gathered at Monkey's feet.

'... warm, snug... even when it's raining and snowing...'

Snug sounded nice. They huddled closer.

'I mean, it's all well and good to have magnificent horns... but, you'll find it impossible to snuggle up to your friends. And, it would be spectacular to fly to the far horizons... but, what happens when it rains? You end up dripping wet on the end of a saggy branch, and life isn't so spectacular then, is it? No.'

One little creature spoke up. '*Where* is the snuggest place on earth?'

Monkey breathed a sigh of relief. 'Well... in the earth itself... deep in the soil, where the temperature never varies, and it never blows or rains.'

The little being seemed satisfied with this. 'Then, I want to be a giant, horned, flying predator with a stupendously loud roar that lives in the earth!'

Monkey massaged the bridge of his nose. His head ached. 'No, you can't be a gigantic horned whatever, because all those things have already been taken... I told you. But you *can* live comfortably in the ground... where you will be very snug... and safe.'

'As what?' asked the little pink creature dubiously.

Monkey took a deep breath. 'Well... as a worm.'

The creature raised one tiny eyebrow. 'And what do they look like? Are they spectacular?'

'Ah, no...'

'Are they dangerous?'

'... not as such...'

'Are they impressive?... in any way?... at all?'

Monkey looked at the earnest little face before him. Then the truth hit him. 'Yes,' he said, looking distantly into the darkening forest, '... yes, you are impressive... because without you, the forest would die, and with it, all of the other animals. You tie the earth and the animals together so that life can flourish. You are the humblest creature with the most exalted purpose in this world.'

The little pink being's chest filled. She blinked away any doubts and made up her mind. 'Then I shall be a worm!' she said proudly.

Monkey leant forward and gave her a little kiss on the top of her pink head. 'Henceforth, you will be Earth Worm... builder of fertile soils and recycler of all living things.'

Newly named Earth Worm squirmed with delight and wriggled herself deeper into the soft soil.

Monkey had a few more wishes to bestow—most of the recipients being less than happy with the outcome;

—the blind, tunnelling mole, who managed to convince Monkey to give him claws except that he couldn't see them.

—the sloth who forgot his piece of fruit and had to accept a pelt like a carpet and claws that were only good for hanging from a branch.

—and the pig, who was absolute last and had to remain pink and round with a snub nose, but who was so disgruntled and squealed so loudly, that Monkey hurriedly gave him a curl in his tail just to shut him up.

... and one other little pink being that staggered out of the forest with the most delicious red berry in her tiny paws.

'I hope I'm not too late,' she said anxiously 'I was looking for the nicest piece of fruit in the whole forest and I think I found it.' She triumphantly held out the berry.

Monkey's heart was filled with gratitude. What a thoughtful gesture. This little pink creature had gone out of her way to make him happy.

But what could he give her in return? All the best features, all the most remarkable traits, the finest qualities, the most awesome attributes... were taken. He had just sent away the pig with nothing more than a curly tail!

Monkey was beside himself with remorse. He was tired, sure... but here was the most selfless little being, who deserved something wonderful, and he had nothing left to give. What could he do?

He dropped his head into his hands.

What could he do?

Monkey felt a little tickle at his elbow. He looked up.

The little pink being was stroking his arm. 'I understand,' she said, '... I was gone a long time, and now, all of the dreams have been taken.'

Monkey was on the verge of crying. '... yes...' he croaked, '... all of the dreams *have* been taken. There is nothing left.'

Every nook and cranny had been filled by birds, insects, reptiles and mammals. Every wish, no matter how bizarre, had been granted—hooks, suckers and stings; venom, stranglers and parasites; hibernators, hermaphrodites, humpbacks... all taken.

There was definitely no chance of granting her a delicate wing or a shapely leg; a lovely eye or a splendid tail. All *those* animals were out there preening and grooming themselves. Even the warthog was making herself more attractive with a thick layer of mud.

Monkey was at a loss.

The little being dropped her hand from Monkey's arm and looked forlorn. 'I will stay as I am,' she said, '... I don't mind.'

91

Monkey shook his head in his hands. 'No... you can't live in the forest anymore—you will be defenceless,' he sobbed. 'Look, it won't be long before all the other creatures actually change into what they believe they are. You will be surrounded by predators—pythons, hawks, hyenas, camels... no, not camels, but lots of other dangerous beasts will be out to get you. It won't be safe anywhere.'

'Then,' said the little thing softly, '... I will hide where no one will find me.'

'No, no, no,' said Monkey impatiently, '... like I said, every nook and cranny has been occupied. There is *nowhere* for you to hide.'

A fat tear rolled down the little pink being's chubby cheek. 'What will become of me?' she squeaked.

Monkey pounded his forehead with his fist. 'Think, Monkey!... think!...'

Then, miraculously, with a last spark of genius, Monkey had an idea. 'I know!' he said.

The little being's eyes widened. She wiped away the tear with a plump finger.

Monkey stood. He looked into the distance. There was just enough light for him to walk around without bumping into a tree. 'There is a place,' he mused, with a knuckle to his lips, 'that no one wants to go near. A place that is safe... and warm... with plenty of food. A place that appears everywhere, all of the time... that is out of the blizzard, out of the hot sun... that is moist and comfortable...'

The little being was beside herself with excitement. 'Oh, where?... where?... where is this perfect place?'

Monkey paused and sat back down. He took a very deep breath and didn't exhale for ages.

A small frown of worry began to grow on the pink creature's brow. 'What's wrong?' she said uncertainly, '... why hasn't this place been taken by one of the *other* creatures?'

At last, Monkey breathed out. 'Ah, well... here's the thing,' he said, and he reached out and held the little being by her round shoulders. 'This place... this perfect place that is safe and secure... is,' his eyes grew large with hope, '... this place is.. under a pile of poo...'

The pink creature's multiple chins dropped. She glowered at Monkey from under her brow. 'Under a pile of poo, you say?'

'Now, hear me out,' said Monkey, holding up his hands in defence. 'I'm aware that, on the surface, this doesn't sound like such a great idea...'

'You're right about that!' said the little being, tightly folding her arms.

'... but... you have to look at the big picture...'

'... from under a pile of poo?'

Monkey was beginning to wonder whether his idea was so brilliant after all. 'Well, yes... from under a pile of poo. But consider this—you will be out of the rain, hail and snow...'

'... but I'll be covered in poo.'

'But it will be your *home*! And, get this—you'll be able to choose your poo!'

'That's a good thing, is it?'

'Well, of course, it is! I mean, half the animals out there spend all day stuffing themselves with grass and most of it doesn't even get digested properly. There's heaps of food in their poo—seeds, flowers, little organisms... and it's all yours!'

Monkey could see that the little pink creature was becoming interested.

She loosened her arms. '... and I'll be completely safe?'

'Completely! Absolutely safe. None of the other animals want to go anywhere near poo... they're always trying to avoid it. "Oops, nearly stepped in some poo!" "Did I just sit on some poo?"'

The little pink creature smiled. She was starting to see the benefits of living under a pile of poo. 'And, you said something about it appearing all of the time, everywhere.'

Monkey clasped his hands. 'Yes, of course! Animals are always roaming around, absentmindedly pooing all over the place. Think about it!... herds of Wildebeest covering the grasslands in steaming, handy homes for you... one elephant poo could be your home for the best part of a year! Then there are horses, bison, giraffes, zebras, antelope... need I go on? Each one of them will make a home for you *every* day! *Every* day you will have a warm, cosy home with ample food, and no one will threaten you or prey on you... you will be left alone to enjoy life with your family.'

The little being laced her fingers and looked down. 'Who will want to be my friend, if my home is a pile of poo?'

'*Oh, boy,*' thought Monkey, '*... tough question.*' He steepled his fingers and nodded thoughtfully. 'Well, the fact is that, in a way, all of the animals will be your friend... I mean, not the sort of *come inside and we'll have a cup of tea* type of friend—oh, well the worm, maybe— but more the quiet, respectful, slightly distant sort of friendship that you will build with all of the animals, because if it weren't for you and the worm, the whole world would soon be metres deep in poo... and absolutely *everyone* is very grateful that you're taking care of *that* problem. And anyway, who wants to be friends with a bunch of preening, self-satisfied, show-offs who only think of themselves? You and the worm will have a wonderful friendship.'

Monkey could detect a growing interest in the picture he was painting. But, there was still the matter of...

'There is a downside, however,' he pronounced gravely.

The little button eyes looked up. 'A downside?... to living in a pile of poo? Whatever could you mean?'

Monkey gave her a look. 'Now, now... don't be sarcastic. But seriously, the trade-off to having the perfect living conditions is that you can't be pretty.'

'Well, I'm not so pretty now,' said the paunchy little creature, '... so, in reality, nothing will change.'

Monkey was moved by this logic and nodded deeply. 'I'm glad to hear you say that. That's very mature of you... yes it is. Your name, by the way, will be Dung Beetle... should you choose to accept.'

It was almost completely dark now. Somewhere out amongst the trees, newly named Bat was trying out his night vision, with only the occasional bump and squeal to be heard.

Monkey held the little pink creature's hand. 'Are you ready to become your dream?' he asked. 'You will either always regret becoming a Dung Beetle, or you will never *ever* regret becoming a Dung Beetle—you will either always hate the idea of living under a pile of poo, or you will celebrate the advantages for all of your life. What do you think?'

The little pink thing thought and smiled. 'Will there be a creature living under *my* poo?'

Monkey laughed. 'Yeah, the worm, I suppose...'

'Well, that's alright then.' She reached out and hugged Monkey. 'I'm ready to become a Dung Beetle.'

Monkey's voice was full of emotion. 'Little pink thing,' he said, '... you will be the luckiest creature in the animal kingdom. The other animals will make a home for you every day. I pronounce you Dung Beetle, saviour of the environment, a friend to all, and the only living thing without an enemy in the world.'

Newly named Dung Beetle felt a great relief, having at last found such a splendid niche... and so convenient, really—her home just dropped from the sky, ready and waiting for her to inhabit. She had never dreamt of *anything* like this.

She whispered, 'Thank you for my dream, Monkey.'

Reunion

This story takes place one starlit night, in a long, winding valley where all the windows of a rambling old farmhouse are lit with a yellow glow. There is a family reunion going on inside, and just about every room in the house is being used at one time or another. Out on the dewy lawn, the cars are neatly parked against the old slip-rail fence, and in the paddock, the herd of Friesians liberate clouds of steam from their bodies as they lie amongst the tussocks of grass.

One of the windows is that of the main bedroom where Mr and Mrs Geddes have slept and made children for over forty years. Their youngest daughter Denise, who has told all of the guests tonight that she has changed her name to Glow, is standing with her head against the door of the ensuite, listening very intently for noises being made by her son, Spume. He is only three, and he is determined to do a wee unassisted.

'I hope you haven't made a mess on Nanna's toilet,' Denise says. She listens closely for sounds of disaster. 'I'm Glow,' she whispers to herself. 'I'm Glow.' She moves to stand in front of the cheval mirror and admires her profile.

She is short and muscular, ideal farming stock, but to the great disappointment of her parents, she has decided to become a hippie and a vegetarian. She is wearing something she has made herself, despite never before having an interest in fashion, nor acquiring any

96

of her mother's dressmaking skills.

Denise pirouettes in front of the mirror, then checks to see how far up her dress it is possible to see if she bends right over. Her legs are unshaven, but it isn't very noticeable because she is quite blonde.

At this very moment, there are three separate conversations going on in the old family home, that have to do with Denise.

'I'm Glow,' she trills unmusically as she flounces the ragged pleats of her earth-fairy outfit.

One of the conversations dwells on the fact that she was driving tractors and hosing down stalls from when she was in primary school. 'She was the youngest by far,' someone mentions, '... and all the other kids had left home. Never had the chance to be a child. Poor Denise.'

'I'm Glow,' she murmurs. She looks closely at the piercings on her face.

In another conversation, amidst a lot of juvenile sniggering, a well-known story is being retold about how some moronic feral had tattooed 'Demise' onto her back and that, as far as anyone knew, she had never become aware of it.

'I'm Glow.' She pulls down the material of her bodice to reveal the name 'Glow' tattooed above her breast.

The last conversation is being held out in the cold, on the veranda, and goes along the lines of; '... this area was once a farming community, and now it's being overrun by shiftless dole-bludgers and new-age pot-heads who are responsible for corrupting the likes of Denise...'

'I'm Glow,' she implores the mirror as she untangles the hairband of leaves and nuts from her dreadlocks. She is about to repeat her mantra when there is a noise from within the ensuite. She moves to the door.

'Spume!' she calls softly, '... do you want me to come in and help you? Yes?'

She opens the door a little, and her son wriggles through, minus his pants, and leaps straight onto the double bed. Denise rushes into the bathroom and retrieves her son's pants and underpants then rushes back out to grapple with him as he jumps up and down on the bed.

'Spume!' she says sharply, in that tone that mothers overuse until it becomes ineffectual, '... don't be naughty—get off the bed—stop jumping on the bed—let me put on your pants—don't run away. Spume! Put your jumper back on...'

But it's too late; the little terror has escaped into the house.

Denise walks to the door to pick up the jumper. As she bends down she notices a woman entering the doorway. She stands erect.

The newcomer is Claudia, Denise's cousin. Tall and elegant, she is wearing a cocktail dress and stilettos and is in the act of rummaging through a glittering purse.

They stop and stare at one another. They speak at the same time—Claudia with the poised smile that she uses daily in her corporate environment, and Denise with the gape of recognition that she hasn't resorted to for years because she knows everyone in the valley.

'My God,' Claudia says, with a beautifully controlled mouth, '... it's you.'

'Y'kiddin' me!' Denise blurts, thrusting her head forward, '... Claudia!'

They appraise each other for a moment longer, then come together, Claudia with a confident stride and obligatory affection, and Denise barrelling in with unbridled enthusiasm. Claudia winces in her cousin's strong grip. They separate, still holding each other's hands.

Denise swings Claudia's arms in and out and says loudly, 'Jeez, Claudia, you look great!'

Claudia takes a step back and looks Denise up and down.

98

She decorously adds to the swinging of the hands and produces a look of excitement. 'Thank you—and don't you look... free... and everything...' then gushes, 'Denise!' because she has, at last, remembered her cousin's name.

Denise gives Claudia another hug 'I didn't know that *you'd* be here!' She takes Claudia by the hand and drags her to the little settee at the end of the bed. Denise plonks herself down in one corner and watches Claudia settle onto the edge of the cushion without once allowing her knees to separate.

Claudia brushes delicately at her forehead. 'I flew in from Copenhagen last week... but I thought I'd come to the reunion.' She looks about the room and spies Spume's jumper lying on the floor next to the settee where Denise dropped it. She reaches down, picks it up and folds it slowly in her hands, 'How long has it been, Denise?'

Denise lifts her foot up to the seat and chops down at her dress to preserve her modesty. 'Whenever it was, I've changed my name since then—I'm, Glow!'

Claudia nods deeply and nestles the jumper into her lap. 'I can see that—you've really found yourself.' She looks at the doorway, 'And, your son?'

Denise nods proudly.

'... is named... Spume?' Claudia probes with narrowed eyes and a furrowed brow.

'Yeah. Lovely, hey!'

'Really. That's so... unusual...'

Denise lifts the other foot to the seat and hugs her knees. 'I think it was in a poem—*the spume and spray of the wild sea.*'

Claudia hugs the jumper to her belly. 'Oh, by Tennyson, perhaps?'

'Dunno,' Denise says with a smile, '... but I hope he grows up like that... y'know—wild and free.'

'Of course,' Claudia pronounces, '... and, just looking at him, he's well on his way.'

Denise looks at the jumper that Claudia is stroking with her thumb and holds out her hand.

Her cousin smiles self-consciously and hands it over.

'So,' says Denise, with unnecessary assertiveness, '... you got kids?... yet?... married?'

Claudia cups her knees. 'No... no... none of the above. Too busy working... making money—you know how it is.'

'Not really.'

'No? Well...'

They stare at each other while Denise folds the tiny jumper against her bosom. 'It's funny isn't it,' she says, '... how we all turned out so different.'

Claudia gives a vague nod.

'I mean, look at you! So sophisticated. And me... a mum already! It's funny where our life takes us, isn't it...'

Claudia tightens her mouth with emotion then suddenly drops her head into her hands.

Denise reaches out to her. 'Claudia... what's wrong? You're not upset because you didn't turn out like me, are you?'

Claudia shakes her head and gives a little sob.

'I didn't think so.'

Claudia suddenly raises her face and dabs at her eyes with the back of her hands. 'No!... I didn't mean... it's not that I wouldn't want...' She hastily opens her purse and pulls out a small packet of tissues. 'Oh, god... what's happening to me.' She wipes her eyes.

Denise smiles. For a suspended few seconds, she isn't at odds with the forces in her life; her face reveals the natural compassion of a soul on its journey. She is suddenly suffused with excitement. 'You know what I'd really like to do?'

Claudia delicately blows her nose. '... no... what?'

'What we did as kids—remember!'

'No.'

'Trying on each other's clothes!'

'Oh, yes...' Claudia stands and walks over to the cheval mirror and inspects the runs of mascara on her cheeks.

'We even swapped uniforms one day...'

Claudia makes little noises of confirmation as she cleans her face.

'... that was so cool. You just had the smartest uniform—with all those pleats—and a tie and jacket—and a hat!'

Claudia looks at Denise in the mirror and stifles a laugh, 'And you just had the daggiest dress!'

Denise shoots up from the settee. 'Shut up!' she says with feigned outrage, '... private school bitch.'

Claudia spins around and holds Denise's hands. 'I'm sorry, Denise—ah, Glow. Sorry.'

They look at each other.

'We're not exactly the same size anymore, Glow.'

'I know—I'm not expecting to be zipped right up. But I want to know what it feels like to be a corporate gunslinger.'

Claudia steps back and looks her cousin up and down. 'And, I suppose I won't mind going feral... just for the evening.'

Denise gives an excited little jump. 'That's the way, cuz. C'mon, help me with this.' She spins around so that Claudia can unzip her. She pulls the dress up over her head and hands it over.

Claudia holds it out and tries to get the pleats to fold properly. 'It's so...'

'Pretty?' Denise interrupts, '... it's just two recycled dresses... but you'd never know.'

'No... no...'

'... and it's going to look great on you, Claudia—and, if I may be frank...'

'Frank?... I'm just getting used to Glow!' Claudia lays Denise's dress over the bed and turns her back.

'Very funny,' Denise unzips Claudia, '... but I was just going to say, that a little bit of hippie will be good for you.'

Claudia steps out of her dress. 'Do you think so? Why?'

'Because you've never tried it—Mummy and Daddy wouldn't have approved.'

Claudia hefts the earth-fairy dress over her head and lets it drop around her thinness. '... hmmm, yeah... got that in one.' She searches around for the ribbons to tie around her waist.

Denise delicately steps into Claudia's cocktail dress. She shuffles to the mirror and carefully wriggles the material up her body. She pulls the hairband from her head. 'Didn't you ever want to be... y'know, alternative or something when you were at uni?'

Claudia undoes the fancy hair clip that holds her bun in place and shakes out her hair. 'No... no. That was never an option for me.'

'Wow! See—you had options. I just had to make do.'

'Well, I didn't really have options.'

The two women exchange hair adornments.

'Didn't you?' Denise piles up her dreadlocks.

'It's not an option or choice if you're told to aim for the top the whole time.'

Denise raises a disdainful eyebrow in the mirror. 'Yeah, right—I suppose it isn't. And?'

'And what?'

'Did you make it to the top?'

Claudia elbows Denise away from the mirror and settles the leafy hairband in place. 'Well, yes—in a way. I'm on my way to the top.'

'Hey, wow!' Denise cries, sitting on the bed, '... we have the same size feet.'

Claudia looks around and smiles when she sees her shiny black stilettos dangling from Denise's toes.

Denise fixes her cousin with a meaningful eye. 'But you're still desperately unfulfilled?'

'Maybe. Are you fulfilled?'

'Shit no! And I tell you this in the strictest confidence, Miss Killer Claudia—but I reckon that I could be a real ball-tearing, corporate shaker and mover.'

Claudia laughs half-heartedly. 'Is that what you think of me?'

'Nah,' Denise staggers on her high heels to the mirror and commences taking out her piercings. 'You're not really a killer. I can't see you in the cut and thrust of negotiating—boardroom backstabbing an' all that.'

'My power dressing wouldn't fool you, huh?' Claudia looks around for some shoes and then remembers that Denise has been barefoot the whole time. Demurely, she sits down on the settee and crosses her legs in the meditation position. She looks over at Denise, 'You're not expecting me to wear any of that shrapnel, are you?'

'Haven't you got any piercings—anywhere?' Denise asks, suggestively.

Claudia has her eyes closed and is trying to look meditative. 'No.' Her eyes flick open, '*No!* Jeez, Denise!... uh, Glow—now you've got me thinking that *I'm* the gauche one!'

'You're the *what* one?'

'Gauche—unworldly. Just joking.' She runs her fingers through her hair then tries to pull the pleats of the earth-fairy dress straight.

Denise turns from the mirror and bestows a look on her. She smirks. 'You look like the compost fairy.'

Claudia's eyes blaze.

Denise laughs and bends down to hug her. 'Are you ready to cut and thrust with the relies?' she laughs in her cousin's ear.

Claudia's arms come up to embrace Denise.' You are *me* now, Glow... you can do the infighting.'

The old house, usually serenely quiet, resonates to ridiculously loud music as the young ones try to fill the void of countryside with a party ambience. Out on one of the side verandas, Denise and Claudia are slumped together on a small couch, both quite tipsy and being very tactile as they share each other's jokes.

Claudia flounces her fairy dress and says, 'I'm feeling all whimsical. I'm all aglow. No! Wait a minute...'

Denise paws at her, 'I'm Glow! You can be... oh, I know! You can be, Whimsy.'

'Whimsy,' Claudia affirms, '... you may call me— Madam Whimsy!'

'Madam Whimsy!' Denise guffaws.

'Our new company policy,' Claudia begins pompously, '... is... oh, I don't know—you decide.'

'But I'm not feeling whimsical.'

'Ve haf vays off makink you feel vimsical.'

The two of them laugh hysterically, spilling their drinks and upsetting the cracker and dip plate on the armrest.

Sauntering along the veranda is roguish old Uncle Mick, third in line to inherit his family's farm, and instead, becoming a car salesman and town councillor. He steps carefully up to the girls, puts his beer down on the armrest and tries to speak as clearly as possible.

'... evening ladies...'

Denise and Claudia hold their laughter. 'Good evening, Uncle Mick,' they titter.

Uncle Mick, encouraged by the girls' politeness, leans towards them with his hand on the back of the couch and tries to think of a conversation starter. 'Oh, I've made friends with young... ah, young...'

'Spume?' Claudia volunteers.

'That's it! Young Spume.'

Denise crosses her legs and flicks the hem of her cocktail dress. 'His name comes from a poem by Tennyson, you know.'

Claudia makes big eyes and discreetly shakes her head.

'Tennyson, hey!' says Uncle Mick, swaying noticeably. 'I didn't know that... but *there's* a name that's easy to remember.' He decides to abandon this topic and go for something more provocative. 'Now, I've been watching you two,' he slurs.

'And we've been avoiding you, Uncle Mick.'

'What? No, ya haven't. No, I've been watching you two...' Uncle Mick's hand slips between the backrest cushions, and he lurches forward into Denise's face. 'Oh, shit!'

'Watch out, Uncle Mick!'

He pulls himself away, accidentally groping at the girls' legs. 'Sorry... sorry... sorry...' He stands upright again. 'Now, what was I ... oh, yeah—I've been watching... ah... '

Uncle Mick decides that he should make himself comfortable. He picks up his beer and sits down on the armrest. 'Right, that's better.' He assumes his suavest persona and attempts to cross his legs. The momentum from this manoeuvre pitches him across the sofa and onto the girls' laps, from where he ingloriously rolls out onto the floor.

Denise and Claudia squeal with horror.

Uncle Mick struggles hastily to his feet, shakes the spilt beer off his hands and runs his fingers through his hair.

Denise bawls at him. 'Just how close do you need to get?'

He tries to pacify the girls. 'Now, now... calm down, calm down... my apologies—your Uncle Mick has had a bit to drink, and I think I must have overbalanced. No harm done—I'm all good.' He pats himself about the body and kicks the beer glass under the sofa.

'So,' drawls Claudia, '... what did you see?'

Uncle Mick looks alarmed and holds out his hands defensively. 'I didn't see nothin', girls—it was an accident. I didn't see anything.'

Claudia rolls her eyes. 'While you were *watching* us, this evening.'

'Oh,' he says, looking very relieved. He steps closer to the girls, glances left and right, and then hunkers down on one knee. 'Well, I reckon that you two have changed sides—know what I mean?'

'Oh, Uncle Mick,' says Denise, sarcastically, '... that's very observant of you.'

He focuses for a moment on Denise's stiletto dangling in front of his face.

'Huh? Uh, yeah—I'm not pervin', mind… but I know what's going on.'

Just at this moment, Cory, Uncle Mick's son, passes by with a full glass of beer in his hand.

Uncle Mick reaches out to him. 'Cory, give us your beer mate. Thanks… we had a little accident.'

Cory turns and goes back inside.

Claudia squirms coyly. 'And—what do you think is going on?'

Uncle Mick takes a sip. 'Now,' he begins pedantically, '… your old Uncle Mick is a man of liberal persuasion, and I've got no hang-ups at all as far as…' he leans closer, 'you two being, y'know—lesbians.'

'We're not lesbians!' the girls chorus.

Uncle Mick grimaces and cringes. 'Bloody hell! Shut up! Look, it's okay, I'm cool with that, but you don't have to shout it out to the whole, fuckin' family.'

Denise thrusts forward. 'We're *not* shouting it out to the family. We're *not* lesbians, dickhead.' She settles back into the sofa and adjusts the cocktail dress over her knees.

'Oh, fine,' says Uncle Mick peevishly. He takes another swig as he eyes Denise and comes to the conclusion that the girls would probably be up for a bit more provocation, 'Suit yourself, Madam Claudia,' he wipes his mouth with the back of his hand, '… but I bet you're not wearing any underwear. Go on! Prove me wrong.'

Claudia looks across at Denise. 'She's not Claudia—I'm Claudia. And she's not Denise—she's Glow.'

Uncle Mick levers himself to his feet and looks groggily at his beer. 'Shit, I must be pissed.'

Claudia, herself a little cross-eyed, persists. 'Why do you think we're lesbians?'

Uncle Mick waves his hand. 'Nuh, I'm not goin' there. You two are messin' with my mind.'

Denise chimes in. 'You started it!'

Uncle Mick peers at Claudia. 'I could have sworn you were the hippie. And you,' he casts a disapproving eye to Denise, '... are that stuck-up career queen.'

Claudia's eyes twinkle with mischief. 'Actually—you are right, Uncle Mick.' She takes Denise's hand in hers.

Uncle Mick's eyes open wide with triumph. 'See! See! Ya can't fool me... I knew you were lezzos!' He takes a celebratory gulp.

Denise uncrosses her legs. 'So... do you want to have a look?'

Uncle Mick wipes his mouth with his sleeve. 'What?'

'Do you want to see?'

'See what?'

Denise parts her knees a fraction. 'Whether I'm wearing undies.'

Uncle Mick, with the glass to his lips, chokes and abruptly holds his hand to his mouth. 'Orr, fuck,' he says, and looks furtively to see who's around. He moves towards the sofa, then straightens suddenly and puts his hand on his hip, 'Oh, sure... as if Saint Claudia—patron saint of boardroom prick-teasers—is going to oblige me with a gander at the office shrine.'

Denise glowers at her uncle. 'We keep telling ya—I'm *not* Claudia.'

Claudia lifts a knee under the pleats of the earth-fairy dress. 'Do you want to see if *I'm* wearing any undies, Uncle Mick?'

He darts an indifferent glance at Claudia. 'Nah—I *know* you're not wearing any, ya mad hippie.'

Claudia gives a little gasp. '*Denise!*'

Denise looks coyly away.

Claudia turns to Uncle Mick with a withering eye. 'Well, she is now—I saw them!'

Uncle Mick clenches his fist and boxes the air. 'See! Ya are, aren't ya? Try and play games with Uncle Mick, hey! I twigged straight away you two were lezzos.'

Denise rolls her eyes. 'So, if we're lezzos, how come you're here hitting on us?'

Uncle Mick's eyes flash with anger. 'I'm not hit... Jesus, you can be a bitch! I'm just saying that I don't care if you're a lesbian—like, it doesn't worry me, y'know? If you choose to be a perpetual vestal fuckin' virgin for those corporate wankers, I don't blame you for turning to other women.' He turns a contemptuous eye in Claudia's direction, 'Though why you'd want to be with her, I can't imagine.'

Claudia suddenly stands, holding on to Denise's hand for support. 'Just mind yourself, Uncle Mick! You really don't know *who* you're talking to—look at my face! You haven't looked at my face all night!'

Uncle Mick retreats a few steps, conscious of the spectacle that is developing.

Claudia lets go Denise's hand and points at Uncle Mick's face. 'What do you see? Huh! Someone you can dismiss and discard? Someone that you feel comfortable ignoring? I won't stand for it!' Claudia sways tipsily.

Denise rises and stands beside her. She holds onto Claudia's shoulders and whispers in her ear. 'Claudia... Claudia—sweetie.'

Her cousin hasn't finished. 'I don't want to catch you looking straight through me as though I don't exist. I earned my stripes—my input matters too.'

Denise pulls Claudia, who is looking rather disorientated, slowly backwards. 'Hey... hey... c'mon—it's only Uncle Mick. You okay? You getting all that stuff off your chest?' She seats Claudia back into the sofa. 'Feeling better now?'

Uncle Mick composes himself as best he can and slinks away. 'Bloody hell, I'm going home.' he says to everyone around.

Denise hugs Claudia close. 'C'mon, let's go to the bathroom.'

Claudia sits disconsolately on the settee in the bedroom.

Denise, kneeling in front of her, gently wipes the runs of mascara from her cousin's face. She dips her head a little and looks up into Claudia's eyes. 'They won't know you when you get back to the office.'

'Poor old Uncle Mick.'

Denise rises and takes the tissues to the bathroom bin. 'Feel good to stretch the claws?' she calls from the doorway.

Claudia puts her head in her hands. 'I'm so pathetic.'

'No, Claudia. What you said, needed to be said.'

Claudia peers up from her hands. 'He's a bit of a soft target. Do *you* do it very often?'

'What? Stretch my claws?'

'No—go without undies. Just joking!'

Denise looks suddenly pensive. 'He never looks at me. Did you notice?' She plonks herself onto the settee.

'Of *course,* I did!' Claudia puts her arm around Denise. 'I was *you!*'

Denise stares into the distance. 'Everyone thinks they know you. You can never change—no matter how much you try.'

The music has been turned down. The harsh light coming through the doorway of the ensuite makes the two women look strangely exposed and vulnerable.

Claudia focuses on the same distant horizon. 'I've spent my entire life shaping myself into something that, I don't know... is not even respectable. I mean, I'm respected for what I do—but what I do is not worthy. I just want to have a baby—and now I can't, because I haven't got what it takes to be a mum.' Tears brim in her eyes.

Denise takes hold of Claudia's shoulders and confronts her. 'Claudia! What are you saying? Of course, you can be a mum—you'll be a great mum!'

She sniffs and composes herself. 'No... not like you.'

'Bullshit! What makes *me* such a great mum? My kid is running through the party with no pants on.'

'Exactly, exactly,' Claudia says with a tiny smile, '... can you imagine *my* child having so much fun?'

The two women sit in silence for a moment.

Denise slowly shakes her head. 'I don't know if I'm doing the right thing. It's like we're on two journeys here—Spume's and mine...'

'Oh,' interrupts Claudia, '... look who's come to visit us.'

Spume has walked through the open door looking worn out and tired. Claudia puts her arms out to him, and he walks straight into her lap.

'Ahh,' Claudia gushes, '... are you looking for your lovely mother?'

Upon hearing Claudia's unfamiliar voice, Spume looks up. His eyes alternate between Claudia and Denise. He reaches out and grabs a handful of his mother's cocktail dress.

'That silly!' Spume says in a sharp voice.

Claudia holds him gently around his middle. 'That's not silly,' she says, playfully, '... your mother is gorgeous.'

Spume suddenly takes off, but not before Denise grabs him. She attempts, with some difficulty, to put on his jumper. 'Spume! Don't be naughty—just let me—there, all done!'

As soon as Denise lets him go, he shoots out of the doorway.

Claudia bites at her lip. 'Deni... er, Glow. You could have done one thing better.'

'What's that?' Denise responds, taking a deep breath after the exertions with her son.

'Glow, seriously—the poor thing hates his name. *I* hate his name. It's a ghastly name.Whatever possessed you to name your child Spume?' She reaches out and takes hold of Denise's hands. 'The family will never give you that chance... to change—you know what I mean?'

Denise bows her head. She remains still, and a tear falls into her lap.

Claudia strokes Denise's forehead. 'Glow—you have to think of your son's journey as well.'

Denise shudders with a big sigh. 'When I found I was pregnant, I went to the beach. It was a wild, wild day and that line from the poem—at least, I think it's a poem— just came to me. I wanted to make that day mean something for me. And now I've gone and named my son Spume!' Denise drops her head into Claudia's lap.

Through the doorway can be heard the sound of people saying their farewells, and through the window comes the sounds of car engines starting.

Claudia looks distant and comforts Denise. 'It's his name, Glow— it's not *who* he is. He's one of the family. We'll work it out. He's a perfect little boy,' she whispers.

A noise at the doorway pulls Claudia out of her trance.

Uncle Mick comes staggering into the room, prematurely unzipping his fly. 'Oops. Sorry ladies—my mistake. The door was open, and I was just gonna...' he points to the ensuite.

Denise lifts herself from Claudia's lap and dabs at her eyes with her palms. The two of them look blankly at Uncle Mick.

He turns to leave, but hesitates and looks over his shoulder. 'Listen, I'm sorry about my behaviour tonight. I've had too much to drink—but that's no excuse. Sorry.' He looks at Denise's teary face. 'And I'm sorry for what I said to you, Claudia... hey—wait a minute... you're not... you're...'

'... the mad hippie.' Denise finishes.

Uncle Mick shakes his head. 'Shit! I don't know what's going on. Anyway, look, don't worry about me I'm not important in your life. I didn't think I could upset you that much.'

Claudia gives a contrite smile. 'It's not you, Uncle Mick... not just you.'

A little boy scoots around the corner, wraps himself around Uncle Mick's legs, and stands there looking up at him.

'Ahh... young Tennyson! Come on up, m'boy and say cheerio to your Uncle Mick.' He lifts the little feller into the crook of his arm and smiles closely at him.

Denise is perplexed. 'Spume?'

Claudia is in awe. 'Tennyson!' she pronounces with joy.

Uncle Mick walks up to the sofa. 'Yeah, everyone—this is my good mate, Tennyson. He and I go back a long way, don't we, son! Yeah...'

'You... you know the poem,' Claudia declares.

'I don't know any poem! You mentioned, Tennyson.' He looks at Denise. 'Sounds to me like a good name, Deni...er, Glow.'

Spume puts his arms around Uncle Mick and whispers in his ear.

'What's that? You want to show me the cat? Okay then.' He bows deeply. 'Tennyson and I must take our leave, ladies.' They turn and walk towards the door.

Denise stands suddenly. 'Uncle Mick!'

He turns. The old man and the boy look back at the two women.

'Thanks,' says Denise.

'Yeah, no worries.' With the little boy's arm around his neck, the two of them disappear into the house.

Claudia stands beside Denise. They look at each other with barely suppressed jubilation. With a little nod of affirmation, they simultaneously shout, 'Tennyson!' and hug each other joyously.

Superior Inferior

Agent Stuart Cranmore walked briskly down the long corridor and wondered whether the Minister for Foreign Affairs would be in his office at this early hour. He could have slowed his pace, but he'd been advised that, in Parliament House, only ministers and those with some sort of public profile dawdled; everyone else was obliged to be brisk. They were working for the betterment of the nation, after all.

When he arrived at the minister's door, it was open. He could see past the unattended reception desk, that the Honourable Craig Thornton was slouched in a double lounge with his head resting in his palm. Cranmore inferred from the minister's creased coat and the empty Scotch tumbler on the side table that Thornton had been there for some time. He didn't bother to knock, but walked straight in, closed the door behind him and pushed the lock button. He already knew that this briefing would take some time and that it was going to be unquestionably private. He wanted to give the impression that he was utterly conversant with the gravity of the situation and that he was doing everything necessary to mend the damage done, and that included locking doors—though that metaphor seemed futile now.

Cranmore walked around the reception desk, making as much noise as possible on the plush carpet.

Thornton turned his head and directed the agent to one of the other lounge chairs. He waited until Cranmore put down his briefcase and settled himself before heaving a big sigh. 'So, Swain tells me that you're the man who kicked off this imbroglio.'

Cranmore's answer was direct and vital. 'Yes, sir. It started with me.'

Preparing to fall on his sword, thought Thornton. He gave a small wave of his hand. 'You can call me Craig.' Then, with a sudden dismissive gesture of his arm, said, 'No! Fuck it. You can call me sir. I don't want any bullshit here—I want to know the facts.'

Cranmore nodded just the once. 'Yes, of course.'

The minister felt around for his glass, then, seeing it was empty, put it back down with a small grimace of irritation. 'Okay—so, tell me, how did we manage to incite the Indonesians to this degree of anger? Because they are *very* angry.'

The minister's steadfast gaze didn't really worry Cranmore; he'd decided already that, after his sacking, he would buy a cheap yacht and poke around the Top End—do some fishing.

Thornton decided that he really did need another drink and got up and went to a little cabinet against the reception wall. 'Now, the ambassador has told me *what* has happened—but what I need to find out from you—and your boss tells me that you're the man— what I need to find out is exactly *how* ASIO got us into this mess.' As he filled his glass, he took a quick glance at Cranmore's briefcase. 'Please tell me that you're not going to corroborate your story with reams of notes. Because, it's notes that got us where we are—so I've kind of lost faith in the paper trail.'

Cranmore shook his head just the once. 'No, sir. No notes.'

The minister put his drink on the table, slid off his coat and loosened his tie. He lowered himself into the lounge and pried off his shoes. 'You'll have to forgive me, Mr Cranmore—I've been up all night. I do appreciate you seeing me this early, and at such short notice, but I haven't been able to relax knowing that what we have done is tantamount to declaring war. Do you realise that?'

'Yes, sir, I do realise that.'

'Cranmore, were you ever in the army?'

'Yes, sir—communications.'

'Right... right... because you're a bit stiffer than the usual spooks I have to listen to.' He reached over to his coat pocket and pulled out a small voice recorder. 'Now, I'm going to record this—as I told Swain, so he's okay with that. Alright?'

The agent nodded. 'Yes, sir. I was told that recording was allowed.'

Good,' breathed the minister heavily, 'Okay, I think... yeah, it's on. You may begin, Mister Cranmore.'

Stuart Cranmore placed his knees together and laid his hands in his lap, hoping that this pose would convey a suitable degree of contrition. 'Well, sir, the beginning of this whole episode is a bit of an embarrassing accident...'

'I should hope so,' interrupted the minister. 'I'd hate to think that our counter-intelligence community concocted something like this on purpose.'

Cranmore gave an obligatory smile. 'Very true, sir.'

'Sorry...go on.'

'Thank you, sir. We were engaged in a brain-storming session with my sector—it's something we do now and again as a team-building exercise with our junior recruits. It's also a useful tool to stimulate ideas and to review where we're at with our assignments. We somehow got to discussing the ways and means by which a potentially hostile neighbouring country might be sabotaged without the need for incursion or force, and, I'm ashamed to say, sir, that I promoted the idea of planting an inferior education policy within that country's government so that, in time, it would weaken their academic and practical integrity.

'We debated on this for quite some time before we came to

the conclusion that it was impossible to contrive an education policy that looked respectable on the outside but was insidiously destructive on the inside. We left it at that—an intellectual exercise meant to stimulate debate amongst the team.

'That very afternoon, I received a summons from Dr Swain. He'd heard about our little exercise and thought that it was the perfect vehicle by which we might train new agents—to give them a harmless practical mission and thereby prepare them for proper espionage work. So, we constructed an assignment whereby one team was to recruit suitable candidates to develop the aforementioned sabotaging curriculum, and the other parallel team was to find ways of deploying it into the host nation.'

Thornton sniffed wryly. 'And this was meant to be an *innocuous* exercise.'

'Yes, sir. It was totally impractical to implement—but the important objective was that it gave our recruits practical experience of managing people in the field, as well as introducing them to the complexities of another nation's government.'

'And your boys immediately picked on Indonesia—couldn't have been New Zealand, or even Tasmania?'

Cranmore nodded ambiguously.

Thornton turned irritably in his seat. 'We've been banging on since *I* was a boy about a potentially hostile neighbour. I always thought we were talking about the Kiwis, what with us getting regularly thrashed in just about every code of sport. It wasn't until I was at uni!—*yeah, seriously!*—that I thought our hostile neighbour might be some other country—and even then, it was some nebulous landmass off the West Australian coast that I never actually tried to put my finger on until I flew out to Christmas Island for some government junket and thought, "Fuck me! There's nothing here". It was only then that I consciously interpreted what hostile neighbour meant! It was always Indonesia—always. Wasn't China—they're

116

not a neighbour. Same with Japan and India. Wasn't New Guinea—they're irrelevant. It was only ever the huge, enveloping island nation of Indonesia, and we have made colossal fools of ourselves for decades with our silly euphemisms about hostile neighbours.'

Cranmore nodded sagely. 'Sir... I'll continue with my story.'

'Please do,' said Thornton.

'Well, I put together an appropriate assignment and presented it to my team. It was, I should emphasise, a practical mission, requiring all of the preparatory phases except the last phase, that of deployment. I played the role of control, and I was to be updated daily. For the rest, the team was on its own—out in the field, using their initiative and training to find the best possible candidate for their purpose. I made the decisions that maintained the illusion of a real mission.'

'If only it were still an illusion, hey, Cranmore? Ah well...'

'Indeed, sir. Now, the end of the school year was coming up, and we had to act quickly. The team found a likely candidate. Tim Sheridan was the Deputy Head at Pacifica College, a private school in an outlying suburb of Brisbane. He'd been released from his job—sacked, for no reason other than that he was expensive and that it was possible to delegate his job to other, aspiring teachers.'

Thornton took a swig of his drink and wiped his mouth with the back of his hand. 'Cost-cutting and retribution?'

'Well, sir, apparently, he was a bit of a drone—utter conservative who had repeatedly missed out on other appointments, and was languishing as a deputy and filling in for bus duty and stuff like that.'

'And *he* was what you were looking for?'

'Indeed, sir. We wanted someone who was conversant with the system... and desperate enough to abase himself to do our dirty work. '

'Did you have to look very far?'

'Sadly, no sir. Apparently, there were quite a few suitable

candidates, but Sheridan was a prime one—disheartened at his dismissal, and desperate—because he was only fifty-seven and still needed to build on his super. And, to top it all off, his wife, Patrice Sheridan, was about to launch a state-wide education initiative that was going to transform Queensland from just the smart state into the intellectual state.'

'Fuck me, Cranmore—do me a favour and try not to mention the word *smart* in your little narrative, there's a good lad.'

'I'll try not to, sir.'

'So his wife is a teacher as well?'

'Yes, sir—works for the education department as a senior curriculum advisor.'

'Oh, so there's a bit of rivalry between them?'

'Absolutely, and this played nicely into our hands.'

'Because you offered him a prestigious assignment...' Thornton deliberately left his sentence hanging.

'... with ASIO. That's right, sir. We discussed remuneration— these exercises don't come cheap—and Sheridan was happy with that.'

'Of course... and how did you know that he could deliver the goods?'

'Sir, based on the brainstorming session that initiated this whole exercise, I privately believed that it was impossible for Sheridan to come up with anything that would do the trick. However, for the purpose of the exercise, it didn't really matter. Nevertheless, the second team would review Sheridan's proposal, which took the form of a video presentation as well as a digital document. Sheridan, obviously, was not actually going to be there to implement this scheme. Based on the contents of the presentation, the second team would devise a way to plant it.'

'So how, in God's name, did this thing *actually* get planted?'

Cranmore held up his hand for patience. 'We're almost there, sir. The combined field exercise was to be assessed by a panel of experienced ASIO personnel who would look into every facet of the mission as well as the manner in which Sheridan's proposal was to be deployed in the host country. The presentation *itself* was just a means to an end. In no way was the panel judging whether it would *actually* affect a sabotaging influence on the nation.'

'No, of course not,' Thornton rolled his eyes, '... that wasn't important—they were just assessing the exercise, right?'

'Correct, sir. The document was just a focal point—a theme if you like.'

'Good-oh. I think we've established that. Tell me more about Sheridan.'

'What we needed was a high-level teacher who could make our proposal credible with the relevant jargon and topical buzz-words—not to mention the raft of acronyms that infests educational doctrine. Sheridan had been cast adrift and didn't know what to do. His wife's career was peaking—he had the whole holidays to share with the daughter that he can't relate to anymore—he didn't want to hang with his friends, not that he has many, only to be reminded that he was unemployed.

'We interviewed him at his house, and he got back to us the very next day—yep, he said, he'd do it—he felt he was the right man for the job... all that sort of puff. It was quite pathetic really. We briefed him on the nature of the assignment and emphasised its counter-productive intent. We told him that the first phase of the operation was for him to put together a compelling presentation that we could use to sell the idea.'

'And he was okay with that?'

'More than okay. It gave him a new lease on life. Within a week, he had booked tickets to Europe—he and the family were going on an extensive tour, mostly around the northern European countries. Ah, sir, I should mention that we'd bugged the house... it's not part of the training, but some of the lads got a bit carried away. Anyway, his whole demeanour had changed. He was assertive and taking control. His wife had just about given up on getting him to go travelling, and now suddenly he was planning itineraries, booking flights, hotels, cars. We all thought that he was beginning to fancy himself as James Bond.

'Of course, it was winter in the northern hemisphere, but Sheridan was promising hot tubs, saunas, skiing—he was beside himself. And now we know why. He was planning on meeting everyone and anyone that had to do with evolutionary education, and he planned a trip that went from Belgium to Finland, Holland to Russia. On the way back, he even called in to Japan and South Korea. He was amazingly organised. While the family went shopping in huge glass-covered malls, he was meeting politicians, teachers, social engineers, social commentators, writers, you name it. He was researching what he thought would be the ultimate dysfunctional education system—so that he could put a similar package together when he returned to Australia.'

'The ultimate dysfunctional education system,' mused Thornton as he drained the last of his drink.

'Absolutely. He came back with masses of data—recorded interviews, videos, books, research papers, lists of web addresses—the works. And he then sat down, and over about a two-month period, synthesised his report.'

The minister shifted his weight in the lounge. 'But I don't get it—if he was supposed to be creating a *counter-productive* education system, why was he interviewing all the luminaries at the cutting edge of new-age educational reform?'

Stuart Cranmore lent forward, rested his elbows on his knees and lightly steepled his fingers. 'That's the incredible thing, sir. Sheridan is so resolutely conservative, so steeped in the dogma of educational tradition, so unimaginative... that he believes completely and unequivocally that any sort of educational reforms will fail—that they will lead to anarchy—chaos. We think that, among other things, Sheridan's sudden enthusiasm for this project was some sort of affirmation of his contempt for anything outside educational orthodoxy. But, in order to find a place where there is vigorous and imaginative thought about the future of schooling, he had to go abroad, because there's nothing happening in Australia. He picked and chose all the best features of all the latest research and practical experience... and accidentally created the most advanced and replete educational template that the OECD has ever seen.'

'Which we've foisted on the Indonesians!'

'That was the intention, sir—in the form of a cultural exchange during a recent intercultural forum.'

Thornton threw up his hands. 'So, if it is as *replete*, as you say it is, what are the Indonesians complaining about?'

'Sir... we had an incident—two incidents, that complicated things.'

Thornton settled back in his seat. 'Ah, the lies beckon. Go on.'

'Sir, just a few more things about Sheridan, if I may? We'd never intended for him to embrace this project as much as he did. As I mentioned, his admission into ASIC gave him a huge lift. It dealt with his self-esteem issues in a very productive and positive way—he'd re-invented himself in a matter of weeks. But all we'd expected from him was a generic document that had some sort of twist to it to make it counter-productive—and as I said, sir, I couldn't think of a way in which it could be done.'

The minister stretched and yawned. 'And it didn't matter anyway...'

'Exactly. Until...'

'... until?'

'Well, sir... word tends to get around at headquarters and...'

'Aren't you people supposed to excel at keeping secrets?'

Thornton interrupted testily, '... that's largely what you do, isn't it—maintain secrecy?'

Cranmore stroked his chin thoughtfully. 'This wasn't anything that secret—it was a training exercise, sir. It's just that various other departments became... well, intrigued by it.'

Thornton gave a laboured sigh. 'Oh, go on then.'

'I was approached by a very senior department head, and it was requested of me that I... how shall I put it... I see this training exercise out to its fullest possible conclusion without actually implementing it.

Thornton held his arms wide. 'But, you *did* end up with a brilliant educational template—even if it was accidental. So where did it all go wrong?'

Cranmore massaged his brow. 'That was the second thing, sir. The Indonesians didn't receive Sheridan's presentation.'

Thornton slowly rubbed his eyes. 'Really. What *did* they get, then?'

'Sheridan was due to hand in his report in early April, in the form of a digital document. As well, there was a video presentation with very good production values, done in one of our studios. He himself is not remotely charismatic, and anyway, we didn't want him to become precious about the whole thing, so we made sure that it was all on video to support the digital document.

'At the same time, his wife, Patrice, was putting the finishing touches to her paper, entitled, *Intellectual Education—Envisaging a Superior State*, which also included a video production because it was meant to be viewed by teachers at all the schools in the state once it had been successfully reviewed.'

The agent paused for a minute to make sure that the minister was still with him.

He was—glowering darkly from under a heavy brow. 'I'm getting a bad feeling about this, Cranmore... seems to be an awful lot of coincidences.'

Cranmore swallowed. 'Yes, sir. It gets worse. Sheridan went shopping to get a solid-state memory stick. . USB... whatever. He came back with a two for the price of one deal or something...'

Thornton closed his eyes at the horror of the pieces falling into place. '... and his wife said, "ooh, you're so thoughtful dear, I just need one of those"...'

Cranmore swallowed again. 'Something like that, sir.'

'So, let me see if I can connect the rest of the dots; Mr and Mrs Sheridan uploaded their respective presentations and then, somehow, in the disorder of domesticity, the two USBs were accidentally swapped.'

Cranmore nodded dolefully. 'Yes, sir, that is what happened.'

The Minister for Foreign Affairs sat absolutely still and, with unfocused eyes, softly said, '... so, the ASIO review panel received the *Envisaging an Intellectual State* or whatever it's called—thought so highly of it as a weapon of corruption and incapacitation, that they gleefully packaged it and duly presented the Indonesian government a gift of our most highly developed educational template. And now, the Indonesians have accused us of attempting to sabotage their nation.'

Stuart Cranmore looked bereft. 'That is how things stand at the moment, sir.'

Thornton nodded slowly to himself for some time then turned to Cranmore with a flicker of rage in his eyes and articulated carefully, 'What the fuck was *in* that report?'

Cranmore sighed audibly. 'This is where there is a lot of confusion. Given that the whole mission was subversive—given that we made a cock-up with the unintended substitution—given that our intentions to the Indonesian government were not altruistic, we *did* end up presenting them with a prized academic model—and they hate us for it!'

'And you have no idea why?'

'We believe that the Indonesians have been suspicious of our overtures for cultural exchange for quite some time,' Cranmore shrugged his shoulders, '... and, as far as we know, our gift of an advanced educational template was scrutinised in great detail by many of Indonesia's leading academics, sociologists and philosophers—and the consensus was that it was a plant, meant to destroy the fabric of their society—ironically, much as we had intended.'

Thornton gave a demanding look. 'So—what was in it that was so inflammatory?'

Cranmore pursed his lips and looked apologetic. 'Sir... we're doing our best to analyse the contents. We've got extra agents working on it, but it's a very tedious document to tease apart. My personal belief is that we are over-thinking what this report holds. Just between us, sir—and it has yet to be confirmed—the top echelon review committee that I told you about...'

Thornton grunted in confirmation.

'... well, one of their agents whispered to me that they themselves took a little while to understand the extreme cleverness of the template as an agent of incapacitation and that, once having got their collective heads around the complexity of the hidden instruments of destabilisation—and, I might add, realising how cunningly this report was disguised as a laudable piece of academia—duly signed off on it, had hard-cover documents printed and included it as part of a cultural exchange package that was occurring at the time.'

The minister raised an eyebrow. 'But *you* think we're over-thinking it?'

'Yes, sir. I've had a pretty good read over it and the reason why it's so difficult to comprehend is because it is so institutionalised— it is so simplistic—based on a spurious ideology of privilege and entitlement—so illogical—so removed from the emerging needs of our society—so contradictory—so blind to the obvious—so...'

'Yes, yes, Cranmore... I get the picture.' Thornton levered himself to his feet and walked over to the cabinet. 'Cranmore, I can only assume that the greatest minds in the Department of Education collaborated on this paper so, you'll pardon me if I insist on just a tad more corroboration than just your gut feeling on this.'

'Yes, sir,' said Cranmore, listening to the clinking of the crystal, '... I was just about to elaborate on that.'

Thornton moved back to his seat. 'Oh, excellent.'

'My boys in the parallel project...'

'... the boys in the parallel universe,' mumbled the minister, '... god, help us.'

Cranmore continued, '... they agree that the whole *Envisaging A Superior State* presentation is just a lot of moronic posturing, *but*, they think it is also a brilliant piece of subversive doctrine—they're just not sure whether it is intentional or not.'

'Whether what is intentional?... the moronic or the brilliant?'

'... either, sir... um, both... ah, what I mean is that the review team is not sure whether the report is just idiotic or deliberately sinister.'

The minister gave a woe-be-gone look. 'They are the two options, are they? The state Education Department is either deliberately confusing schools or they are deliberately upsetting them.' He took a hearty swallow of his drink.

Cranmore wasn't about to let himself look foolish. He held out his hands as though to encapsulate an idea. 'Sir, I wouldn't inflict this on anyone, but if you'd care to read the *Intellectual Education* document for yourself, then you will see how incomprehensible it is. And, at the same time, how crippling it would be to our society if it were to be implemented.'

Thornton looked pensively at his half-empty glass. 'So, the Indonesian Cultural Academy saw it for what it was—a piece of junk, and saw what it would do if ever they embraced it.'

'Precisely, sir. If I may, there is one letter that I think needs to be read, even if only in part, because it conveys the level of antipathy that we can expect from our Indonesian counterparts, and it also casts some light on the... ahh, worthlessness of the educational proposal.'

Thornton rubbed his eyes. 'As long as it hasn't got the word *smart* in it, I'm all ears.'

'No, sir. It's from the secretary of the Indonesian Academy of Culture.' Cranmore lifted a paper from a file in his briefcase. 'I'll skip over their feelings of insult etcetera and get straight to what they thought of their "gift"... and, just to prepare you, sir, he really was very upset.'

The minister slumped against the back rest of the lounge and listened without a movement as Cranmore read from the page.

'... you are a discredited nation that fuels itself on excesses—you live with the delusion that you are superior even in the absence of any such verification. What you were one hundred years ago was not due to your education system—the seeds of genius sprouted in the fertile soil of opportunity. What you have *become* is due to your education system—greedy, self-obsessed and combative consumers craving the inspiration of other cultures.

'If you are foolish enough to implement your education plan you will crystalize your youth in sameness and mediocrity—you will become unable to interpret the future, and you will be dominated by those who can.

'We do not want what you offer us; we will take what we need by cultivating your dependence on us; and we will take what we want by exposing your vulnerabilities.

'You have lost the principles to live by—not even your children inspire a credo of happiness as you claw over each other for child-care places. You have no guiding faith, only a neurotic attachment to a divisive religion. The only manifestation of a formal guiding declaration in your society is the incomprehensible and facile education policy that you have gifted us...'

Cranmore looked up from the page. 'And he goes on to lambast us about our arrogance and presumption.'

The two men sat in silence for some time.

At last, Thornton gave a big, shuddering sigh. 'Thank god, I'm old,' he said, '... and if I can just maintain my delusions for a few more years, I'll die a happy man.'

The agent smiled. His phone burbled. He looked quickly at the screen and put it back in his pocket. 'Sir?'

Thornton was far away with his thoughts but managed a vague grunt.

Cranmore put his hands together and assumed a thoughtful pose. 'Sir... there is a possible silver lining to this whole debacle.'

Thornton cast him an inquisitive eye.

'You see sir, when the USBs became swapped, Patrice Sheridan presented hers to the state review panel.'

'... and that contained Sheridan's loopy rantings about an educational dystopia,' interrupted the minister.

'Well, yes,' said Cranmore, '... and no...'

Thornton suddenly came alive. 'My God! Cranmore... are you telling me that I am going to be held accountable for destroying a *state's* education system as *well* as starting a war with Indonesia?'

'No, no, sir... not at all.'

There was a knock on the door. Thornton flinched.

Cranmore got up and walked across the room. 'That will be the Minister for Education, sir.' He unlocked the door and opened it. The Honourable Andrea Monk entered, smiled and walked over to Thornton.

The Foreign Minister didn't bother rising. 'What the hell is going on?' he said too aggressively.

Andrea Monk slipped off her coat and threw it over the back

of the lounge chair that she lowered herself into. 'Good morning, Craig. You look as though you've done a day's work already...' and she deliberately lingered on the empty tumbler.

'Want one?' said Thornton.

The minister shook her head sweetly.

Cranmore resumed his seat. 'Ah, sir, if we're going to play the advantage here, we have to keep our eye on the ball.'

Monk sighed with exasperation. '... please let's not speak in sporting metaphors. I don't need to be reminded that sport is the only sad form of inspiration in this country.'

The agent nodded just the once. 'Of course, Minister. What I mean to say is that we have a short time in which to take the initiative. Ms Monk?'

Andrea Monk cleared her throat with a delicate cough. 'Sheridan's video report came as quite a shock to the state reviewing panel—it was brilliantly done...'

Cranmore gave Thornton a smug little pout of affirmation.

'... and,' continued the minister, '... the research and the scope of the study was truly exceptional. In fact, never before has such a comparative, international study been done. Not that I'm aware of—we've tended to be a bit isolationist here in Australia and our education system has become somewhat self-serving. Needless to say, Sheridan's presentation came out of left field. The panel was pretty much expecting some dreary new iteration of past policies—the milieu of schooling in Australia has been steadfastly conformist and incapable of change.

'But Sheridan was advocating student-initiated educational pathways, independent trainers and educators responsible for their own modules, classes and practicals held not just in schools, but throughout the community and industrial complexes, open-ended days, unrestricted urban travel, lowering the allowable working age to twelve—a whole raft of totally radical changes. The education authority would have some sort of oversight on each student, and facilitators—read ex-teachers—would monitor the journey of each student. As I said, it's all fastidiously researched from models that seem to be gaining traction elsewhere in the world.'

Thornton and Cranmore exchanged a quick look, each understanding how Sheridan would have seen such a scheme as a road to ruin for any nation mad enough to implement it.

Thornton felt obliged to show some initiative but could only manage, '... wow... that *is* pretty radical...'

Cranmore stepped in. 'The thing is, the state reviewing panel, being made up of career teachers, sat around looking at each other, transfixed, each waiting for the moment to make a politically expedient move.'

'Yes,' said Andrea Monk '... this sort of situation required a level of courage that none on the committee possessed—whether to discard it or to embrace it. I'm sure they could all see the merits in such a scheme, but it was way beyond their scope and experience to sign off on something like that—which is why our country's education remains stagnant—we are systemically incapable of accepting change.'

'So, what is this panel doing at the moment?' asked Thornton with round eyes.

Monk nodded towards Cranmore. 'Fortunately, we had a spy team on hand. You go, Mr Cranmore.'

'We only became aware of the switch when our parallel team started commending us on aspects of the Indonesian sabotage video that we did not recognise. We became alarmed and asked to see a copy of what they had. Well, we just about shat ourselves, but even then, we couldn't let on that there'd been a mistake. It took us a little while to work out where this new presentation came from, but we eventually traced it to Patrice Sheridan. It was just, as you said sir, a domestic mistake... somehow the two USBs got switched.

'So, the ASIO review panel that was assessing the mission, assumed they were looking at a cleverly disguised instrument of sabotage, but which was, in fact, the state education department's master plan. We had to slink back to the office and wonder what those boffins could see in it with respect to destroying a nation's culture.

'We were in deep shit. The Indonesian issue was obviously out of our hands because the ASIO board took control of Patrice Sheridan's masterpiece and were hell-bent on planting it during the cultural exchange ceremony. However, we felt that we had a responsibility to find out how Tim Sheridan's baby was faring in the hands of a bunch of school teachers, so we sent a surveillance team out to monitor the situation.

'No one knew the provenance of that report—certainly not Patrice Sheridan and her team. Tim Sheridan had remained pretty hush-hush about the whole thing during their travels. His wife knew he was working for ASIO, and he told her he was being paid to travel the world. She got caught up in the mystique that her otherwise boring husband was creating. Be that as it may, we knew that his video presentation could in no way be supported by the supposed creative team behind it so, when we found out about the switch, we had to hustle into position quick smart—and it's just as well that the review committee was gripped in a hiatus of indecision because it gave us time to, ahh... create an alternative solution.'

Thornton screwed up his eyes and massaged his temples. 'What sort of *alternative* was it necessary to create?'

Cranmore was showing signs of fatigue by now and he exhaled in a long sigh. 'Sir, we had to get Sheridan's vision approved. Not to do so would have meant the definite disclosure of substitute material and the likely revelation that we, ASIO, had been tampering with... well, everything. We had to remain out of the picture; we had to make it look as though Sheridan's work was a true outcome of the state's progressive educational reforms, developed by imaginative and critically informed senior teachers.'

'And? Did you manage to achieve the impossible?'

'Sir, my team and I have spent the last two months getting close to the panellists—accidental meetings at their favourite coffee shop, serendipitous encounters in the supermarket, opportune conversations at kiddies' football, chance remarks in random settings, random...'

'Oh, for god's sake, Cranmore—I get it! You spiked their conscience—excellent. But did you get them to vote?'

'Yes, sir, our coaching campaign worked. They voted to adopt the report in its entirety.'

'Oh,' said Thornton, with some surprise.

'Mind you, sir,' Cranmore continued with a hint of joviality, '... our team sat up long hours discussing the future of Australia, and how education might best be reformed, and came to the happy conclusion that Sheridan's contribution was just what the country needed. So, our hearts were in the right place.'

'Yes... good for you, Cranmore.' He stood up and looked at Andrea Monk. 'Well, this calls for a celebration. What about it, Andrea?'

Monk nodded. 'Yes, please. I think I need it... now that I know ASIO is in charge of the school curriculum.'

Thornton ambled over to the drinks cabinet. 'So, Andrea, I presume that you are in on this because of the connection between the two education policies.'

Monk looked out of the window towards the distant hills. 'It's just that there is a story brewing about an insulting gift of an educational nature having been made to the Indonesian government, and it is beholden of me to be conversant with the shape of our supposed ideology in this regard. God knows, somebody has to be. As well, we have one state in Australia that is about to launch a proposal for the most radical overhaul of education since ancient Greece, and I—

we—the Federal government has got to establish a position on this so that we can make the appropriate noises of accord.'

Thornton handed Andrea Monk her glass and resumed his seat. 'So, this is the silver lining that you were referring to, is it, Cranmore? A new vision for our country.'

'That is correct, sir.'

'Well, that's very magnanimous of you, because you know that both of us are going to get the boot, don't you.'

Cranmore nodded stoically. 'I'm afraid so, sir.'

Monk swallowed a mouthful and smacked her lips. 'What I'd like to know is, who was the real genius behind taking advantage of the cultural exchange?'

The agent looked at the floor.

The Minister for Education was obviously a lot looser than usual for this time of the morning. 'Oh, come on, Cranmore... we can keep a secret, can't we, Craig?'

Thornton snorted wryly. 'I'm not so sure that I can be responsible for my actions if I find out who the real perpetrator is.' His phone tinkled melodiously. 'Yes?' Thornton listened to the message. 'Very good, very good... thank you.' He turned to Cranmore. 'Well, old son... you and I are going to fight another day. My secretary has just informed me that the Indonesian government has just sent an official communique thanking us for our bountiful benevolence during the cultural exchange. Also, some mention of a reprimand for the secretary of the cultural academy for shooting off his mouth in an unauthorised capacity.'

Cranmore nodded deeply. 'Really... well, sir... that *is* good news.'

'Yes, indeed... but you know what it really is?'

Cranmore furrowed his brow.

'What it really is,' continued Thornton, '... is that the Indonesians either believe that we are incredibly naïve to believe in *An Intellectual Country*, and that they are simply humouring our stupidity and waiting for us to implode in hopeless ineptitude, or, that they believe we are a scurrilous bunch of hypocrites intent on deceiving our neighbours at every opportunity, and that they are doing their best to maintain good relations—take your pick. Because the only other option—that our educational gift to them is a useful and much-appreciated exchange, is highly unlikely.'

Andrea Monk sighed. 'Well, if that's all, then I'd better be getting to work.' She and Thornton looked expectantly at Cranmore.

Stuart Cranmore felt relieved enough at the unexpected outcome of this episode to entertain the thought of taking a little risk. He surveyed the two ministers with a meaningful eye. 'If you wouldn't mind switching off your recorder, sir.'

The minister acknowledged Cranmore's request with a raised finger. He reached across the seat and grabbed the recorder. He looked at it closely for a few seconds and pressed a few buttons. Thornton's face darkened. 'Oh, what the,' he began, then suddenly threw the recorder into the corner of the couch. 'The fuckin' thing hasn't even been on. Jesus, how difficult does it have to be?'

Cranmore attempted some levity. 'Happens to us all the time, sir.'

Thornton took a big breath and settled back in the couch.

The agent continued. 'In our organisation, we don't always observe the hierarchical structures that are commonplace elsewhere—we tend to give our personnel opportunities to demonstrate their capabilities at quite high levels. One of these characters, who I have known for quite a while, is Jack Radley who, possibly because of his charismatic name, has become a bit of a favourite with Swain, and was permitted to grace the assessment panel. He's an impulsive idiot who, on one occasion when he spectacularly failed an assessment, still passed because Swain believed that the answers were merely academic and that what he admired most was that Radley was prepared to strenuously defend his wrong answers.

'Swain is of the opinion that in our line of work, truth and correctness are contextual and that reality changes with each new perspective. He thinks that a good agent is one with a steadfast ability to stick to his story.

'Well, the board was most surprised when Radley suggested that we actually go ahead with the plant—his reasoning being that, as far as he could make out, the document had all the hallmarks of a well-intentioned curriculum and all the prerequisites of a sabotaging system, and so, he deduced, if Australia were to cripple itself by implementing such a scheme, then the least we could do would be to burden our potential enemies in the same way. This line of thinking was pursued rigorously and, well, the panel concluded that, at worst, the Indonesians would think we were idiots, and at best they might implement the scheme and spend decades trying to reform their chronically incapacitated youth from a confused perception of reality and a spiralling sense of entitlement.'

Andrea Monk plonked her glass onto the cabinet. 'Jesus!... is that what ASIO thinks of our education system?'

Cranmore took hold of his briefcase and stood up. 'ASIO has never had to concern itself with our education system other than selecting recruits with advanced reasoning abilities and neglected moral development. However, I think we owe the panel some gratitude for having weighed our curriculum for what it is—they had the advantage of not being affected by any agenda other than what the outcome might be—and, they thought it made a good weapon of mass destruction.'

Thornton choked back a laugh. 'So we have created a superior inferior education system!' He rose slowly to his feet and followed the other two to the door. 'Stuart,' he said, with a hint of deference, '... you and I... and Andrea, have done pretty well out of our education. Wouldn't you agree?'

Cranmore stopped at the door. 'Sir, I'm not sure what I could be. All I know is that I would be happier doing something simpler than my current job. How about you? What are you going to do after politics?'

Thornton's close brush with disaster had taken the edge off his natural hubris, and he gave Cranmore's question more consideration than he normally might have. Still, he couldr't think of an answer, and he looked Cranmore square in his eyes. 'Don't know... don't know,' he said and gave a vague shake of his head.

The agent held out his hand. 'Case in point, sir. Your education has left you chronically uninspired.'

The Minister for Foreign Affairs took Cranmore's hand in both of his and shook it slowly.

'If I might make a suggestion,' Cranmore smiled, '... you could put together a module—documents and a video. Call it, *A History of Australian Foreign Affairs*. Make it available on the education program and see how many kids show an interest in it. It's the way education is going to go—you could find yourself hosting workshops on diplomacy... history... stuff like that.'

Thornton gave a little grin. 'Might not mention this last episode though.'

The two men parted with a nod.

As Cranmore walked down the corridor with Andrea Monk, Thornton could hear her saying, '... are you contracted to your job for long?... I'm just asking, because...' but her voice faded into the distance.

135

The Other Twin Towers

The sun rises on the drab monotony of an inner-Sydney suburb. Two decrepit blocks of units, known as Twin Towers, glow briefly in the orange light. They have serrated the urban skyline decades before the cataclysmic events of 9/11.

It is October, 2001, and the new millennium has already defined itself in distant New York; it is the age of terrorism, and one Australian is about to embrace that particular zeitgeist.

Barney Evans scratches his belly through his singlet and slouches against the mailbox wall as he reads someone else's morning paper.

The headlines scream: TERROR AUSTRALIS

Barney shakes his shaggy head in disbelief and whistles softly through his teeth. One of his tenants, Terry Crane, shuffles out of the entrance in his slippers.

On spying Barney, he rolls his eyes. 'Reading my newspaper again I see.'

Barney is consumed by the story.

Terry leans over the mailbox wall and pulls out someone else's paper. 'You know, for once I'd like to read my paper and know that your grubby hands haven't been all over it.'

Barney spreads the paper over the concrete structure and slaps at the main article. 'Look at this, Terry, look at this... bloody terrorists are establishing themselves in Australia!' he searches with his finger, '... here—*ASIO is warning all Australians to be vigilant and prepared!*' He looks at Terry with a fatalistic mien. 'They're amongst us now, mate... foreign and hidden—like raisins in an Anzac biscuit.'

Terry breathes a heavy sigh. 'Listen—there are a couple of things I need to discuss...'

Obviously not in a listening frame of mind, Barney rolls up the newspaper and waves it conspiratorially in Terry's face. 'Between you and me, mate, I've got to tell you that I've always had me suspicions about them Osmans.' He points with the rolled-up paper at a particular mailbox slot. 'Know what I mean but, Terry?' He stands back a little with a grim and superior look on his face. 'I mean, it doesn't take a genius to work out that we're a target.' He indicates the *Twin Towers* plaque hanging askew on the wall. 'It's too much of a coincidence that the,' he hesitates briefly with emotion, '... Twin Towers in New York are destroyed... and now, a Muslim family has moved into my units.' He nods at the Osmans' mailbox. 'Hmmm?... what do you think?'

'I think you're a bloody idiot, Barney... this place is more likely to collapse if one of the pigeons makes a bad landing. Anyway, they're Turkish... not terrorists.'

'What's the diff?'

'Jesus, Barney... it's not 1915... we've moved on since then—I hope. Listen, Sharon is having a lingerie party this afternoon, and it'd be nice if she could have a shower before then... so, if it's not too much trouble, could you fix the hot water in between being vigilant and prepared?'

Three other tenants have come out for their newspapers and are standing around the mailbox wall.

'Oh, yes, please fix the hot water, Barney... it's getting ridiculous... we're all having cold showers.'

'... and when are you going to fix the gas? You said you'd have the gas fixed, and it's been a week now... when are you going to fix it?'

'... and my window, Barney... can you hurry up and fix my window before I get burgled again.'

'You too, huh!'

'Twice!... this is the second time! Whoever he is must be nesting somewhere in the building.'

Barney glowers under the assault from his tenants, irritated that there isn't a little more patriotic vim. 'Give me a break, will you.' He slaps the rolled-up paper against the wall to punctuate his speech. 'Why am *I* the only urban kelpie? Wait until the terrorists move in... if they haven't already.'

This causes a few raised eyebrows.

'Yeah!... yeah, you think I'm joking? Well, read it for yourselves, ya pack of whingers... living your cosy little lives with every luxury under the sun... completely unaware that there are agents of darkness waiting to bring us to our knees... waiting to destroy everything that is precious to us,' he waves his arm to encompass the two blocks of units. 'Go on!... read it for yourself.'

The tenants tentatively scan their papers.

Mustafa Osman comes down the path to the mailbox wall and checks his empty box.

Barney gives one last, petulant swat with the now shredded newspaper. 'Everything's fine when there's a roof over your head! But one day, you'll be like a periwinkle in a concrete mixer, and then you'll ruin the day you've caused me grief.'

Mustafa nods deeply and eyes his paper. 'Is that my paper, Mr Evans?'

'What?... oh, yeah...' Barney smooths the paper as best he can and hands it over without looking at him. 'Some of us are prepared to man the rampants and goad our lions.'

The tenants titter at Barney's muddled idioms. They retreat up the path to the entrance way.

With a sympathetic look, Terry squares up to Barney. 'Mate... I

138

don't expect every luxury under the sun... just hot water.'

The other tenants turn. '... urgently please, Barney.'

'. . and the gas...'

'... and my window... I'm not buying another DVD player until it's fixed.'

All four tenants make their way back along the path.

Barney looks sullenly after them, completely unaware that Mustafa is waiting patiently behind him. Shifting his gaze to the brass name plate, he lifts the corner so that it sits horizontally. Grabbing his singlet, he makes a wad and spits generously into it. He commences polishing the plaque.

Mustafa coughs.

Barney jumps. 'Jesus!... you scared the shit outa me.'

Mustafa bows apologetically. 'I'm terribly sorry, Mr Evans... I didn't mean to startle you.'

'What do *you* want?'

'Well, actually, if you could possibly see your way clear... I was wondering whether or not...'

Barney is suddenly moved to articulate his train of thought. He points with an accusing finger. 'You know, it's going to become very difficult for you to sneak around like that in the very near future.'

Mustafa blinks. 'I'm sorry?'

Barney taps at the paper in Mustafa's hand. 'We're onto you lot... ASIO, mate... top bloody intelligence organisation... and they're enlisting the help of every bona fide bloke in the street—and that includes yours truly,' he thumbs his chest, '...and I'll be sussin' you out to the max, son. I'll be sniffin' that close you won't be able to fart without me knowing about it... um, in a manner of speaking.'

Mustafa smiles awkwardly. 'I see... well, if you are too busy at the moment, we can always use the toilet out the back. It is just the cistern that needs a new washer, but I can do that myself, it is no trouble. I can just as easily repair it myself. Sorry to bother you, Mr

Evans.'

Mustafa makes his way back to the building entrance. Bits of his paper fall to the pathway.

Barney looks darkly after him. '*Sorry to bother you, Mr Evans...* yeah, I know your game, mate—keep a low profile and don't attract attention to yourself. You don't fool me for a moment. I know a time for patriotism when I see it. From now on, my senses will be on full alert... every nerve will be keenly tuned... I'll miss nothing and be aware of everything. I'll be a shadow in the hallways... I'll sleep like a coiled spring. I'll be all sweet and charming on the outside, but like an assassin on the inside...'

He wipes his nose with his singlet and leans with pot-bellied poise against the wall.

Barney's nefarious sidekick, Hazim El Shahoud, creeps out of the shrubbery and saunters to the wall.

Unaware, Barney continues with his little fantasy. 'I can be the ultimate agent because nobody suspects me...'

'Of what!'

Barney squeals. 'Jesus Christ!... Hazim. What?'

Hazim gives a bemused pout. 'Of what?'

'What?... of what, what?'

'Nobody suspects you of *what*... having any brains?'

Barney straightens his singlet. 'Hey, just you watch it, okay... just remember who's the brains behind our little enterprise.'

'Sorry... sorry... no offence intended. But, did I just overhear something about a DVD player a while back?... 'cos I can unload one to unit seven.'

Barney slumps back against the wall. 'No, nothing yet... they just want me to fix the window before they buy a new one.'

Hazim nods uncertainly. 'So fix it... just make sure that I can easily *unfix* it... because I can sell it as soon as I get one.'

'Yeah, yeah, okay. Listen... make sure you keep the stuff from each tower separate, y'know... we don't want neighbours *accidentally* spying their old wares in somebody else's unit.'

Hazim waves a careless hand. 'Yeah, sure... no worries.'

'Which reminds me,' says Barney, looking thoughtfully at nothing in particular, '... Sharon Crane is having a lingerie party this afternoon, and as far as I know, she's invited everyone in Twin Towers. Is there anything in their place that's going to cause trouble?'

'That's unit two, isn't it?'

Barney nods.

'Nah, they haven't bought anything.'

'Okay, good. I wonder whether the Osman ladies will be going? Shouldn't think so. Do Muslim women wear lingerie, Hazim?'

'How the hell would I know? When I get married, remind me, and I'll let you know. That's another unit we haven't done yet, by the way... supposed to be a fair bit of stuff in there too.'

Barney leans forward with interest. 'Really? What sort of stuff?'

Hazim searches Barney's face. '... stuff... y'know... stuff...'

'Like WMDs?'

'... what?'

'WMDs—weapons of mass destruction.'

'No... DVDs. *Weapons of*... what *are* you on about, Barney?'

Barney retreats in disgust. 'Am I the *only* person that ever reads a newspaper? I am talking about terrorists in Australia, targeting places of cultural significance, like this,' he indicates the units, '... inserting themselves omnivorously into the fabric of our society and waiting patiently for the chance to strike. I hope, Hazim, that it has not gone unnoticed by you, of the link between the Twin Towers in New York and the Twin Towers here which, in view of their age, have become a cultural icon and, consequently, a desirable target. But what is most disturbing, my friend, is that as we speak, enemies of the state are plotting to destroy us, and it is our job—no, our bloody duty—to ferret out any submersive elements.'

Hazim gives a doleful sigh. 'So, what has the Osman's DVD player got to do with this?'

'Nothing, you moron! Bloody hell, can't you see the obvious? We declare war on terrorists, and shortly afterwards, the Osmans move into Twin Towers. For all we know, they could be storing up plastic explosives...'

'... inside their DVD player?'

'Will you forget about the... look, yes, maybe... inside a DVD player, inside their fridge... I don't know. The point is that we have to be vigilant—that's what it says in the paper... we have to hone our powers of observation.'

Hazim gives another big sigh. 'Well, okay... but, if you do happen to *observe* a DVD player in their unit, let me know because I can easily move it.'

Barney massages his brow. '... yeah, okay... I'll let you know.'

Hazim slaps the wall. 'Great. Okay... gotta go.'

Barney rests with both hands against the wall. The brass plaque is sitting awry again. He repositions it reverently, but it returns to a skewed angle.

'Why is everyone around my ankles like a pair of ruptured Jockeys? And suddenly, when there's a call to arms, they're about as visible as a hip flask in the council chambers.'

Barney leaves the plaque to dangle and walks up the path to the entrance.

* * *

Sharon Crane, dressed in a frilly, black cocktail dress, prepares hors d'oeuvres on the kitchen bench. She looks over her shoulder and listens. 'Justine...' She waits for a reply but gets none. 'Justine... come on, I need your help here... they'll be here any minute.'

Justine marches out of her bedroom into the kitchen looking

both defiant and vulnerable at the same time. She stands and looks at the food on the bench. Her jeans sit at her hips, and her stretch top is a tad skimpy. She hoists at her jeans to try and cover some of her midriff. They slide back down, exposing the band of her underwear. Her Mum discreetly looks her up and down from where she is slicing cucumbers and gives a resigned sigh.

'Here, look... just slice these thinly and put them on top like that.' She goes to the sink and washes her hands. She dries them with a tea towel and, with held breath, appraises Justine's make-up. 'Um, sweetie... you're a little bit Gothic... are you sure that's appropriate?... and a bit exposed... I'm just thinking that with the Osmans coming... I don't want them to feel embarrassed at all.'

'Mum!' Justine says with indignation.

'I'm sorry, darling. It's just that they're from a very different culture. They're not as liberal as we are.' She surveys her daughter's expanse of bare skin. 'They're very... well, traditional... you know what I mean? Why don't you put on that nice skirt, or that dress that Nan got for you?'

Justine flings around. 'Mum!... that dress is *so* a present.'

'Oh, don't be silly, Justine... it fits you beautifully, and it looks great on you. Anyway, you're not comfortable in those jeans—you haven't stopped pulling at them. I don't know how you can wear them, honestly! They do nothing for you—I mean, not so much you... it's just that they accentuate all the wrong parts of a woman... they cut you in half just where you're at your widest—the hips, and they expose all of your belly and, well, you're quite slim, but some of your friends... I mean, do they *want* everybody to know how fat they are?'

Justine puts her hands on her hips. 'It's called a doughnut!'

'More than likely it's caused by doughnuts, but I feel bad enough criticising your fashion sense—don't get me started on your diet.'

'No—I said it's *called* a doughnut.'

'What is?'

'That ring of fat that girls have above their jeans.'

'You're joking!... and they're proud?... of having a doughnut?'

'Mum!'

'Well, it's most unflattering. All the time I see your friends hoisting their jeans to cover their undies and pulling at their tops to cover their bellies. What's the point of exposing yourself if it makes you uncomfortable?'

Justine juts forward. '*Mum!*'

The doorbell chimes. Sharon brushes at her dress.

'They're here. Just finish those for me, love.' She gives Justine's arm a quick squeeze and goes out of the kitchen.

With desultory movements, Justine decorates the last of the hors d'oeuvres. The sound of voices and greetings comes from the lounge. She stares moodily into space and unconsciously tugs at her jeans. She freezes suddenly in mid-adjustment. Slowly, her face crumples into tears.

Sharon breezes into the kitchen carrying a plate of edibles. She clears a space on the bench, unaware that Justine is crying. 'Love, can you make a bit of room? Oh, and can you put those drinks in the fridge... bottom shelf.'

Justine sniffs.

'Justine... what's the matter? Oh, darling.' Sharon puts her arm around her daughter. 'What's the matter?... hey? Come on, don't take what I said too seriously. I don't mind if you wear what you want, but we can't cry about it now... we've got a party to host. The Osmans will just have to take us as we are.'

Justine does her best to compose herself. 'But, I don't want to wear stuff that everybody thinks looks ridiculous.'

'I didn't say you look ridiculous... it's just the fashion. I remember some pretty weird fashions when I was sixteen.'

'I know... I've seen the photos.'

They laugh and hug each other.

144

Fatima Osman, with a plate in her hand, walks slowly into the kitchen. She is dressed in hijab—a headscarf and a light cover-all topcoat. She bestows an indulgent smirk on mother and daughter. 'Oh dear, is someone upset?'

Sharon smiles back. 'Justine is upset because I criticised her outfit.'

Fatima puts down the plate and holds out her arms. 'Come here, Justine...'

Justine accepts Fatima's invitation and moves over to her.

Fatima embraces her. 'You know... you mustn't let fashion dictate your *style*.'

With her chin buried in the Muslim woman's garment, Justine gives an anxious look. 'I'm not sure if I have a style.'

Fatima holds the teenager at arm's length. 'You should always be confident about what you wear.'

Justine looks askance at Fatima's attire. '. . um, really?'

'I know what you're thinking.'

'I'm sorry... I've never actually met someone who wore...'

'This,' Fatima runs her hand down her clothing, '... is generic hijab—a scarf and a loose gown. In Turkey it is called, *tesettur*.' She loosens her scarf and shakes out her hair. Her curls are glossy and abandoned. 'Unfortunately, clothing is much more than a fashion statement, Justine.'

Justine self-consciously puts her arms around her midriff. 'I feel really silly now.'

Fatima laughs as she stuffs the scarf into her coat pocket. 'Don't feel silly about the way you dress—you should have a *motive*!' She turns to the bench and begins to unwrap the plate.

Justine moves next to her and creates some room. 'Okay... comfort then?'

'Sure! Why not. But not when you're sixteen.'

'How do you know that I'm sixteen?' Justine says playfully.

Fatima brushes the crumbs from her hands above the sink and begins to unbutton her coat.

'Kemal told me.'

'... oh...'

'Would you mind helping me with this?' Fatima presents her back to Justine and lifts her coat at the shoulders.

With her face slightly flushed, Justine lends her assistance.

Underneath, Fatima is wearing a full, knee-length skirt in black and grey, and a gorgeous, embroidered short-sleeved top. She turns to Justine, who is holding out the coat, and rummages in one of the pockets. She pulls out a pair of heeled dress sandals, and winks at the young woman. 'Coats can be so handy.' She leans with one hand on the kitchen bench and buckles them on. 'When you can, you must dress for your pleasure—otherwise you may as well join the army.'

Justine looks with amazement as Fatima straightens and flounces the voluminous material of her skirt. A little frown creases her brow. 'Why do you wear... tesettur?'

Fatima tosses back her hair. 'Because it keeps my hair clean. You have no idea how dirty the air is in down-town Istanbul.'

'Really?'

'... that... and to make a point.'

Justine can't stop herself from grinning at the wonderful transformation that has occurred in front of her.

'Wow... you look lovely, Mrs Osman.'

'When I'm dressed like this, you may call me Fatima.'

'... Fatima...' Justine says softly, still holding out the coat.

Fatima delves into another pocket and extracts a small make-up bag. 'I wear hijab because it shouldn't make a difference.'

Justine nods uncertainly. '... it shouldn't?'

'No, it shouldn't.' Fatima carefully adds a touch of lipstick and rouge from a compact. She rolls and purses her lips and studies Justine from close by. 'I have contacts... but I'm not wearing them.'

146

She puts the make-up bag back into the pocket and pulls out a pair of gold rimmed glasses. 'For special occasions!' she puts on the glasses. 'I think these give me an air of piquant intellect.'

Sharon re-enters the kitchen with Fatima's mother, Merve, who is wearing chador—the much more restrained robe that reveals only the face.

Sharon does a double-take when she sees Fatima. 'Wow!... you've changed.'

Fatima holds out her skirt. 'No, I'm still the same person.'

'You know what I mean!' Sharon laughs.

Justine grabs at her mum with her free hand. 'Doesn't she look gorgeous, Mum!'

Sharon holds her daughter close. 'Fatima... I know you work, but I haven't been told what you do.'

'I work at the university.'

Mother and daughter nod with awe.

'... in the cafeteria.'

'Oh, well, that's a nice place to work.' Sharon says solicitously.

Fatima loosens a button to reveal a little more décolletage. 'I'm hoping to get into the political science faculty... but I have to jump through a few loops first.'

'Hoops,' says Sharon with a smile.

'Oh, I beg your pardon—hoops.'

As the women prepare the trays of food, Merve utters something in Turkish to Fatima. Sharon carries a tray out into the lounge room and steers Merve along with her.

Fatima selects something from a tray on the bench and offers it to Justine. She takes one for herself. 'My mother is scolding me for mixing modern styles with traditional folk dress.'

Justine's eyes sparkle. 'And, I suppose, that top button *is* there for a reason...'

Fatima laughs and scatters crumbs all over the floor.

Justine continues in order to give Fatima time to compose herself. 'She doesn't mind that you wear modern...'

'No... no, not at all,' interrupts Fatima with a dismissive wave, '... who minds? Then again, I did lose my job in Turkey because I wouldn't wear religious dress. And jumping through *hoops* to get a job wearing *that*,' she points at the coat draped over Justine's arm, '... will arouse some prejudice. But, on the whole, people don't mind.' She licks her finger. 'Isn't cuisine one of the most divine aspects of any culture?'

Justine shrugs. 'I wouldn't know—I'm Australian.'

Fatima snorts and gives Justine a hug. 'You're amusing, Justine. I believe that food, music and dance can bring us all together.'

'... and fashion?'

Fatima eyes the teenager with a raised brow. 'Well, now isn't that interesting—it's okay not to like Turkish Delight, or to be unmoved by Mozart, but if you don't wear the uniform you will be singled out.'

'Then, I'm confused. Why do you insist on covering yourselves if you live in a country where it is not necessary?'

Fatima gently lifts her coat from Justine's arm and places it over a chair back. 'Simply—my mother wears chador because of her faith. In Turkey, in the fifties and sixties, religious dress became outlawed and, for some families, including my mother's family, it meant that they had to make difficult changes to their beliefs...'

'... but now, she can dress in the way her religion wants her to?'

'Yes... yes... more or less. She is at an age now where she wants to savour that little triumph, even if, in this country, it is a completely meaningless gesture.'

'And you... why do you cover yourself?'

'Because I have the freedom to.'

'Are you religious?' Justine says impulsively, before realising her mistake. 'Oh, I'm sorry—it's none of my business.'

Fatima smiles wistfully. 'That's just the thing—I'm not religious...

not specifically.'

Confusion furrows Justine's brow.

'Something as abstract and as ephemeral as fashion, should not become a political issue—*that,* is ridiculous.'

Something about the way that Fatima has shaped their conversation propagates a growing logic in Justine's young mind. 'So, you're claiming your right... to be yourself... even if it means being judged.'

'Well done, Justine. What would be the point of me teaching political science if I felt too intimidated to wear hijab?' she gestures with empty hands. 'So, paradoxically, in this free society, I find myself dressing for a principle. It's very boring.'

They regard each other with growing admiration.

Fatima puts a finger to her mouth. 'You know, I've been thinking about a little project that I just haven't had time for—do you sew... clothing?'

Justine nods enthusiastically. 'Mum's teaching me.'

'Good... I'm thinking of creating a little hybrid vigour in the fashion world... you know—Eastern tradition meets Western chic.'

Sharon pops her head into the kitchen. 'Come on, girls! I think we're about to play a few party games.'

'Ooh yes, let's...' Fatima says encouragingly.

Sharon does a little shimmy. 'Sort of get us in the mood!'

'*Mum!*'

Fatima throws back her head and hoots loudly. She ushers Justine through the doorway.

The crowded lounge room pulses with excitement as neighbours chat and eat. The large coffee table in the centre of the room is piled with glittering boxes overflowing with lace and straps and shimmering fabrics in vibrant colours.

Fatima stands behind her mother and runs her hands down Merve's gown as they survey the display. 'Sharon... I think we require your expert opinion. It's surprising how much you can wear underneath one of these things, and I hate to think of what crimes against fashion my mother might be committing.'

Some nearby women laugh. Sharon moves over and strokes Merve's hand. 'We don't have any fashion police here. Just you go your own, sweet way.'

Through the open front door, old Mrs Bloom enters uncertainly from the entrance hall into the lounge room.

Sharon reaches out to her. 'Hello, Mrs Bloom... are you lost, or have you come to join the party?'

Mrs Bloom clutches Sharon's hand. 'Oh, no dear... well, a little... I might if I may... if it's not too much trouble...'

'Of course not... you're very welcome.'

Mrs Bloom pumps enthusiastically at Sharon's hand. 'Oh, lovely, dear, lovely... but do you mind if I phone my unit first? I want to check that my answering service is functioning correctly. May I use your telephone?'

'... um, of course you can. It's in the kitchen...' but Mrs Bloom has already headed in that direction.

Fatima leans towards her host. 'You know, Sharon, Mrs Bloom needs to be watched—for her own good I mean!'

'I know, I know,' Sharon says sympathetically, '... she's becoming quite...' and she bats at her head to indicate dottiness. 'I invited her, but it was just a gesture... being so, you know, forgetful and everything. I'm sure there's nothing on the table that would interest her.'

A tight huddle has formed around this particular conversation.

Gloria, from 2B, says, 'The other day I was taking in my groceries from the car, and I'd left the front door open—y'know, I was going backwards and forwards—anyway, I'm starting to unpack stuff in the kitchen, and the next thing I know, she comes wandering out of the bedroom mumbling something about not being able to find something or another...'

'Oh, I know,' says Penny, from 3A, '... she did the same thing in my place when I was carrying up my washing baskets. Scared the life out of me.'

Everyone tut tuts and nods their support.

Fatima edges in. '... getting rather cemented is she?'

'Oh, yes,' Penny interjects freely, '... she even ends up in the wrong *tower* sometimes.'

'Completely strange,' Gloria adds, '.. poor thing.'

Fatima looks over her shoulder towards the kitchen. '... hmmm... I'm not so sure.'

Sharon claps her hands. 'Well, I have to say, Fatima, how surprised we all are—and delighted—to see you here... I mean, you being so devout and all... so faithful to your, um... I didn't think that... well, I wouldn't expect you to... with your hijabs and everything...'

Fatima waves her hand airily. 'Oh... no, no! In fact, we have the ideal opportunity to wear lingerie. It's just that we wear it *under* our clothes... unlike some fashions.'

A titter of nervous laughter ripples through the group. Some furtively scan their attire to see whether they are guilty of a fashion faux pas.

'Really?' says someone, '... I didn't know Muslim women...'

'Well,' Fatima continues, '... I can't speak for *all* Muslim women— there are half a billion of us—but there are a good many, from Turkey, where I come from, that still practise many of the traditions of feminine beauty from the time of the Ottoman empire.'

'Wow!... wearing lingerie,' someone impulsively tenders.

'... hmmm... yes... and much more.' With her eyes, Fatima gathers in her audience. 'They were the women of the harem, and they would dress themselves in the finest and most sexually alluring garments. They were privileged and highly educated, and they bathed and nurtured their beauty with essence and oils. They would engage in full-body depilation...'

'... full-body what?' Penny asks with round eyes.

'Shave! All over. It's very liberating...'

The women unconsciously lower their gaze on Fatima, then abruptly resume eye contact.

Fatima holds out a slinky, red teddy from a box on the table. 'Ooh, I like this,' she says, and cants her head for a new perspective. She has everyone's undivided attention.

Sharon injects herself into this slightly awkward hiatus. 'Yes!... it *is* lovely. I think it would look really nice...' but she suddenly laughs self-consciously and puts her hand to her mouth. 'You know... I had no idea that those times were so sophisticated. I was going to play some party games to break the ice, but that seems a bit silly now. Why don't you tell us more about the harem, Fatima?'

The others concur with vigorous nods and expectant eyes.

Mrs Bloom reappears, shuffling aimlessly into the lounge room and looking gormlessly about.

Sharon stands on tip-toes and addresses her over the heads of the guests. 'Mrs Bloom... did you manage to... with your answering machine?'

Mrs Bloom grins with large and perfect teeth. 'Yes, dear... yes. Oh, it's such a confusing thing... don't you think?... all this modern technology.'

Everyone in the room is hushed, out of deference to the old lady.

She clutches at the arms and elbows of others as she wends her way to the door. 'It's not often that one gets to hear one's own voice... it's quite a revelation. I thought I sounded a bit vague, you know... a little, well... *doomed*, actually. I don't sound like that to you though, do I?'

The group responds with a rush of denials.

Mrs Bloom at last reaches the door and looks back. 'No, I didn't think so... it's my hearing, you know...'

'You won't stay for our little party?' Sharon asks tentatively.

Mrs Bloom clings to the door frame. 'Thank you, darling, but no... it looks very tempting, but I'm never certain about which bits I should cover and what I'm allowed to expose, so I simply cover everything—it's safer that way. But you have a lovely party, my dears—oh, golly, when I was your age, it was nothing but party, party, party. I was a wonderful dancer, you know... quite the belle of the ball...' She grins one last time, slides out into the hallway and scurries out of sight. She narrowly misses Barney, lurking near the door with a glass of beer in his hand. With a malevolent squint at him, she lurches on her way.

Barney steadies his drink. He rolls his eyes at Mrs Bloom's departing form then turns back to the door, just as somebody closes it from inside. He glances furtively over his shoulder then sidles carefully to the door and places his ear to it. An evil smirk comes to his face. He sculls the last of his beer, puts the empty glass to the door, and plants his ear to the glass.

In the lounge room, the congregation adjusts to Mrs Bloom's sudden absence.

'What do you suppose she meant by 'doomed'?' Penny says in a piercing little voice.

They all ponder this for a moment.

'Oh, I suppose,' Gloria says uncertainly, '... she senses that, you know... the time is coming.'

Sharon snorts with disdain. 'Don't you worry, she's as tough as nails... she'll be with us when *this* place is nothing but a pile of *rubble!*'

On the other side of the door, Barney nearly drops his glass with shock.

A soft rumble of murmurs commences as the women resume their conversations.

Sharon calls out over the top, 'Fatima, why don't you tell us more about depilation, and how liberating it is. I'm getting all excited.'

A swell of eager voices give their approval.

Barney straightens in alarm. He stares with wide eyes down the length of the hallway. He shakes his head in disbelief. A strong voice on the other side of the door comes to him. He hastily repositions the beer glass.

Fatima looks at her neighbours with a gleam in her eye. 'Aha!... that is what the women of the harem did best—stirring excitement!' She reaches out and languidly pulls a set of satiny Cheeky Line briefs from one of the boxes. 'You see, the Sultans invested *massive* amounts of money in the harem. Why? So that he could be titillated each night? So that he was sure to have a son—an heir? No. To be selected for the harem was a great honour, because it allowed a woman to do something for her country. It allowed her to be part of the great power play that all nations are engaged in. Constantinople was at the centre of art and science for the best part of a thousand years, and it was not a large army of soldiers that protected the soft cultural heart of that society—no, it was a small army of women.'

The lounge room is deathly quiet.

On the other side of the front door, Barney holds the beer glass with two hands to stop it from trembling.

Fatima holds the briefs to her face and stretches the glossy fabric to cover everything below her eyes. 'The great empire of the Ottomans was maintained by the women of the harem. How? Because they shared the beds of the most influential men of the time. The Sultan generously gave away beautiful and talented women to all foreign dignitaries—generals, ambassadors and princes—and the concubine would report back anything of interest that she might overhear at court or in bed or anywhere in between. She was the perfect spy and, like a spy, she was trained in the arts that would make her effective, or, in her case, irresistible to men.'

'A spy,' Penny sighs, '... how amazing.'

154

'So,' Gloria drawls with a puzzled brow, '... the harem girls weren't there to pleasure the Sultan at all?'

Fatima guffaws. 'What? Are you crazy? No doubt he bonked himself stupid every night. I mean, why wouldn't he? But that was a fringe benefit. The real purpose for nurturing those girls—the real reason so much money was spent on them—was to place them in the corridors, or rather, the boudoirs, of power.'

Penny looks vacantly into the distance. '... and to think that my fantasies about being a harem girl were only ever about being a sexual slave...'

'Ooh, I know,' Gloria says with a little shiver, '... can you imagine Q introducing the latest in technology.' In her best British accent, she says, 'Pay attention, Bondina... now, this little fellow is inserted here...'

The room erupts in laughter.

Fatima extracts a Floozie Bra-let from a box and holds it against herself. 'This is the only technology we require to fulfil our aims. It is more explosive than dynamite... it stays hidden under your clothes and you need no special training to use it. It's a small price to pay—it's worth the ultimate sacrifice...' She simulates a sexual grind.

Barney can barely contain himself. He straightens and fidgets indecisively. He looks left and right and accidentally drops his glass. He scurries after it, scoops it up, and hastens down the hallway.

* * *

Barney bursts into his unit and slams shut the door. He scrabbles with the locks, then leans with his back against the door, breathing heavily and staring anxiously into the distance.

'... right!... emergency...'

His eyes drift to the wall phone. With his mouth set in grim resolve, he propels himself forward, lifts the receiver and punches nervously at the buttons.

'... oh, shit!... too many zeros. Calm down... calm down... now, how many zeros in triple 0?... oh, right—three...'

Barney fretfully wends and winds the cord as far as it will allow. Suddenly, the connection is made—it's a woman's voice.

'Emergency Services...'

Barney holds the phone with both hands close to his mouth.

'Yeah, this is an emergency!'

'Do you require ambulance, fire or police service?'

'... ah, actually, I need to speak to ASIO... it's about a national security issue.'

'I can't give you that service, sir.'

Barney blinks with indecision. 'It's about a terror cell that I've uncovered—all women actually—they're planning to blow up my block of units.'

There is a longish moment of quiet on the other end.

Barney leans out to check that the door is closed. 'They're recruiting ah, Caucasians... y'know, Christians... whites, like you and me.'

'I'm Filipina.'

'Oh, right... whatever. Look, they're having secret meetings disguised as lingerie parties, but I know for a fact that they're suicide bombers.'

'... ri...ght...'

Barney gives a smug little snort and leans with one arm against the wall. '... and they're using the latest in depilation technology.'

'Hair removal?'

'What?'

'You said that they're using the latest in hair removal technology.'

Barney shakes his head with incredulity. 'I think they're planning on removing more than a few hairs, madam! Whatever it is, it's bloody explosive and doesn't require any training to use... you connect the dots!'

The operator's voice assumes a noticeable haughtiness. 'Do you mind if we monitor this call?... it's just a formality.'

Barney begins his pacing again. 'I don't bloody well care what you do with this call—as long as it reaches someone of authority... do you understand? I'm being vigilant, right! I'm becoming an integral part of the information gathering arm of ASIO! Didn't you read the paper this morning?'

'Ah, not that part—but I'll tell you what, we'll send someone over right away, okay?... because I've got to free up this line just in case a real... I mean, another emergency comes in.'

With a nervous look over his shoulder, Barney cradles the phone. 'Okay... that's better. Now, how will I recognise him—or her! Can you make it a her?'

'Who?'

'The ASIO agent, ya dill!'

'Oh, right. Ah, well, he'll find you... he'll know who you are. I've got to go now... I think the phone is being tapped.'

'Right...' Barney gives a little conspiratorial salute with his free hand, '... gotcha...'

He hangs up the phone and stares boldly into the distance. He nods slowly. 'Right... well, that went pretty good.' He looks across at the bar fridge. 'I think that deserves a beer.' He goes over and pulls out a stubbie and grins at the little joke forming in his mind. 'How would you like that, Mr Bond?' and in his best Connery says, '... shaken, please... not stirred...'

He chuckles indulgently to himself and says it once more for effect. '... shaken, please... not...' but he nearly drops his beer when there is a sudden knock at the door, '... shit!'

Anticipating another complaining tenant, Barney strides fatalistically to the door. 'What is it now?—wood rot?—mildew?—subsidence?—vermin?'

He reefs open the door.

A nondescript, middle-aged man in a bland jacket stands dutifully in the hallway. 'Hello... ah, my name is Dennis Gordon, and I'm the building inspector.'

Barney catches himself, the echoes of his ranting still audible. 'Oh... right, right. So, what's the problem? Everything's fine here... yep, no problems at all...' He tries to assume a suitably casual stance.

Mr Gordon bows his head and takes a step forward. He looks up at Barney. 'Look, Mr Evans,' he commences with great gravity, '... I've decided to visit you personally about the imminent demolition of your building. Now, according to our records, this building is to be condemned unless you and I take extraordinary measures to prevent it from happening.'

Barney slumps, peeved at being bullied by the authorities yet again. He folds his arms and scrutinises the inspector.

But something unexpectedly clicks for him—it's as though this man *blends* into the décor of decay around him. *This must be the ASIO agent, speaking to him in coded euphemisms.*

Barney's heart gives one pump of pure adrenalin. '... the imminent... condemnation... of this building...' he drones unevenly.

Mr Gordon looks grimly apologetic. 'Yes... yes, it must be a shock for you.'

Suddenly conscious of maintaining the façade, Barney straightens incongruously. With a fixed stare, he says, 'No... ah, no... not at all...' and, realising that he needs to convey his collusion in the matter, he gives a prolonged wink.

Mr Gordon eyes him warily. 'Really? Well, it is my earnest advice to you that you carry out a thorough inspection of all units for any sort of anomaly that ah, might render this building unfit for human habitation. Do you understand?'

Rigid with concentration, Barney processes this advice. '... thorough search... anomaly... unfit for human habitation...'

With a questioning eyebrow, the building inspector leans forward. 'Mr Evans?... are you with me?'

For Barney, this exchange is what he has subconsciously been willing to happen. 'Oh, I'm *right* with you.. absolutely.' He gives another exaggerated wink.

The building inspector breathes a heavy sigh. 'Right... good then. Well, I'll stay in touch.'

With a furtive glance down the hallway, Barney leans forward conspiratorially.

Mr Gordon feels obliged to turn his ear to Barney's mouth.

Barney whispers hoarsely, 'Can I just say... you blokes are *amazingly* quick.'

With a confused nod, Mr Gordon veers off down the hallway.

Barney closes the door and punches the air in triumph. '*Yes!* The game is in play—the terrorist mastermind versus the master spy.' He stills in mid-fantasy. This is the moment where all his failures and frustrations are behind him. He beholds a vision. 'Barney Evans— ASIO Operative.'

Hazim, having entered Barney's kitchen through the window, is calmly seated at the dining table watching his boss. With steepled fingers and a cynical smile on his face, he gives a little cough.

Barney jumps. 'Jesus!... Hazim. Why are you always sneaking around like that?'

Hazim gives a careless shrug. 'It's what I'm good at.' He waves an admonishing finger. 'Now, you wouldn't be planning to dob me in, would you, Barney?'

'What?'

Hazim gives a nod towards the door. '... talking to Mr ASIO.'

Barney chuckles with relief. 'No, my friend... no, no, no. You are more of the public nuisance type of criminal. *We*, are after the international terrorist type of criminal.'

'We?'

Unable to contain his excitement, Barney hastily pulls out a seat and sits down at the table.'Hazim! I'm an official agent for ASIO!'

'You're shittin' me.'

'Hazim, this morning I uncovered a terrorist cell so dangerous that the ASIO bloke was knocking at my door within thirty seconds of me hanging up the phone.'

'I don't believe it.'

'It's true! Absolutely true. We have a national security issue right here in Twin Towers, and it's my mission to, ah… assess the status of the situation at this junction.'

Hazim leans back in his chair with a dubious cast of his eye. 'So… how long have we got?'

'How long?'

'Yeah. How long have we got to lift all the good stuff before the planes…' he spreads his arms in a swooping gesture.

Barney stands abruptly. 'God!… I don't believe you, Hazim. Hundreds could die and all you can think of is their whitegoods.'

Hazim gives a dispassionate shrug of his shoulders.

Barney moves across the floor and comes to rest behind him, softly gripping the back of the chair. He ponders a train of thought that has been set in motion. '… of course, you do have a good point there.'

Hazim smiles evilly.

Barney breathes in sharply. 'Wanna beer?'

Hazim simply holds out his hand.

Barney scuttles to the fridge and pulls out a couple of bottles. He hands one across, gazing out at a distant horizon as he twists the top. Things are definitely falling into place for him.

This unfamiliar win/win situation makes him positively expansive. 'You know, Hazim, it surprises me how well we work together… know what I mean? I mean, you being from Iran an' all—don't they chop your hands off for theft in Iran? I read that somewhere... don't they?'

'I don't know, Barney. I've never lived there.'

Barney takes a swig and waves his beer about. 'Well, how do you... y'know, steal from people? Isn't that against your religion? Don't you have a difficulty with that?'

Hazim plonks his beer on the table and smacks his lips. 'Get real, Barney. I have the same difficulty with that as you do—none whatsoever.'

Barney laughs weakly and gives Hazim a little pat on the shoulder. 'That's true. Well, like I said, we are so very similar—in the best possible way, I mean. Human nature—it's a beautiful thing.'

Hazim looks at his watch. 'So... the Osmans' place. It might be time to make a move... what d'ya think?'

'No!' says Barney, emphatically slicing the air with his hand, 'We can't go in there—not just yet. I've got to suss the place out first—it could be dangerous.'

Hazim gives Barney a pointed look. 'WMDs?'

Barney wordlessly indicates that this could be a distinct possibility.

Hazim drains his beer. 'So, when are you going in?'

'Dunno... tomorrow morning. They'll be taking Kemal to soccer.'

'Oh, yeah.' Hazim looks at Barney from the corner of his eye.

There is a knock at the door and the two men reflexively stiffen. They look at each other before Barney responds in a tremulous voice.

'... it's open!'

Kemal lets himself in and stands deferentially by the door. 'Excuse me, Mr Evans, but my father was wondering whether you might have a new washer for the outside toilet.'

'A new washer for the outside toilet!' Barney retorts bumptiously, 'Well, today is your lucky day, Kemal, my son, because not only are you privileged to be presiding in the country with the best beer in the world—isn't that right, Hazim?'

'Give him the bloody washer, Barney.'

'Yeah, alright. We're havin' another one, Kemal. You up for a beer?'

Kemal looks behind him at the open doorway. 'Er, no thank you, Mr Evans.'

'Too early for you? You'll get a thirst for it soon enough... like Hazim here—isn't that right! Gets as dry as week-old road kill, don't you, mate. Sure you won't have one?'

'Yes, I'm sure. I'm not actually allowed to drink.'

Barney's face suddenly darkens. 'Yeah, right. You're quite happy to come through the door with the whole extended family, but it's not your kind of party—is that it?'

Kemal wrings his hands. 'It's just that I'm still under age.'

Hazim explodes in laughter. 'He's got you there, Barney!'

Looking nettled, Barney walks over to a cupboard. 'All right, then... let's see about this washer.'

Mustafa appears in the doorway. 'Excuse me... I was just ... oh, Kemal, there you are.'

Barney trawls with his finger through a plastic container. 'It's okay, Mustafa... we haven't sold your son into slavery.'

'Oh, ah... yes, very funny.'

'Not that I'd expect the same degree of civilised behaviour if, god forbid, your kind are ever in control.'

'Oh, you needn't worry about the washer, Mr Evans. It was just the corpse of a mouse that was preventing the plunger from performing correctly. It is working satisfactorily now.'

Barney's chest swells. 'Ah, well... there you are then—everything in tip-top shape at Twin Towers.' He squares up to Mustafa with smug defiance. 'My family were First Fleeters, you know. You know what that means?'

Mustafa gives a thoughtful pout. '... um... that they stayed just a little while?'

Barney's eyes flash. 'No, it doesn't! It means that we're still here and bloody proud of it... ya mad Dervish!'

Mustafa clasps his hands apologetically. 'Yes... yes, I see... you have a lot to be proud of. Well, thank you.' He turns to leave, but faces Barney from the doorway. 'You know... for migrants, it is best to leave our pride in our homeland—it is an unnecessary burden in a new country. Our children will make us proud.'

When Mustafa and Kemal have gone, Barney turns to Hazim. 'What the hell was that all about? Did you understand any of that? You're proud to be an Australian, aren't you?'

'Bloody oath, mate!' Hazim says, pointing to his empty bottle of beer.

Oh, right.' Barney meanders to the fridge. '... *our children will make us proud*... just because I didn't have any kids.'

Hazim grimaces and shakes his head. 'It's a... it's a tragedy, Barney. Are you sure they're at soccer tomorrow?'

'Huh?... oh, yeah.' He hands Hazim his beer. 'Anyway, how does he know that I don't have any kids?'

'He doesn't, Barney... you're reading too much into it.'

Barney looks vacantly at the door. 'Still hittin' below the belt but... as it were.'

* * *

The living room of the Osmans' unit is quiet and dark. The curtains are drawn and only faint road noises intrude. A sharp snap emanates from the kitchen. Outside on the balcony, peering over the kitchen window sill, Hazim puts down his jemmy and slides open the pane. With possum-like nimbleness, he wriggles inside. He heads straight for the lounge room and begins unplugging the television and DVD player. Mid-way through untangling the cords, there is a knock at the front door. He freezes and waits. Then, there is another sound—someone is inserting a key into the lock. Torn between finishing the job and running, Hazim flees into the kitchen. At the last second, he spies a large, black box sitting on the dining table. With a deft lunge, he grabs the parcel, sits it on the window sill, then climbs outside. He lifts the lid and has a quick peek inside. With a disappointed smirk, he replaces the lid and lets the box drop at his feet.

At the front door, Barney lets himself inside. Leaving the door ajar, he cautiously manoeuvres himself from point to point, waving his arms about with Kung-Fu readiness. He searches fruitlessly until he comes to the open window in the kitchen. With a quizzical brow, he leans out. Upon spying the box, a look of horror overcomes him. He straightens, clutches at his throat and stands, stricken, in the middle of the room. Then, with one parting glance at the window, he races for the door and leaps out.

The room is quiet again.

From behind the curtains, Mrs Bloom steps out and adjusts her attire. She calmly walks out through the open doorway.

* * *

The morning sun burns into the pitted concrete of the mailbox wall as Terry Crane shuffles out in his slippers to retrieve his newspaper. He pulls it out of the slot, cradles it lovingly in his hands and sighs audibly. A few other tenants make their way into the glare of the already hot day.

'Pristine condition, hey, Terry?' asks one tenant.

'Pristine condition,' confirms Terry, '... not a grubby fingerprint on it.'

The other tenants chuckle.

'Barney has been rather conspicuous by his absence, wouldn't you say?' says one.

Terry thoughtfully rolls the elastic band off the paper. 'Yeah, I suppose so… makes a nice change. Can't say I blame him… after that bomb fiasco.'

The others nod and still, each remembering how the day had unfolded for them—after Barney had raised the alarm about a terrorist bomb in the Osman's unit.

That Sunday afternoon had been their initiation into the nation's response to the anomalous. Sirens had wailed from near and far and, within ten minutes, the street had become gridlocked with emergency vehicles of all descriptions. Loudspeakers blared, firemen raced throughout the towers, pounding on doors and insisting on immediate evacuation irrespective of states of dress. Evictees were herded by imperious police towards detention buses, where they were left unguarded with no air-con—until the residents took the initiative to stroll back to the footpath. There, they shuffled for space with other bystanders and tried to get a glimpse of the heavily suited bomb-disposal expert who was making final adjustments to his rig amidst the madly flashing strobe lights that the police always seem to leave on, and which greatly adds to general alarm.

A hush fell over the streetscape when the bomb-squad man entered the building. Not a sound rose from any lip nor from any shoe on the pavement. The silent, frenzied flashing of the strobes held the crowd in suspense.

Then, a ripple of expectation spread—the bomb-squad man was returning from his mission.

He emerged through the entrance door holding out extendible tongs and, held in its vice-like grip, there dangled the shimmering satins and twisted straps of a colourful assortment of lingerie.

Standing in silence around the mailbox wall, the tenants regard each other with suppressed mirth as they recall the outcome of the episode—the entire street erupting in a roar of laughter—and Barney, mingling with officials whose favour he'd been cultivating moments before, standing open mouthed in utter bewilderment.

'He's become a bit difficult to find lately. It took me ages before I could tell him about the pigeons.'

'Nothing will get done... nothing will change... except if you live in unit five.'

'Yeah! Is that true, Terry? Are the Osmans getting preferential treatment?'

Terry shrugs. 'Seems like it. I know Barney is spending a lot of time in there, but don't ask me what he's doing.'

'God only knows why he became a landlord!'

'He inherited the place,' Terry replies.

'Fair dinkum!'

'Yep... his old man built this place. But he died when Barney was somewhere in his twenties.'

The other tenants reflect for a moment on this bit of information.

'So, he's always been a landlord?'

Terry nods. 'As I understand it, yes. Apparently he was headed nowhere good.'

'Like, criminal, sort of?'

'Yeah, yeah... his father was a crook—y'know, council kick-backs, that sort of thing.'

'How do you know all this, Terry?'

Terry laughs. 'Mrs Bloom.'

'Ahh...' the others acknowledge as one.

'So, he kind of landed on his feet then,' someone suggests.

Terry gives a sardonic grimace. 'Do you think so? I don't know that Barney would see it that way.'

'What do you mean?'

'Well... do you think he likes having to be around us? Families—people with holiday plans—who visit each other's units.'

The group slowly meanders back to the entrance.

'Why doesn't he just sell the place then?'

'Too late now. They're both beyond redemption—the buildings, I mean. And Barney too, I suppose.'

The men ascend the stairs.

'I d like to know what he's doing in the Osmans' place.'

* * *

Barney is in the Osman's unit, lying on his back under the kitchen sink.

Fatima gathers her handbag and car keys from the dining table and stands for a moment with a contemplative look. 'It was an honest mistake, Barney. You were quite right in reporting it as a suspicious object—although I have no idea how that box came to be outside on the landing.'

Barney makes some conciliatory noises from inside the cupboard, and lifts his head to peek out.

Fatima sighs. 'It's terrible that we are creating such a climate of fear.'

Barney wriggles out from under the sink and discreetly inspects the contents of some nearby drawers while Fatima's back is turned.

'If it's any consolation, it was as embarrassing for me as it was for you—having all my high-performance underwear waved about to everyone in Twin Towers.' She toys with her keys.

Barney resettles himself under the sink.

'Well, I've got to go to work. Kemal is in his room if you need anything. I do appreciate it very much that you are doing so many repairs.'

'Not a problem, Mrs Osman... not a problem. I won't be much longer.'

'Alright then.' Fatima calls out to Kemal. 'Bye, my love... I'll be

back at six. Come and give your mother a kiss—don't be shy now.'
She winks at Barney.

Kemal rushes out of his bedroom. 'Okay, Mum... okay.' He gives
his mother a peck on the cheek.

With an exaggerated Middle-Eastern accent, Fatima says, 'Is that
how you Aussie boys kiss?'She blows her son a little kiss and lets
herself out.

Kemal fidgets indecisively then turns to look at Barney's torso
sprawled out onto the kitchen floor. He is rather disadvantageously
exposed with his legs apart and the red of his underwear visible.

Barney chuckles. 'There's no end to the embarrassment that
women will create for you in life, son!'

Kemal averts his eyes.

Barney leers out from under the sink. 'I could tell you a few
things about the wooing of the fairer sex—a few tricks to get your
end in. You with me?'

Kemal swallows. '... er, no thanks, Mr Evans.'

'No, I'm just saying that sometimes it's hard to get the low-down
from your parents, y'know? They're too embarrassed to tell you
about their own fumbling in the dark.' A tool clatters to the floor
under the sink. 'Maybe they've never had anyone else, know what
I mean?'

Kemal asserts himself. 'They haven't—they had an arranged
marriage.'

A whole bucket of tools clatters to the floor. Barney extricates
himself from inside the cupboard with maximum noise and haste.

'You're kiddin' me! An arranged marriage? Bloody hell, that's...
that's... that's not match making—that's match fixing! It's un-
Australian.' He sits on the floor, covered in grime.

Kemal moves to the lounge room windows and draws back the
curtain.

Barney is still shaking his head in disbelief. 'I'll tell you what, mate, you must be counting your lucky stars that you ended up in Oz, hey! Am I right? An arranged marriage—that's bloody wrong, isn't it. It should be banned, mate... should be outlawed. You can't stop people's freedom to choose. It should be banned.'

Kemal is still cautiously peering through the window.

'Australia—well, you know for yourself—is a lot more tolerant, and we wouldn't put up with bullshit like arranged marriages. We embrace our freedoms—and we've got the steroids in our police force to make sure it stays that way.'

Kemal turns suddenly. 'Are you married, Mr Evans?'

'Three times, mate! I've stepped up to the nuptial crease on three occasions... and been bowled for a duck each time.'

'What did you like about them before you married them?'

Barney's brow creases in a taken-aback frown. '... what did I?... I didn't think I'd have to explain something like that to a red-blooded, good lookin' feller like you, Kemal. Doesn't it perk you up when you see a woman with all the bits in all the right places? Stirs my loins, mate, I can tell you.'

He repositions himself under the sink, creating a visual horror as his shorts ride up.

Kemal parts the curtains again and looks anxiously out.

Outside, Justine approaches the mailbox wall, looking behind her with a secretive glance at the window.

Kemal hastily turns towards Barney. 'Mr Evans... I just need to see someone briefly. Will you be okay if I go?'

Barney lifts his head. 'Huh? Oh, okay, yeah... that'd be good—I mean, sure, son, go ahead, I'll be right.'

Kemal hurriedly leaves through the front door. Barney waits for a discreet while then rolls out of the cupboard. He stands in the centre of the kitchen, flicking his fingers with indecision, and then darts off into Kemal's bedroom.

                                    *   *   *

Kemal strolls to the mailbox wall and casually looks deep inside
the slot. The box is empty. He stands straight, looking a little lost.
Justine, leaning with her back against the front of the structure,
surreptitiously passes him a sales catalogue, which Kemal takes
with a whispered 'thanks'.

The two of them studiously examine their respective catalogues.

Justine nonchalantly turns a page, 'Why didn't you come last
night?'

Kemal turns to a new page, featuring specials on barbecues. 'I
couldn't get away.'

'I waited for ages. I think people were getting really suspicious of
me lurking outside for so long.'

'I'm sorry, Justine. My uncles were over last night, and we had a
big meeting about a building project that they're thinking of doing,
and I was sort of included in the whole thing. Mum would have been
really suspicious if I had left.'

'I really wanted to talk to you, Kem—I really needed to talk to
you.'

Kemal looks over his shoulders at the Twin Towers, then quickly
skips around to the front of the mailbox wall. He puts his arm around
Justine, and together they sink down and lean against the concrete.

'I need to talk to you too, Justine. I... I think we might be moving
away from here.'

Justine throws her hands to her mouth. 'Oh, no... Kem!'

'I'm not sure what's going on—I was thinking about you the
whole time. It was something about us moving until we're ready to
move into the new units that my family is building.'

Justine is distraught. 'Where? Where are you moving to?'

Kemal clasps Justine's hand in his. 'I don't know. I was trying to
think of a way to get down to see you, and it was just my uncles

                                    170

talking about this new architect-designed building, and showing me a model of it, and wanting me to paint the site board or something, and I just didn't have my mind on it... so, I don't know...'

Justine grips Kemal's hand in both of hers. 'Kem, I don't want you to leave—I'll go crazy if you're not here.'

The two of them shuffle closer together in the shade of the mailbox wall, Kemal looking dejected and Justine looking forlorn.

At the entrance door to one of the towers, Mrs Bloom makes her unsteady way to her mailbox.

Justine rests her head on Kemal's shoulder. 'Oh, Kem... I don't want anything to change.' She studies Kemal's hand in hers. 'What's a site board?'

Kemal stares across the footpath. 'I don't know... oh, a board with model buildings on it and a space for the new construction. It's supposed to show shadow fall on nearby buildings... stuff like that. It's in my room. I'm supposed to paint it—all white, or something. Uncle Mehmet took the main building home with him to make some modifications.'

Justine raises her lips to Kemal's cheek. 'I'll come and live with you, Kem.'

They turn to each other and kiss in a delicate embrace.

Mrs Bloom, meanwhile, fusses with her mail on the other side of the wall. By chance, she peers over and spies the two teenagers. Lingering with her elbows on the wall and with her chin cupped in her hands, she observes the young lovers. 'Ahh, the sweetness of love's first blossom,' she croaks with an indulgent smile.

Kemal and Justine clutch at each other in fright.

Mrs Bloom attempts to calm them by showing more of her teeth.

Justine smiles back uncertainly. 'Mrs Bloom—please don't tell anyone.'

Mrs Bloom tut-tuts. 'Oh, I wouldn't dream of it. I was young too, you know—it seems like only yesterday. Was it yesterday? No, of course not. Yesterday was recitals with Mr Wiesenthal. It must have been the day before. Oh, I've forgotten... what was I saying?'

Justine squirms to face Mrs Bloom, but remains below the height of the wall. 'Mrs Bloom, you mustn't tell anyone about us, will you?'

'Good heavens, no! I know how to keep a secret.' She taps the side of her nose.

'Oh, good, good... excellent.'

'I used to work for the Mossad, you know,' says Mrs Bloom, with a glance over her shoulder.

Justine gives a suitably dramatic little gasp. 'Really! How exciting.'

'... and dangerous.'

'Of course.'

Mrs Bloom leans closer, '... but the struggle goes on forever, you know... we have to hang on with tooth and nail.'

'... ri...ght...' Justine says, risking a peek over the wall. 'Hang on to what, Mrs Bloom?'

'This!' Mrs Bloom waves her arm to encompass the Twin Towers, '... our home.'

'Oh, yes, of course.' Justine gives Kemal the nod for a quick escape.

Mrs Bloom's hands shake with emotion. 'I am the last bastion against the threat of the new terrorism.'

Kemal puts a cautionary hand onto Justine's shoulder. 'The *new* terrorism?'

'Oh, yes!' Mrs Bloom cries, momentarily forgetting the secretive nature of their little discourse, '... it's very insidious... it comes from *within*,' her last word uttered in a hoarse whisper.

'Within?' Kemal says, as Justine makes impatient big-eyes at him.

'Yes!... from within here,' Mrs Bloom points at the two buildings behind her.

'Twin Towers?'

'Precisely! You see, when you live in a culture of fear, you are forced to make alliances with all the wrong people, and eventually they will disappoint you because they were never your friends in the first place.'

Mrs Bloom walks around the mailbox wall and, with some difficulty, settles herself in between Justine and Kemal, 'The *new* terrorism,' she continues, encapsulating the idea with her hands, '... is ever so subtle. It works on the mind in the same way as the old terrorism in that it generates distrust and unreasonable fear—it makes us less able to function effectively—it makes us compliant to the demands of the aggressors.'

'The aggressors? And who would they be?'

Mrs Bloom spreads her hands. 'Well, that's just the thing! It could be anybody—everyone is capable of it. You see, terrorism is not an ideology—it has always been reactionary, but when it is supplanted into the political landscape, we orientate ourselves to take a side and we forfeit our impartiality—our freedoms—liberties—our independence...'

Kemal resists Justine's gentle tugging at his hand. 'I don't understand—how is this playing out here, at Twin Towers?'

'Well,' Mrs Bloom turns to face Kemal with a furtive squint to her eye, '... I know for a fact that a number of people are plotting to evict us... make us homeless... take away everything we have...'

'How do you know all this, Mrs Bloom?' With her head virtually on his shoulder, he can smell the floral scent of the old lady's perfume, stronger than ever.

'I told you—I was a secret agent. I learned how to spy. I learned how to tap phones.' She winks shrewdly.

'You... you've tapped phones?'

Mrs Bloom gives a superior cast of her head. 'I've tapped every phone in Twin Towers. I monitor every call that gets made... and I happen to know that the council wants to demolish the Towers. A chap by the name of Dennis Gordon has repeatedly rung Mr Evans about this conspiracy.'

Justine has slipped down against Mrs Bloom. She puts a frightened hand to her shoulder.

'Did you say, *every* call?'

Mrs Bloom reaches over and pats Justine's hand. 'Don't worry, my dears—to conspire for love is not a great sin, but to love to conspire—that's all I have left at my time of life.'

The old lady clutches hold of the young ones either side of her and levers herself off the ground. 'We'll just have to promise to keep each other's secrets... yes?' She pinches their cheeks. 'You have given me hope for the future—shalom, my dears.'

Mrs Bloom shuffles away, picking up the mail that she'd left on top of the wall. She heads back to the tower entrance then pauses as she passes the open door to the Osmans' unit. She peers inside, but hastily resumes her course when she hears someone approaching.

Hazim strolls into the entrance way and pulls up short when he spies the Osmans' open door. He slyly scans in all directions. Out on the footpath, Kemal and Justine are walking hand in hand down the street. He goes to the doorway and calls softly. Not getting a reply, he glides quickly into the lounge and begins unplugging the entertainment stack. He soon has all the components free and bundled. He hefts the lot in his arms and is about to exit when Barney emerges from Kemal's bedroom. Unable to see over the pile of electronics and hoping to avoid detection, Hazim stands perfectly still.

Barney is visibly distressed. He has the site board in his arms and he totters about, moaning and keening. He bumps into Hazim. 'Ahh! Hazim!'

Hazim sighs with relief. 'Oh, it's you! What are you doing here?'

'Oh, Hazim... Hazim...' Barney says in a disconsolate whimper.

Hazim makes a quick change of plan. 'Open the kitchen window for us, will you, Barney!'

Momentarily at a loss, Barney slopes off into the kitchen and puts the site board on the dining table. He sniffles and sighs loudly as he slides open the window.

Hazim rests his booty on the sink. 'Good onya, mate. Here, help me lower this out.' He leaps out of the window.

Barney passes across the gear as Hazim gently stacks it on the landing.

'It's the young feller, Hazim,' Barney wails, '... it's been him all along.'

'Kemal?' Hazim jumps back inside.

'Yes, yes... Kemal. He's a bloody terrorist.'

Hazim looks about the kitchen. He heads for the food processor. 'And how do we know this, Barney?'

Barney throws up his hands in anguish. '... because,' he turns suddenly to the table and grips the site board. 'Here, I'll show you.'

Hazim plonks the processor on the sink and goes over.

Barney indicates with a quivering finger. 'See! This is the main road... the shopping centre and the indoor sports complex... the park... and here...' his voice breaks with emotion.

No Twin Towers.' Hazim says, looking at the empty space in the middle of the board.

'Exactly!' Barney squeals, '... this is what they're planning, Hazim. There *is* going to be a second apocalypse. *Now* do you believe me?'

Hazim stills for a moment as he comes to terms with the scale of the issue. Then his eyes rove about the room, resting on anything of value. 'What are you going to do?' he says, mechanically.

Barney lowers his head into his hands. 'I don't know, Hazim... I don't know...'

Hazim suddenly has an idea. 'The ASIO guy! Ring him—aren't you an official agent? That's what you said!'

Barney spreads his hands in defeat. 'I don't have his number... he only ever contacts me.' He lifts his doleful face, '... although, I suppose I could try emergency services again.'

'That's the spirit,' Hazim says, '... you give them a tinkle, and I'll just carry on here for the moment.' Then a thought occurs to him, 'You don't suppose Kemal has gone off to, y'know... blow us up already?'

The two of them dwell briefly on this likelihood.

'No,' Barney says, looking into space, '... his mother said she'd be back at six.'

Hazim looks at his watch. 'Plenty of time!' He hustles off in the direction of the television.

Barney goes to the wall phone and purposefully dials triple 0.

The same woman as before takes his call. 'You have reached emergency services... do you require ambulance, fire or...'

'I need to speak to ASIO,' Barney interrupts.

There is a short silence. '... not you again...'

'Look, it's for real—the terrorist threat is emerging before my very eyes.' He turns to face the dining table.

'Like last time... when they stole your lingerie.'

'Listen here, missy—I am literally staring at a space where my building used to be!'

The phone is silent for a moment. 'You're kidding me.'

Barney looks obliquely into the mouthpiece. 'No! I'm not!'

Just then, Mrs Bloom meanders into the room, still clutching her mail. She approaches Barney, on the phone with his back to her. 'Oh, heavens, wrong unit,' she says glibly, '... I've done it again. Honestly, I'm becoming so simple that it occasionally frightens me.'

Barney turns to her.

Mrs Bloom does a double take. 'Oh! It's you! What are you doing here?'

Barney cups the phone and glares at her. 'More to the point—what are *you* doing here?'

'Don't try to intimidate me, you horrible scoundrel.'

The phone squawks. 'Hello... are you still there?'

'Yes, yes... sorry... just dealing with one of my tenants...'

'Injured, are they?'

Barney scowls. 'Huh?... no, I wouldn't say injured exactly. Demented, yes—mad even...'

Mrs Bloom commences beating Barney with her mail. 'Don't you dare call me demented. I used to be a spy, and I know exactly what you're up to, you heartless, heartless man...'

Barney cowers and does his best to protect himself with the phone.

The consultant's voice rises with concern. 'Is the patient becoming hysterical? I can hear commotion.'

Turning his back on Mrs Bloom, Barney tries to sound in control. 'No!... it's alright. It's just an old lady—she seems to be upset about something.'

Mrs Bloom swats at Barney with surprising aim. 'I know that you are conspiring to throw us all out...'

The voice on the phone gets louder. 'I should think she would be upset if her house is lying in ruins around her ankles!'

Barney dodges and frowns. 'What?'

Mrs Bloom punctuates her rant at Barney with well-placed kicks. 'After all these years of putting up with no hot water, leaky gas, cockroaches...'

Barney protects his groin whilst still trying to hear the phone.

'... her house!... blown up by terrorists...'

'Oh!... no, no. The building is not actually destroyed just yet. It's only the model that they've destroyed—but the intention is obvious. Get off me, you crazy woman!' he roars at Mrs Bloom after copping a knee to the thigh.

This provokes the old woman to a new level of violence. '... and did I ever complain? No! I always paid my rent... never caused any trouble...'

'Then who is that attacking you?'

Barney is down on one knee. '... this? Oh, this is just Mrs Bloom. She's normally very sane—well, reasonably sane—at least, not as insane as this. I'll just ask her what the matter is, hang on...' Barney grabs hold of Mrs Bloom's raised leg. 'For god's sake, woman! Will you stop hitting me. What's gotten into you?'

Mrs Bloom retrieves her leg and fixes Barney with a malevolent glower. 'I know what you're up to, Barney Evans—you and that so-called building inspector... plotting to evict us all just so you can bring in new, rich young tenants. Do you think that I don't know that this city is growing—that there is a shortage of housing. You're cashing in!'

With palms in surrender, Barney stands and backs away from the old lady. 'Now, Mrs Bloom, please... I assure you that I am not the one you should be worried about. The whole picture is, well, even worse than what you're thinking.'

'Oh! And how is that?' She straightens her attire.

'Well, you may find this difficult to believe—and I don't want to alarm you unnecessarily...'

'That's not likely!'

'... but, this building is a confirmed target for destruction by terrorists.'

'What nonsense! If it was, I would have known about it.'

Barney gives a patronising blink. 'Really, Mrs Bloom. Well, perhaps you can tell me why it is that...'

During the whole episode with Mrs Bloom, Hazim has been madly stripping the place of everything he can lay his hands on—even the curtains. He has been hoiking his booty out of the kitchen window and has now come to the last remaining chair. Barney, confident of his superior position in the confrontation with his tenant, and with a look of disdain, aims his bottom at the seat. Hazim, in a blur of movement, whips it out from under Barney just as he is about to settle on it. Barney crashes to the floor in an ungainly sprawl.

178

Mrs Bloom looks down her nose at him. 'You're a disgrace! I'm going shopping.' She turns on her heels and leaves the room, leaving the door open.

The phone has sprung back to the wall on its coiled cord. 'Hello?... hello?... is everything okay?'

Barney rolls onto hands and knees and glares at Hazim. 'Shit! Hazim! What the hell are you doing?'

The plaintive voice on the phone travels clearly in the empty room. '... hello?... are you still there?'

Barney rolls over to the wall. 'Yes, yes... I'm still here. Look, this is not a good time for me. I might have to call you back later, okay?'

'I'm afraid I'm obliged to conduct a caller-awareness-protocol before you hang up.'

Barney frowns. 'A what?'

'It's just a little test... to assure the emergency services that you haven't sustained concussion or become disorientated, and that you're not hallucinating as a result of trauma.'

'I only fell off the chair.'

'Is it night or day?'

'Wha?... it's day.'

'Good. Are you with someone at the moment?'

'.. um, er...' Barney looks over at Hazim who is attempting to reef the kitchen sink out of the bench top, '... yes, I'm with someone at the moment.'

'Excellent. And what is this person doing as we speak?'

Barney raises his eyebrows. 'As we speak? Ah, this person is lifting the kitchen sink out of the bench top.'

'Uh huh... lifting the sink... um, that's rather unusual, isn't it?'

'Well, yeah... it is a bit. Even for him.'

'.. ri...ght... and what would this person be doing now?'

Barney sighs with exasperation. 'Well, now this person would be staggering over to the window and would be attempting to throw

179

the sink out. Now! Can I go?'

The consultant takes on a mollifying tone. 'I think it would be a really good idea if we became friends, don't you think? We could talk to each other...'

The sound of the main entrance door slamming alerts both Barney and Hazim. Barney hurls the phone away and rockets to his feet. The two of them rush for the window. Barney spies the site board on the floor, grabs it and thrusts it outside before he clambers out of the window.

Fatima's melodious voice comes from the hallway. 'I'm home early, Kemal.' She lets herself in through the half open doorway and stares at the completely bare room.

The phone swings ominously on its cord. '... you could tell me where you live and maybe I could come and visit you in my special van... you'll like it... it has flashing lights and a siren...hmmm?... what do you think?'

* * *

A dejected Barney enters his unit, dragging the site board behind him. He slides the board onto the dining table, plonks down heavily on a chair and stares expressionlessly into space. His hand moves to the empty space amongst the other model buildings.

There is a knock at the door. Barney obediently rises and shambles across the floor. With a resigned sweep, he opens the door.

Dennis Gordon, the building inspector, clutches tightly at his clipboard. 'Ahem, good afternoon.'

With admirable stoicism, Barney looks him in the eye. 'Really?'

Mr Gordon composes himself. 'I'm sorry to have to bring you, ah, bad news...'

'Oh!... *bad* news. Well, at least that will make the rest of my day seem good in comparison... when I could have done with your assistance... when I could have benefited from that organ called ASIC, who, when the shit hit the fan, left one of their men in the field completely at the mercy of a demented old woman.'

Mr Gordon's eyes wander about in confusion. 'Mr Evans, it is not my decision alone, but the council has decided that your buildings, Twin Towers, are to be condemned as unfit for human habitation, and I hereby serve you with notice for the evacuation of your units by the end of the month.' He hands Barney a writ.

Barney adjusts to this new reality with commendable composure. '... so, you don't actually work for ASIC...'

Mr Gordon bestows a contrite little pout. '... no...'

'.. and you haven't been running me at all ..'

'.. no...'

'.. and there probably isn't any terrorist threat to Twin Towers...'

'.. I shouldn't think so, no...'

Barney holds up the writ. '... and Twin Towers is now worth bugger all...'

Mr Gordon inclines his head in thought. '... I'm afraid so... what with demolition costs and...'

With a raised hand, Barney imperiously demands Mr Gordon desist.

The building inspector smiles tightly. 'Well, until the end of the month then, Mr Evans.'

Barney closes the door and walks back to his seat, oblivious of the fact that Hazim, having climbed in through the window, is already seated at the table.

'What are we gonna do, Barney?' Hazim asks timidly. 'Can I get you a beer? I'll get you a beer...' He fetches two beers from the bar fridge and delicately places one in front of Barney.

The room is ever so quiet.

Barney stares resolutely into space. He turns to Hazim. 'Have you ever broken into Mrs Bloom's unit?'

181

'Are you kidding? That place is like Fort Knox—not a chance of getting in.'

Barney smiles devilishly. He stands, goes to his tools cupboard and pulls a set of keys out of a drawer. 'This'll help.' He absentmindedly fondles the keys. 'There's a piece missing from the puzzle... and I think she's that piece.'

* * *

Justine and Kemal lean side by side in the shade of a shop awning.

Kemal scans the mall. 'How are we going to find her?'

'Kem... how difficult can it be to find a doddering old lady in canary yellow dragging a shopping trolley behind her?'

'Yeah, I suppose. Are you sure this is her shopping day?'

'I'm certain of it—Tuesday, pension day. It's the quietest day of the week.'

'How do you know about that?'

'My Nan. It's a time of the week when the queues aren't too long, and oldies can move about without being run over by yuppies.'

'Why isn't she here yet? Do you think she's sussed us out?'

'How could she, Kem?... we only thought of it this morning. Look, stop worrying—this isn't the Cold War. We're not doing a dead letter drop. We're not going to be bustled into a van by the Nazis.'

'... Stasi...'

'What?'

'Stasi. They were the East German secret police—during the Cold War.'

'Whatever. We are simply going for a stroll, in a free country, and we are going to accidentally bump into Mrs Bloom while she's doing her shopping—it's not a conspiracy.'

'... well, actually, it is a conspiracy—that's what we're doing—conspiring.'

'Kem! She's the only one that can help us. I want us to help her carry her shopping. We've got to get into her unit. We've got to get her to help us!'

Kemal puts his arm around Justine.

* * *

The door to Mrs Bloom's unit opens slowly. Barney pokes his head inside followed closely by Hazim. They enter and listen intently. Barney locks the door again.

'I can't believe it!' Hazim declares. '... she hasn't got a telly *or* a DVD player.'

'Shut up!' Barney hisses. He moves to the middle of the room.

Hazim tip-toes behind him. 'What are you expecting to find?'

Barney harks back his head. 'I'm just getting the vibes at the moment.' He rubs his jaw, 'She knew about the building inspector, that Gordon bloke... that was odd.'

Hazim holds up empty hands. '... not even a phone in this place.'

'Really? Where should it be then?'

'Here somewhere,' Hazim points at a large, enclosed wall unit.

Barney snaps his fingers and points. 'Bingo!'

The two of them investigate the cabinet closely. Suddenly, there is a click, and the whole front face slides open. Inside it is crammed with leads, reel to reel tapes and other electronic paraphernalia.

Hazim gawps with amazement. 'Unbelievable! She doesn't listen to music—she listens to us!' He reaches out to inspect something.

Barney pulls back his hand. 'Don't touch anything! If she is a spy, she'll have your prints faster than you can lift a piggy bank.'

'Oh, yeah... look, Barney, these cassettes are arranged in unit order.'

Barney bends down for a closer look. 'Everyone's phone calls— the Cranes—the Johnsons—the Osmans. A sleeper, Hazim, waiting for the moment to activate.'

Hazim grimaces anxiously. 'Not another conspiracy theory, Barney. She's just eccentric!'

'*Eccentric*, my arse! What's this? A cabinet with the unsold fifty percent of Telstra hidden behind it. She's a spy alright... no doubt in my mind at all.'

A light suddenly illuminates on one of the panels.

A voice comes through the speaker. 'Hello, Julie my love—it's me...'

'Oh, Kevin my darling—I've been waiting for you...'

'Julie, Julie... I'm so aroused by the thought of you. I'm at my window, behind the curtain... you can see me from your unit... go to your window... can you see me?'

'I'm going over, you hunk of man... I can't—oh, my goodness, Kevin!I *can* see you... oh, my... anyone would think that was just a little prickly pear on the window sill...'

'This is what you do to me, my pikelet...'

'Oh, Kevin, my love fountain. If I sit like this on the bench top, can you see that I'm completely bare underneath? Come to me Kevin, come to me—I want you...'

'I can't, my sweet... I can't walk like this. You'd better come over here...'

'Yes, yes... don't wither, my little cactus flower.'

The light on the console goes out.

Barney and Hazim are gobsmacked with hilarity. They are bent double with laughter.

Suddenly, Barney grabs Hazim by the arm. Voices can be heard in the hallway. The two of them quickly slide the cabinet closed. They look anxiously in all directions, then decide to dive behind the couch.

Keys scrabble against the lock of the door before it swings open.

Mrs Bloom enters. '... and wasn't that a lovely stroke of luck, meeting you at the shops... yes, it was...'

Justine and Kemal follow the old lady into the unit.

'Just put the things down on the table, my dears. Well, well, well... I'm home a whole hour early. Now, I'm sure both of you would like a nice big drink of cordial after that long walk, wouldn't you? I know I would...'

Justine steps forward. 'Mrs Bloom... it was really no accident that we bumped into you this afternoon. We want to talk to you.'

'Oh, that's lovely, dear... but you needn't go so far out of your way. You can visit me here any time.'

'Thank you, Mrs Bloom... we will. But we were hoping that you might be able to do us a favour.'

'Of course, my dear. When you get to my age, it's a rare privilege to be able to do anyone a favour. Fire away!'

'Well, you know how Kemal and I feel about each other—and Kem's family is starting a building project, and they're going to move away, and we might never be able to see each other again...'

Kemal puts his hands on Justine's shoulders. '... we were wondering if you could help us... if, maybe, you'd heard anything at all with your, um...'

'... with my taps?' Mrs Bloom adds.

'Yes, with your taps.'

An amazing transformation comes over Mrs Bloom. It is the consummation of years of duplicity. Though she can no longer be sure of why she engages the skills she learnt so long ago, she has a desperate longing to bring it all together, and the strange events around her are a sure sign that she has been right all along.

Mrs Bloom straightens to her full, still short, height and walks to the wall cabinet. 'I'm sorry to say, Kemal, that your family is part of the conspiracy to turn us all out into the street.' With a click, she slides the façade along, exposing the recording apparatus.

Justine and Kemal stare goggle-eyed.

185

'Whoa...' Justine murmurs.

'I won't pretend to understand everything I hear, but this is the latest call made by your father, Kemal, to a solicitor.'

Mrs Bloom selects a cassette and inserts it in the player. She turns to the teenagers.

'As far as I know at present, they want to buy Twin Towers and demolish it. I'm not sure about the reasons why.'

Justine looks distraught. Kemal stands motionless, staring at the cassette player.

Mustafa's voice emanates from the speaker. '... surely it can not be worth that much... I mean to say, the place is ready to collapse down at any moment...'

The solicitor's voice breaks in. 'I know, I know, Mr Osman... but until we can, how shall I put it, motivate the council to declare it condemned, the price will reflect its investment potential. Now, as soon as it gets a death sentence, it's not worth anything—less even than the value of the land, after you factor in demolition costs and the like...'

Barney and Hazim peer over the back of the couch while the others are facing the cabinet.

Mustafa continues. '... so, how do we motivate the council?'

'Oh, you leave that with me... we have a man in place taking photographs of all the faults in every unit. He owes me a few favours... a client of mine... a small time crook by the name of Hazim El Shahoud...'

Alarm shows on Hazim's face. Barney's hands reach for his throat. They disappear behind the couch with a few soft bumps and scrapes, but their commotion is masked by Justine's cry of anguish.

'Kemal! Is this true? Is your father employing criminals to... to destroy our homes? Oh, Kemal!' She rushes to the door.

Kemal intercepts her. 'Justine! Wait... wait, don't you see?' He walks her back towards Mrs Bloom. 'The site-board! It was here—Twin Towers! I didn't get to see it properly because I was too confused by everything. But now it's clear to me—this is the building project that my family is involved with. They want to build a new Twin Towers!'

This is fascinating news to Barney. He pops his head up from behind the couch, momentarily distracted from murdering Hazim.

Mrs Bloom switches off the cassette player. 'Well, bless my microphones! You know, Justine, darling, it's not Mr Osman's fault that his solicitor engages in unethical practices.' She pauses for a moment with a finger on her lips and surveys the surveillance equipment in front of her. 'I wonder whether this El Shahoud character has any photos of my unit? I shouldn't think so...'

Justine separates herself from Kemal. 'So, let me get this straight—we're all going to have to move away while the old building gets demolished and a new one is built.'

Kemal gathers his thoughts. 'Yes... yes. And then we all move back again—I remember now—a new Twin Towers! That's what they wanted. That's what they were designing—new units for everyone. That's what Dad said... but I wasn't listening because...' he looks at Justine.

'Oh, Kem!' Justine rushes into Kemal's arms.

Fatima Osman opens the front door wide and walks slowly into the room. She scrutinises the open cabinet. Her gaze then travels to Mrs Bloom, then to her son and lastly to Justine. She appraises the teenager with a critical eye. 'That is a lovely dress, Justine.'

'Thank you, Mrs Osman.'

'Did you make it yourself?'

'... with a lot of help from Mum.'

'It suits you very much. It's elegant... and assertive.'

'Thank you. I wanted to try something new—sort of, define myself. If you know what I mean.'

'I know what you mean, and it's working well. What do you think,

Mrs Bloom?'

Hunched and open-mouthed, Mrs Bloom has reverted to her dotty façade. 'Oh, I think the young generation is a wonderful thing… so full of life and vitality. Goodness, I remember when I was your age, we used to…'

'Mrs Bloom?' Fatima interrupts.

'Yes, dear?' Mrs Bloom smiles with ample teeth.

Fatima lifts a brow. 'I have been watching you for some time now. In this society we tend not to take old people very seriously… we allow them all sorts of indulgences if it will keep them out of the way. But, where I come from, we can't afford to waste such a resource, so old people do what they can… and I know the difference between senile and guile.'

Mrs Bloom straightens herself once again. 'It's nothing serious, Fatima. It's just,' she turns to the cabinet, '… my secret indulgence.'

'There is too much secrecy in the world already. Keeping secrets has never once made the world a better place. All it does is create intrigue and something for men to fight over.'

Kemal steps towards his Mum. 'I'm sorry, Mum. It was us—me, that imposed on Mrs Bloom. I was worried about what was going to happen… to all of us…' he reaches out for Justine's hand. 'It was stupid of me to go about it this way.'

Justine takes Kemal's hand in both of hers. 'It was my idea, Mrs Osman. It just seemed daring, and I thought she might be able to help us… and now we've just caused trouble.'

'You have no idea how much trouble, Justine. Our unit has been completely ransacked—everything has gone.'

The three others show their shock. There is a stunned silence.

'But, there are bigger issues to deal with,' Fatima continues, '… there is one major obstacle in our way forward, and that is the incredibly stupid, Barney Evans.'

The couch give a little lurch, but everyone in the room is too prcccupied to notice.

'... for some unaccountable reason, we—the company and the local council—can't seem to get through to him that we want to make him an offer that would be of benefit to all of us...'

Mrs Bloom gives a huge, smug smile. 'Well, it so happens that I may be able to help you... if that won't create too much intrigue,' she looks pointedly at Fatima. 'You see, from my spying on Mr Evans' calls, I've deduced that he thinks he is a secret agent tasked with an assignment to winkle out terrorists here in Twin Towers.'

Justine and Kemal gasp in amazement.

Fatima gives a derisive snort.

'It's true,' Mrs Bloom says, steepling her fingers, '... he believes that the building inspector is an ASIO operative sent to control him.'

The others laugh heartily. The backrest of the couch bulges.

Fatima's tenseness dissolves into a comfortable smile. 'I must say, I was quite suspicious of his sudden helpfulness... ugh! The man is quite appalling. Well, it looks as though it might all fall into place despite his stupidity—actually, because of his stupidity. I have just learned that Twin Towers is condemned and that it must be vacated by the end of the month. Our bid will be much lower now... but, we'll have to keep that a little secret.'

Mrs Bloom admonishes Fatima with a finger. '... tut, tut...'

Fatima laughs. 'Come on,' she heads for the door, '... I need some help to move our belongings off the landing and back into the unit.'

All four of them exit the unit.

Barney stands up from behind the couch, his face bereft.

Hazim's face appears. '... what are we gonna do, Barney?' he croaks.

Barney stares impassively ahead and makes his way to the door.

* * *

189

Barney, looking very inebriated, emerges from his bedroom, holding a bottle of spirits. With a mad smile on his face, he splashes the liquid liberally about.

'... fix this for me, Barney... when are you going to make those repairs?... you said it would be fixed by now... fix this, fix that. Yeah, I'll fix it alright... I'll fix it for me...' He splashes liberally all over the couch. 'Nothing that a nice little insurance payout won't fix. Then I'll go and live on the Barrier Reef and just refuse to sell what's left of this to anyone. They wanted a pile of rubble, and that's what they're going to get!' He throws the empty bottle into the bedroom. From a high shelf in the kitchen, he grabs another bottle and cracks it open. '... keep it all a little secret, huh... well, I've got a little secret too...' he talks to the open bottle, '... and you're going to help to make me comfortably off...'

He laughs maniacally and throws the bottle into the bedroom where it smashes against the wall. From his pocket, he extracts a box of matches and walks into the room striking a light.Moments later, there is a flash and a muffled explosion. Barney re-emerges in a cloud of smoke, coughing and batting at his clothing.

A red glow grows through the doorway.

'... this will fix it... this will make it better... think you can diddle Barney Evans, hey?... think I don't know what's going on?... how "incredibly stupid" am I *now*?'

There is a loud knocking on the door.

Barney turns in surprise. 'Oh!... a knock at the door—I must answer it before it burns down. Wait!... don't tell me—it's the smoke... no?... well, the smell then. Is that what you've come to complain about?'

Coughing and fanning at his face, Barney flings open the door. 'Oh, it's you.'

Dennis Gordon sighs deeply. 'Good afternoon, Mr Evans.' A billow of smoke wafts through the door. 'Is ... is everything alright?' He fans the air with his clipboard.

Suddenly conscious of his newly devised plan becoming exposed, Barney steps out into the hall and shuts the door behind him. 'Huh?... oh, yeah... everything's fine. It's just my toast... burning... to a crisp... as we speak...'

Mr Gordon half nods. 'I see. Well, marvellous. I bring you good news, Mr Evans.'

Barney remains transfixed in the doorway. 'Well, that's terrific, Mr Demolition.'

Mr Gordon averts his eyes. 'Look, I do want to apologise for that, but I was only doing my job.'

'As am I, mate,' Barney says with a clipped giggle.

'Yes, of course... but the issue here is that a case of impropriety has emerged in the proceedings regarding your building, and as a result, the demolition order has been revoked—Twin Towers has a clean bill of health... well, at least for the time being.'

Barney has slowly absorbed what he's heard. He blenches and, with a stricken look, feels around behind him for the door handle. Mr Gordon makes a dignified bow and hurriedly moves off.

Barney shoves open the door. Smoke swirls and eddies around him.

Hazim is standing in the middle of the kitchen with a look of terror. 'Barney!... I told them everything, mate... about the crooked solicitor... the bribes...'

Barney races straight to the bedroom door and looks inside. 'Don't just stand there, you fool! Get an extinguisher!'

'... he was blackmailing me, Barney...'

'Never mind that now! Get me the extinguisher from the hallway!'

Hazim scurries to the door and disappears outside.

Barney has another look into the bedroom, but is driven back by the heat. '... for god's sake, hurry!'

Hazim returns with the extinguisher. Barney snatches it from him, pulls the pin and aims it through the doorway. Nothing happens.

Barney shakes it violently. 'What's wrong with this thing?'

Hazim puts his knuckles to his mouth. '... it's out of charge, Barney... none of them have been recharged for twenty years...'

'Nooo...' Barney wails and falls to his knees. He suddenly has a thought. He hurls the extinguisher into the flames and staggers to his feet. 'Use water, Hazim... from the kitchen. I've got to ring emergency services. God, I hope the phone still works.'

Hazim races to the sink and begins filling up saucepans while Barney punches frantically at the phone.

The female operator answers immediately. 'You have reached emergency services... please state...'

Barney gushes into the mouthpiece. 'Emergency services!... yes, that's what I need. Hurry, it's an emergency...'

The line remains silent.

'... hello!... what's wrong with you, this is an emergency!'

The operator's voice is sabotaged with emotion. '... I can't believe you're doing this to me... why?... my job is stressful enough without you harassing me...'

Barney gesticulates wildly at Hazim to get a move on. 'I'm not harassing you, woman! Get a grip on yourself, and send a fire truck down here... pronto!'

'Fire this time, is it?'

'Yes, fire!... a bloody inferno, and it's out of control...'

'Oh, an *inferno*! And how did it start?'

'... how did it? Ah, well... it... it...'

'... spontaneous combustion, was it?'

Barney writhes with frustration. 'What does it matter? It's raging as we speak... I need help...'

'Yes, you do! You could do with a good hosing down.'

'Oh, no... look, I didn't phone for emergency counselling...'

'And I didn't ask for a serial attention seeker. You're a bloody nuisance, and if your place is on fire, you deserve to burn up in it! How dare you give me the run around. How dare you inflict your silly phobias on me. I'm here to help people in real trouble and you're just no end of trouble, and if your place burns to the ground and I get sacked from my job it'll have been worth it. You're a disgrace... a disgrace to all of humanity...'

Hazim emerges from the bedroom covered in soot. 'It's too late, Barney! We've got to get out of here.'

Barney is strangely subdued. He cups the phone. '... yeah... yeah... you go, buddy...' he waves to the door, '... I've just got to fix something...' he points to the phone.

Hazim hesitates for a moment, but a flaming crash behind him spurs him to the door.

Barney slides down against the wall. The lights go out. He cradles the phone. '... there go the lights.' He puts his head to his knees. 'You still there?'

The operator sighs heavily, '... yes, I'm still here.'

'Look, you're right—I have been a nuisance. I've been more than a nuisance. I've been responsible for a lot of bad things... creating a lot of bad feelings... creating a lot of trouble. And, you know what the funny thing is?'

'... no... what?'

'The funny thing is that I didn't actually *do* anything—I did nothing. Nothing to help anyone. And now it will all end in nothing.'

'... your place really *is* on fire?'

Barney snorts. 'Yeah, it really is. But, it's okay... it'll save on demolition.'

'Oh, my God! I'm dispatching a fire crew straight away.'

Smoke roils around Barney and he coughs vigorously. 'Oh, thanks... it *is* getting rather warm...'

'You've got to get out of there! The roof might collapse.'

Barney looks up. 'Frankly, I'm amazed it hasn't already.' He slumps to the floor. A fire alarm begins clanging loudly.

'Are you still there! Hello!...'

'Yeah, I'm still here.'

'You've got to get out!'

Barney breathes heavily. 'Looks like I'm not going to make it to that resort on the Barrier Reef after all. Do you look good in a bikini?'

'... no... I'm short and dumpy.'

Barney closes his eyes. '... no matter... I still love you...'

* * *

The early morning sun imbues the marble mailbox with a salmon pink. Either side of the structure, also in marble, is a curved sculpture that encloses the negative space of a Turkish dome. Leading onwards, along a glimmering quartz path bordered with pointed cypress pines and a rampant ground cover, is a stone terrace that precedes the columned foyer. Rising spectacularly into the sky in a series of supportive arches, the façades of the newly built towers glow orange in the dawn.

Barney Evans steps down from the terrace and strolls along the path to the mailbox wall. Wearing rush slippers with a mild curl to the toe, he is resplendent in white knee-length shorts with a colourful jubba over his white shirt. He stops at the wall and admires the bronze plaque that spells in large, raised letters—TWIN TOWERS. Pulling a large cloth from his back pocket he bends down and commences polishing the already shiny bronze.

Terry saunters down the pathway and gives a cheery wave. 'Mornin', Barney!'

'Mornin', Terry... it's gonna be a good one.'

Terry shields his eyes from the sun. 'Not wrong!' He pulls a newspaper from his slot.

A few more residents approach the mailbox and exchange

morning pleasantries.

Terry turns to the back page of his paper. 'Are you going to the show this afternoon?'

Barney returns the cloth to his pocket and pulls a paper from the slot marked 'Evans'. 'Wouldn't miss it for quids, mate.' He scans the headlines; they scream: GLOBAL WARMING.

'Look at this, Terry... look at this,' Barney slaps at his paper, '... if they're right about this global warming, then the hottest parts of the world are gonna get even hotter, right?'

Terry grunts in the affirmative.

'.. and the hottest parts of the world is where all the terrorists live, right?'

Terry looks up from the sports page. 'So?'

Barney spreads his hands in appeal. 'So... problem solved. They've just bogeyed in the sand trap.'

Terry grins. 'Hey, that wall next to the outdoor oven is looking really good.'

Barney acknowledges Mustafa as he bends to extract his paper. 'I'm getting a fair bit of assistance from the master of mosaics, here.'

Mustafa straightens his paper. 'Well, we have had a few thousand years of practice.'

Barney nods slowly. 'Oh, I was wondering... do you mind if I take the afternoon off? Y'know, to see the fashion um, thing.'

Mustafa smiles broadly. 'Of course, of course... you do not need to ask. We are all going. Are you wearing anything? Oh, excuse me— modelling anything?'

Barney snorts. 'No fear, mate. I don't think it's possible to dress this keg with legs and make me look distinguished.'

The others laugh. They turn and walk back up the path, leaving Barney alone at the wall. He has a curious smile on his face that widens when Justine comes tripping towards him. She is wearing a beautifully tailored pleated robe that swishes elegantly behind her.

She props provocatively against the side of the wall and eyes Barney.

Barney raises a brow. 'You still meeting Kemal here on the sly?'

Justine gives a lipstick pout of consideration. 'Nooo... well, yeah... sometimes. For old time's sake.'

Barney stands back and appraises the young woman. 'You really have adopted the whole um, Muslim thing, huh... with your long garments and... sorry, I don't mean to intrude.'

Justine sashays with her hands on her hips. 'It's okay, Barney... it's not really a Muslim thing though. I'm just taking the best of all fashions, from all eras and cultures, and I'm making my own style.' She does a little pirouette, 'What do you think? Is it sexy?'

'It's as sexy as hell, Justine... but isn't it a bit warm for today?'

'I'm not going to have it on for long.' She opens her robe dramatically to reveal a stylish one-piece, boy-leg swimming costume. 'The fabrics are so much better today than they were in the nineteen twenties. I'm going for a swim with Kemal.'

Justine delves into a pocket of her robe and extracts a small parcel. 'Mum wanted me to give this to you. Do you know what it is?'

Barney accepts the parcel in both hands. 'Yep, I know what it is.'

Justine leans on the wall with her chin in laced fingers. 'You know, Barney... I was kind of worried about... y'know, growing up and having to reveal myself—physically. You know what I mean?'

Barney looks solemnly at his feet. '... ah, no...'

'... well, it's just that we make such a big deal about exposing our bodies, you know... it's like our bodies are our resume in society... which isn't very enlightening, is it?'

'... no, I suppose not.'

'... but, like this, I can feel secure...' Justine hides coyly behind the collar of her robe, '... or I can feel sensual...' she exposes her leg to her upper thigh, '... and I can be sexual...' she leans forward and attempts to press her breasts together with her upper arms. 'Well, you know... it's a work in progress.'

'I think it's working,' Barney says softly.

Justine smiles sweetly. 'Oh, I designed something special for the M.C. tonight—that's you, by the way.'

'Me!'

'We all voted, Barney... you can't get out of it. We'll have a run through, don't worry.'

Justine turns on her heels, flings her robe in a languid arc and heads back up the path.

Barney sighs hugely and pulls the cloth back out of his pocket and wipes his brow. He kneels down in front of the plaque and gives the square rim a good polish. 'Whoa! That little girl will either bring peace to all Mankind... or fire up World War Three...'

Mrs Bloom peers over the wall. 'Having an engaging conversation with yourself, Mr Evans?'

'Good morning, Mrs Bloom. And whose place have you mistakenly entered this morning?'

Mrs Bloom rears a little at Barney's familiarity. '... I... I... well, actually, you know, Barney, it's becoming very tedious...'

Barney rises from the plaque and leans against the wall. 'Uh huh... tedious... what, everybody mad on security now?'

Mrs Bloom brushes away the idea. 'No!... no, quite the contrary. People see me prowling about and they call out from their kitchens and ask me whether or not I'd like a cup of tea!'

'That's very neighbourly of them!'

'... well, yes, I suppose it is. But, the other day, Sharon Crane informed me that my order had arrived—*whilst she was on the phone to someone*!... I don't want other people to know that sort of thing about me!'

'You shouldn't be tapping her phone!'

Mrs Bloom petulantly averts her face. 'What's so *very* annoying is that no one uses the home phone for... well, calls of a revealing nature. These days they've all got mobiles!... and I can't tap into those.'

Barney smiles softly at the old lady. 'That's too bad. It's too bad, because I owe my life to your nosiness, don't I?'

Mrs Bloom regains her superior demeanour.'Well, I was trained in that sort of thing, and when I intercepted your call, the old reflexes just came into play, and the next thing I know, I'm fighting through the smoke and dragging you out of your unit. Everything in between is a complete gap.'

'I thought most of your day was a complete gap.'

'Ha, ha... very funny, Mr Shouldn't-play-with-matches. Oh, and speaking of getting burnt... you should reconsider that e-share portfolio—it's a scam... you'll lose everything. If you want my advice, come up and see me. Who do you think financed all of this, hmmm?'

Barney stares goggle-eyed after Mrs Bloom as she meanders back up the path. Then, with a cautious check in all directions, he pulls a mobile phone from his pocket and punches in three numbers.

He waits intently with the phone to his ear.

'You have reached...'

'Hi, it's me...' Barney interrupts.

'Barney! You know you're not supposed to ring me on this number.'

'I know, but it's an emergency.'

'Oh, yeah... what sort of an emergency?'

'Oh, palpitating heart... on fire... little fat nude guy firing arrows at random...'

'... hmmm, sounds like an emergency. You might need the full treatment. Shall I come over at once?'

'You'd better. I've got a little something for you... and, um, I do mean little.'

'Oh... well, that'll be something I have to wear then.'

'How did you...?'

'Men!... you're so transparent. I must go. I'll see you soon.'

Barney pockets the mobile and leans with his bottom against the wall. He looks out to the road, his face at peace with the world. He pats his belly. '... transparent—that'd be a good start.'

Fatima walks down the pathway towards the mailbox wall. She quietly rests against it with folded arms.

Barney gives a little leer. '... now, this would be Fatima Osman, taking the opportunity on a quiet Sunday morning to come down to the mailbox and smugly size up poor old Barney, and tell him what a prize fool he has been... except, that you won't. You won't, because you are too...' he waves his hand about as he searches for the word, '... civilised, I suppose, to gloat... too...'

'Grateful,' Fatima interjects.

'Grateful? Well, why not. Because of my ridiculous behaviour, you are the proud owners of a very desirable piece of real-estate... and I'm not.'

Fatima suppresses a smile. 'Oh, Barney.. you can't help being what you are.'

'Thank you kindly,' says Barney stoically.

Fatima makes her way to the front of the mailbox wall. 'You are what you are... in the most sincere and inevitable way—as destined as any tremor of the Earth. You help us to shape our life and our existence... and you help us to see ourselves.'

Barney looks across at Fatima. 'Okay, that bit I don't get—how do I help you to see yourselves?'

'It's simple. Think of how much has happened to us all in Twin Towers. We've all grown, and you were part of it.'

'And for that, you're grateful?'

Fatima smiles wistfully. '... strangely, yes. But I'm relieved that it's all over. What I'm grateful for is that everything has worked out... well, for most of us.'

Barney holds up a hand. 'Hey, Fatima... it's worked out for me, believe me. I'm much happier now. The old Twin Towers is a part of me that has gone forever.'

Fatima swats Barney on the shoulder. 'Hah! I know *you* are all right, Barney Evans—I was thinking of Hazim!'

'Oh, yeah... Hazim. Well, with good behaviour, he'll be out in a year... less.'

Fatima looks askance at Barney. 'Do you still believe in terrorism?'

Barney looks perplexed. '... *believe*... in terrorism...?'

'Yes... do you think it exists?'

'Well, yeah! On the telly I see buildings being blown up by terrorists, so, I suppose yeah, I do believe in terrorism. You?'

Fatima eyes Barney carefully. 'Yes. I see people believing in terrorism, so, yes, it exists.'

'Wait a minute—what are you saying—that terrorism is all in our minds? That it only exists because of... of... Look, I happen to know a bloke who was really badly injured because of a terrorist act, okay!... and I wouldn't want to be the one to try and convince him that it's all in his mind. Know what I'm saying?'

Fatima closes the space between them. 'Barney... terror is only ever a word away. Look at you, living in a country with such sublime peace—and you let your prejudices and misunderstanding take you down a road to ruin. How much harder must it be to attain peace in old cultures with long histories? In poor countries with too many people? We must see terrorism for what it really is—an act of war by people who can't fight on conventional battlefields, and whose acts of terror are no more irrational than the terror unleashed by carpet bombing or chemical or nuclear warfare. When we understand that we are at war, we will ask why... and then we can make the changes towards creating peace. But as long as we think of ourselves as innocent victims, we will be deluding ourselves, and our righteousness will only fan the flames of conflict.'

Fatima faces Barney. 'I'm sorry, Barney... I'm lecturing you, and I shouldn't.' She leans back against the wall. 'I was accepted by the university, by the way.'

Barney nods and smiles. 'Good for you, Fatima. I'll have to drop by one day and hear what *dogma* you are *foisting* on the new generation—right use of words?'

'Yes, correct use of words. But I hope that that is not what we're doing. The community today is highly informed, and educators must focus on turning over attitudes before it gets to the stage of turning over cars.'

'Uh huh... let there be riots of the mind before we take to the street. I get it.'

Fatima looks into the distance. 'You know, it has often been said that peace is the time to prepare for war—and to our shame, we do. It's outrageous—we live in a country of such peace and affluence... and we spend obscenely on what the government euphemistically calls defence. In such a time of abundance and prosperity, that cannot last forever, it is our chance to prepare, not for war, but for an enduring peace, and it is offensive for us to think of our neighbours as potential enemies. While we bankrupt ourselves buying weapons, our populous neighbours are building the world's tallest skyscrapers and reinventing themselves as industrial giants, never thinking of invading our desert island. If we are in fact victims of terrorism, it is as much in our mind as it is in reality—it depends on our interpretation of the violence... and it is this that will establish our relationship with the rest of the world.'

There is a prolonged silence. A currawong chortles on the footpath and cars sigh past.

Barney's brow creases. 'There's one thing I don't get, Fatima. Why did you keep the name Twin Towers? I would have thought that you'd have every reason to want to change it.'

Fatima laughs. 'Oh, no, Barney! I would never want to change it... it is the perfect name.'

'Yeah? And why would that be?'

'Well, it has to do with duality... it is a metaphor for the structure of existence...'

Barney throws up his hands. 'Whoa!... sorry I asked.'

Fatima faces Barney and teasingly cants her head. '... you know what I mean—positive and negative... yin and yang... the spirals of DNA... the fact that we cannot live in isolation—we are not monoliths... we can aspire to great heights, together... the twin towers of balance. See?'

Barney nods and scratches his belly. 'You and me, Fatima... opposite in every respect— perfect balance.'

'Yes, Barney... yes, I think so...'

Fatima smiles and walks back to the towers. Barney follows her progress from the corner of his eye. He reaches into his pocket and pulls out the tiny parcel. Prying open a corner of the folded cardboard lid, he withdraws a bright red teddy. He holds it out and admires it, then refolds it and puts it back into the box. He glances at his watch, leans expectantly forward, and looks up the street.

* * *

The lights in the auditorium dim, and the murmur of the audience fades. Barney strides purposefully to the dais, his robes swishing luxuriously with each step. He spreads some notes in front of him and clears his throat.

'Good evening, everyone. Welcome to *Chic-Chadore*, a fashion show that infuses sartorial elements from all over Eurasia to create a hybrid vigour in style and function. First, I will make mention of my attire tonight, a comfortable polished cotton ensemble we call *Bisht Dressed* which, as you can see, comprises a lush embroidered tunic to the hips... that on me, is about here... over loose-fitting *Thobe or not Thobe* trousers in cream denim, which, I don't mind revealing to one and all, are "not to be" later on tonight. And now, I will just take off my *Ghutramunda* head gear, before my brain melts, by loosening the tasselled, leather Igal which we call… an Igal, because we haven't thought of any smart Ockerism. There, that's better…

'Okay, our first model is… Susan Jones. Put your hands together, that's the way… Susan won't let a sunburnt country ruin her fair skin when she's wearing this elegant outfit in organza and twill-weave cotton that we like to call *Back of Burqa*. Lovely, Susan. And after the show, you must have a closer look at the henna designs on Susan's hands.

'Next is Gloria… all set to party the night away, but being delightfully coy about her arrival behind her *Happy Hijabby* veil. She is totally demure and comfortable in a *Dishdash-Partybash* cloak… which will easily hide a six-pack, ha, ha… just joking. Cheerio, Gloria.

'Okay, men… do you want to look urbane and mysterious all at once? Kemal will show you how, sporting a *Can-Do-Kandura* casual ensemble of collarless tunic in breathable synthetics… oh, wow!… this is unscripted. Yep, so easy to slip off your top, and you're ready to *Pyjama Party* in ankle-tied Aladdin trousers… hey! Is that a six-pack that you've… oh, right, it's all you… okay, you can leave the stage now… stop showing off.

'Are you planning a weekend in the great outdoors? Penny is, and no pesky flies are going to spoil her view of Oz because her *Khimar Country* veil will protect her, and her *Out-and-about-Abaya* doubles as a warm wrap, a pillow, a picnic blanket… you get the picture… no amorous opportunity will slip you by when you've got this little number at hand. Thank you, Penny… yep, it's alright, there's no need to demonstrate… give her a hand, folks.

'Now, you're never too old to embrace *Chic-Chadore*… never too old to reinvent yourself. Give a big hand to Florence Bloom as she comes out wearing… Holy Jesus!… sorry… wearing her *Nifty Niqab*, the provocatively revealing face mask with a modern touch—integrated sun glasses… making her look every bit like…

like Hannibal Lecter and Darth Vader had a bedroom tryst. I'm not sure about this one but, hey, I love the *Jillaroobab* fitted coat which I'm sure will contain all the odds-and-bobs that a new-age senior citizen is likely to need. Thank you, Mrs Bloom... and will someone please restrain her until we're all back in our units.

'Come on out, Justine. Ladies and gentlemen... we present, *Cha-Cha-Chadore*... this one combined with a deep indigo outer and a lurid pink inner lining, perfect for the beach with the ability to transform into a stunning gown through the simple expedient of tying the *Pash-Me-Pashmira* scarf around the waist... hey!... how about that... and only moments ago she looked like a rug merchant. This is a very versatile ensemble for captive teenagers embarking on their first school social.

'Wait for it! Ladies and gentlemen, the woman who made all of this possible... wearing a *Killer Khaleeji Kaftan*... Mrs Fatima Osman. Yeah, give it up... how stunning is that? Personally, I didn't know kaftans were figure hugging... ooh, Mrs Osman. Now, I've got permission to tell you that underneath this gorgeous garment, the sensuous and lovely Fatima is wearing a *Wine La-La-Lace Mesh Panty* and a satin *Peek-a-Boo Push Up Bra*...

The applause crashes like waves as the models make their way along the cat-walk. The evening is filled with laughter.

Outside, the moon shines brightly. The city looks grey and old.

The Twin Towers, pale and reflective, soar into the night sky.

The Road to Perfection

Travelling down a country road in his battered MG roadster, Tommy is escaping yet another domestic crisis with his partner, Maddie. His mind flits to images of her arguing with him on the front porch—of her pointing at him accusingly and then hugging herself tearfully. He can hear her strident pleas above the roar of the wind.

'I know what I want from our relationship, Tommy... but *you* can't work out what it is!' he hears over and over again.

He grips the steering wheel harder with frustration.

Hells bells! Why is it up to me to work out what she wants? Things were going fine...

'... if you loved me, Tommy... if you loved me—you'd want me.' He can't escape the exasperation in her voice.

I want her! Have I ever given her reason to doubt that I want her?

Tommy reaches across and switches on the radio.

'... it's twenty-four degrees and you're with Drew Bayliss on the Country Music Hour, and it's a great day to meet a stranger...'

... meet a stranger? I live with a stranger! Where did that suddenly come from anyway? Talking about... about... wanting stuff! I've barely sipped my tea and the first thing I hear is that note of dissatisfaction...

'... is this all you want, Tommy? Don't you ever think that there's something missing? If you loved me, Tommy, you'd want to know what's missing... but you don't care. It's like this is enough for you...'

205

Jeezus... how the hell would I know what's missing? I'm not searching for anything more. There's nothing missing... just stuff getting in the way!

The garrulous note of the MG's exhaust enters Tommy's thoughts as he changes down the gears on the approach to the old wooden bridge. As the tyres rumble over the decking, Tommy looks through the wispy casuarinas to the flowing water in the creek. It's dark and green in the shadows of the tree canopy, and for a moment, Tommy understands how simple things can be.

The scruffy roadster hits the sealed road on the other side of the bridge and Tommy floors the accelerator. The echoes boom off the road cutting.

His mind returns to the argument.

'... if you loved me, Tommy—you'd want me...'

For god's sake!

He turns up the volume on the radio, determined to expel the echoes in his head.

'... the latest release from a new Australian band—the *Sunburnt Celts*'

I've got a bad feelin' this isn't gonna work,
I haven't got a suitcase and I've only got one shirt
I was too busy arguing to pack a proper kit
Now I'm shootin' down the highway, and I'm regrettin' it

You say you know what it is you want
And you'll shout it to the world while we're standin' on the lawn
If I'm self-centred... well, you're pretty selfish too
'Cos I can't find a way to say that I love you

You say that I'm complacent—hey, is that so bad
It's just that I know what I've got and it's more than what I had

206

You say you want perfection—I don't know what you mean
To me our love is perfect, how much better can it be

The MG roars up a gently winding hill. The wind noise, the taut
trumpeting of the engine and the jangle of the instrumental coming
through the speakers, are hypnotic. The day is sunny, and Tommy is
dazzled by the reflections off the chrome frame of the windscreen.
At the top of the hill the road is bordered by large gum trees that
throw mesmerising shadows onto the car. Tommy allows himself to
settle into the seat. Maddie's sunglasses are on top of the dashboard
ledge, tucked against the windscreen, and for a moment, that visual
cue starts a new train of thought.

What if they were someone else's glasses?

The tree shadows flash by—dark, light, dark, light...

... someone who knew what I want...

... dark, light, dark, light...

... yeah... what I want...

... dark, light, dark, light...

He stares, unfocused, out onto the road.

... what do I want?...

A flash of light in the rear-view mirror catches Tommy's eye.
Behind him, catching up fast, is another MG—red, just like his.

... can you believe it!

He watches it surge through a corner.

Wow!... so shiny...

The roadster rapidly fills his mirror. Tommy marvels at the gleam
of the grill, the decal on the bumper bar.

*... unusual... not motoring association... a butterfly?... no!... a fairy.
A fairy?*

Tommy's eyes flit between the road ahead and the mirror.

Hello!

The driver of the MG is a woman—white scarf with black polka-dots—long, white driving gloves—50s sunglasses with tiny wings on the upper corners.

Whoa... how close do you want to get, sweetheart!

Tommy notices the indicator flashing, and as he looks ahead to check that the road is clear, the sparkling MG comes alongside him, passing him with impressive power and shimmering, wire-spoke wheels.

Tommy risks a quick look to the side.

Cute!

Smooth, creamy arms—sleeveless polka-dot dress—wisps of shoulder-length blonde hair fluttering at her neck.

Carmine lip-stick. Carmine? I didn't even know that was a colour.

The sun gleams off the boot of the MG as it re-enters the lane ahead of Tommy. He can't help smiling. The woman's gloved hand rises in a cheery wave. Tommy lifts his hand from the steering wheel and returns a little salute. Soon the MG is far ahead, and at the next bend, it has disappeared.

The countryside opens out into rolling paddocks. Sunlight is everywhere and the grass is almost iridescent. Tommy scans the bends ahead but there is no glint of red.

Polka-dots! How very evocative—evocative? Where did that come from? What does it even mean?

'... anything you want it to mean, Tommy...'

That's not Maddie's voice.

The gearbox whine, the rush of air over the windscreen and the hum of the tyres soothe Tommy's thoughts.

Is that what another woman would sound like? Is that what she sounds like?

With a habitual glance, Tommy checks the fuel gauge.

Getting low.

Tommy makes up his mind to get some fuel at a service station up ahead. He checks his mirror and flicks on the indicator. As the turn-off approaches he runs down through the gears with little blips of the throttle. Each staccato rev cheerfully reassures him. He searches ahead for the bowsers and spies the glossy red MG parked in front of the glass façade of the cafeteria.

Sweet.

Tommy runs alongside a bowser. He surveys the interior of the café, but the reflection on the panes makes it difficult to see inside. As he fills up, he runs his eye over the mysterious MG.

Never seen one so flawless... is that what's wrong with me? My flaws? Is my beat-up car a metaphor for what I am? A what-a-for? Why am I coming up with these stupid words?

Some petrol gushes onto the concrete.

Shit!

Tommy gets back into the sports-car and parks it next to the other MG. He goes inside and pays at the counter. The woman is in the dining area, seated at a table and resting her chin in her elegantly bridged hands. Without any hesitation, Tommy walks over. Coyly, she raises her eyes as he nears the table.

'Hello, Tommy,' she says with disarming familiarity. Her voice is soft and clear. She casually opens her hands to indicate that he should seat himself. 'My name is Avril.'

Without a word, Tommy sits down at the table. Avril smiles at him then turns to look out the window at the two roadsters parked side by side.

'Ah, want,' she says, with perfect lips, '... it's the purest emotion.'

I didn't know want was an emotion.

'... it's the purest emotion—the stronger the want, the purer it is.'

Tommy would like to say something in return, but he is spellbound by Avril's beauty.

'You shouldn't know too much about me, Tommy,' she looks straight at him, '... but you must tell me more about the woman in your life.' Her lovely smile reveals just enough of her teeth to convey

209

some wickedness. 'Are they her sunglasses on the dashboard?'

Avril stirs her coffee. Tommy hadn't been aware that she had one.

'Tommy and Maddie,' she says emphatically, with a finger against her lower lip. 'You're lucky, Tommy—most women keep their sunglasses with them.'

Tommy looks towards his car and rests his eyes on Maddie's sunglasses sitting on the dash.

Suddenly, Avril is leaning over him, putting her lips to his ear. 'Want,' she says, her voice deep and languid, '... is never edifying—unless it is for someone. Then it becomes love.'

Tommy thoughts clamour in his head.

Want... love... love is an edifying want... what?

'How pure is *your* want, Tommy?' she says, then sneezes delicately in his ear.

Jeez... she just sneezed in my ear.

Tommy's gaze stays fixed on his car.

How pure is my want? I dunno...

Tommy turns to face Avril, but she is no longer there. He cranks his head around and scans the shop area, but she's nowhere to be seen. Out the back of the building is a covered patio area, and Tommy eases himself out of his chair to have a quick look around. When he turns to go back into the dining area, he notices that Avril's MG has gone.

She just sneezed in my ear... and vanished.

Back on the road, Tommy can't stop reliving the bizarre encounter with Avril.

'How pure is your want, Tommy?... atishoo!'

He holds his hand to his ear to better recall her sneeze above the noise of the wind.

The road winds on endlessly.

Carmine lips... car—mine... that's funny!... she knew my name...

and Maddie's.

Rounding a bend, Tommy notices the red MG stopped in the middle of the road. In front of the sports car is a workman with a stop sign. Tommy eases up behind Avril, his thoughts in tumult.

Avril! No road-works signs—odd. Guy's got a red Mohawk—weird. Not wearing a hat. How long has she been stopped here?

Tommy can see that Avril is looking at him in the rear-view mirror. He feels a little embarrassed and lifts his hands in a gesture of helplessness. She holds up her mobile phone with one hand and makes a phone gesture with the other.

Keeping his eyes on Avril, Tommy hastily extracts his phone from his pocket.

Avril indicates the number zero, and then holds up four fingers.

Tommy madly punches in the numbers, trying not to miss Avril's signals and trying not to make a mistake. Suddenly his phone is dialling. He clamps it to his ear and stares out through the windscreen. The burring in his ear stops.

Hello, Tommy... where are you staying tonight?'

Tommy hadn't planned on staying anywhere; he hadn't *planned* on grabbing his keys and leaving the house in a huff. He had nothing with him—just his wallet. He just needed some space to think things over.

And now, he is sitting on the edge of a bed, looking at himself in an antique cheval mirror. Avril is behind him, kneeling on the bed. Her arms are around his shoulders, her mouth right by his ear.

'... want isn't sane,' she says, just above a whisper, '... it's not like a need. Our needs are not very glamorous... but our wants reflect the contents of our soul.'

The timber-lined room in the old pub has very high ceilings, and the single yellow lightbulb casts a mellow reflection. Tommy looks into Avril's eyes. She is irresistibly sensuous and she smiles at him with a drowsy impudence.

'... we can do anything you want, Tommy... anything you want.'

Tommy eyes himself in the mirror and wonders what it is that he wants.

The ring on Avril's finger has a tiny whorl of opal that somehow catches the weak light and transmits a ray of blue. It's like the blue of a wave, and Tommy has a sudden image of Maddie, holding her surfboard. She is tanned and laughing at him as she runs towards the water.

'Maddie,' Avril says, '... she is your ideal.' She strokes Tommy's chest and nuzzles her mouth closer to his ear, 'Want is an ideal. It may be illogical and irrational, but that is what makes it so beguiling. You can't justify want—but you can't ignore it. It's the nature of love.'

Tommy closes his eyes.

Avril hugs him around the waist. 'We all have the perfection of want,' Avril's mellifluous voice laps at Tommy's consciousness, '... our duty is to turn it into love.'

Tommy wakes up alone in the bed. He turns and looks at where Avril was sleeping. The pillow is plumped and smooth.

He quickly dresses and walks downstairs to the front door. The two MGs are parked side by side, rear against the kerb.

Avril is standing by the driver's door. With a coquettish smile, she pirouettes lightly and leans seductively on the bonnet. She is gorgeous; her lips are so perfect, her shape so curvaceous, her feet so prettily enclosed in her sandals that Tommy can't help but stare at her. Demurely, she juts her chin at him and wraps her arm over the windscreen. The hem of Avril's petticoat is just visible above her shapely knee. Her dress billows lightly in the morning breeze. The polka-dots are entrancing. She is so lovely, so delicately perfect that it comes as a shock to Tommy when he realises that she is not what he wants.

The morning sun glints off Avril's winged sunglasses. Tommy squints. He has a vision of Maddie, walking towards him holding out two ice-cream cones.

'... which one is yours, Tommy?' she says, '... this one?' and she takes a big lick, '... or this one?' and she licks the other. She smiles with ice-cream on her chin.

Tommy laughs at the memory.

He feels Avril standing very close to him. Her hands splay on his chest. Tommy refuses to open his eyes. He stands there with his arms by his side, knowing that she is going to say something, hoping that it will bring him closer to Maddie.

Avril tucks her chin into Tommy's neck. He can feel the hot breath from her nostrils on his ear.

'Goodbye, Tommy,' her voice is low and smooth, '... think of me when you cross the bridge.'

Tommy can feel her lips on his earlobe.

'Remember... you have the perfection of want. Want is inexplicable—you don't know why you want her. If we didn't possess want, Tommy, we would be happy enough just to eat and sleep. It only makes sense when want becomes love... we all *need* love.'

Tommy remembers that, when he and Maddie were first together, that is all they did—eat and sleep... and want each other.

He opens his eyes. Avril is just opening the door of her MG. She turns and smiles at him. Tommy smiles back. The starter motor whines and the engine roars into life. Avril tightens the scarf around her head, shifts into first gear, and with her white gloves lightly on the steering wheel, turns the sports car out onto the road. She gives a little parting wave before the roadster growls away.

The water ripples faintly below the bridge. Tommy stands at the splintery timber rail and looks down into the cool, green shadows. His MG is parked on the decking with the dented door wide open.

... which one is mine?

He gives a little snort of laughter.

I want the perfect one... the one who wants me.

A butterfly alights on the hand rail. Tommy's eyes widen. Its wings are white with little black polka-dots. It flies off suddenly into the wispy branches of the casuarinas.

... thank you, Avril...

Tommy lingers for a while longer, listening to the sounds of the bush. The butterfly flits erratically through the trees and down to the flowing water.

Tommy turns to his car and climbs in. He looks at Maddie's sunglasses on the dashboard and gives a wry chuckle.

Won't hear the end of this—"You drove off with my sunglasses!"

Tommy starts the car and eases off the bridge in the direction of home.

The Worst Gig in Heaven

Meredith walks obediently to her harp. With a disgruntled look, she seats herself, sighs and looks at where a watch should be on her wrist.

Oh—bad habit. What's the point of measuring eternity?

She reluctantly commences playing Bach's, 'Jesu, Joy of Man's Desiring' but stops suddenly.

Crap! I never desired this. Just my luck to ascend when the last harp player is being carted away with a nervous breakdown. Understandable though, I suppose... he'd been at it for two hundred years.

Trust me to open my awe-struck gob when God says, *'Are there any harp players amongst you?'* I should have twigged then that he isn't that bloody omniscient.

'Oh, lovely, Meredith!' says he, all matey and unctuous... leading me up the garden path with his arm around me.

'It's the musicians, you see,' he says, looking at me as though I'd know—or care.

'... everyone is happy in Paradise—their labours are over and they went for nothing but to ramble in the garden of Eden. Except for the musicians—they want to play music.'

Yeah... and God gets the shits because he didn't invent it!

I mean, artists and stuff, they're always copying God's work—and he loves that. He gives them any amount of paint and brushes

215

and chisels and mallets and they're up there banging out one piece of art after another. No idea what he does with them all. Probably hides them in the jungles for anthropologists to find—'*Oh, will you look at this! A giant Olmec head in the middle of nowhere.*'

But play a note of music!... and God will suddenly be there coughing omnipresently.

He reckons it imposes on the peace. And like, Henry Moore doesn't? Carving great holes in blocks of granite... chipping away incessantly.

2Pac is there picking up on the beat, and he's like, '*Yo... heavy... bangin'... rock... bro...*' or something, and God's like, '*Move along, 2Pac... why don't you go and pat the lions...*'

He's that jealous!

We're not allowed to have any musical instruments up here except the harp, 'cos God reckons he invented it. Well, who's going to argue with the ages?

The other day, a bunch of whinging rockers went and petitioned God.

'*Why did Hell get all the good stuff, man?... like electric guitars and drums and shit...*' and, God, like he is pretty patient and all, says to me, '*Meredith, I want you to escort these gentlemen to the fringes of hell... just for a peek.*'

So, I did. Well... two words—AUDIO SHRAPNEL.

When we get back, God's all smug and righteous and says, '*Remember what Pete Townsend said about heavy metal music,*' and we all go, '*... yeah, yeah... it's like farts—you love your own, but you can't stand anybody else's,*' and God's pissing himself he thinks that's so funny.

The problem is that God thinks everything is heavy metal—Elvis... heavy metal—Bing Crosby... heavy metal—Gregorian chants...

heavy metal. The guy lives in an audio waste land.

I mean, on Earth we're hell bent on accessing music to the extent that the iPod is only one step away from being grafted to our brain… and then, you get to heaven and it's just endless serenity. It's very, very quiet.

I know what you're thinking—what about the animal calls? The bird song? The dawn chorus of a million of God's creatures heralding the rising sun? Well, there's no dawn because there's no night—it's always around 3:30 in the afternoon here. And animals have voices so that they can compete for mates or perches or whatever, and up here there is no competition so there's no need to squawk and make a spectacle of yourself. Most of the animals just groan a lot from being overfed.

So, as I was saying, God corners me one day and says, '*Meredith, there are more and more musicians coming up here every day, and I don't know what to do about it…*' and I'm thinking, 'Well, you're the one that invented the coca plant and the poppy.'

So, he's like, '*Perhaps if you play them some of their tunes it will cheer them up…*' Yeah, like Sid Vicious is going to go all misty-eyed if I play *The Filth and the Fury* on the bleedin' 'arp.

Anyway, that's what I've got to do… every time one of these petulant and disgruntled musos happens along, I've got to trot out their party piece.

Speak of the devil—oops, shit… not supposed to say that.

Meredith watches as Ludwig van Beethoven ambles towards her. She readies her harp and begins playing his symphony number five, plucking the distinctive introduction with vigour and aplomb. With his shaggy head bent forward, he walks straight past Meredith without the slightest acknowledgement.

Meredith's brow darkens. She deliberately injects some discordant notes into her playing and waits for a reaction. Beethoven shambles on. Meredith grabs at the strings and purposefully twangs a handful.

Still deaf as a post. Not missing out on anything up here but.

Oh, here comes Elvis! I have to say, the fruit agrees with him... though I think he was hoping for more like the Burger Kingdom of heaven. He's looking a little sad.

With feeling, Meredith plays 'Love Me Tender'. She smiles as Elvis walks up to her. He sings the last few lines. 'I'll be yours through all the years, 'til the end of time...'

Elvis nods approvingly. Meredith is unable to speak just for the moment.

'I'm looking for the Bayou,' says Elvis with a lovely deep lilt to his voice, '... do you know where I might find it?'

Meredith shakes her head.

'Oh, that's alright Mama... any way you do...' he sings to her with a wink and walks on.

The thing most of them miss up here is the groupies—they just never get used to being by themselves. They all skip a heartbeat when they're received by a host of glittering angels, but that very quickly becomes awkward! Except for the likes of Liberace, who is still trilling with ecstasy somewhere around.

Oh, here we go...

Meredith commences playing 'Stairway to Heaven'. She smiles as Jimi Hendrix approaches her.

'Hi Jimi...' Meredith says in a little chirp, but Jimi barely responds, giving only a blithe smile and a languid peace gesture with his fingers. He continues on his unsteady way for a bit, then stops to stare and

laugh at an emu.

Yeah... he's out of it. God made a deal with him. *Stairway to Heaven* becomes the signature tune on ascension, in return for a stash. Apparently, Jimi tried to tell God that he didn't write it, but God wouldn't hear of it. The angels were no help either, and now I know why—they're always mooching joints.

Oh! Hot gos'! The word is, the Rolling Stones are due here soon. It seems they make some sort of suicide pact... something to do with getting so incredibly ugly, that all it takes is one more mirror lined dressing room and they all agree to OD. God wants me to get some of their material up and running.

Meredith acknowledges the presence of Janice Joplin who is standing behind her with a hand on her shoulder.

'Do you want me to play it?' Meredith says, looking over her shoulder.

'Yeah,' says Janice wistfully, '... it's the nicest thing that anyone ever said...'

Meredith plays 'The Rose'.

I suppose you're wondering why so many dope smoking, drug addled, dissolute, drunks managed to get into heaven.

Well, it's all got to do with God's data base. Apparently, the word *love* and the word *heaven* are the most frequently used words in song lyrics and titles and, based on that bit of info, God has admitted this host of musos. I bet he regrets it now... I mean, what was he thinking? The only thing they enjoy is jamming and they're not allowed to. Harpo's got a good gig though—he plays for the chorus girls.

Wow! Here comes Marlene.

'Hi, Marlene,' Meredith says a little obsequiously, 'God still not speaking to you?'

Marlene Dietrich raises a dismissive eyebrow. 'He still hasn't reviewed his plan...'

Meredith sighs in admiration. 'I wish I could stand up to him the way you do.'

'Do you know, 'Falling in Love Again'?' says Marlene huskily.

Meredith props herself against her harp. 'Sure... are you going to sing?'

Marlene nods.

When they finish the song, Marlene strokes Meredith's hair then walks away.

Wow! You'd think that we'd all be equal up here, but that's not the case. Some mortals bring their aura with them—can't say ego. We don't have egos; we have auras. That way, if God has the biggest *aura*, we're not judging him.

Oh no—here it comes again. Ever since he found out I was from Australia, he's had it in for me... still cranky after all these years.

Frank Sinatra strides up to Meredith with a demanding mien.

She hastily applies herself to her instrument. 'Okay, already... I'm playing, I'm playing.'

She plays 'I Did It My Way' with an accentuated and pedantic beat, but Frank has spied someone he knows and wanders off.

Yeah, and up yours too. So fucking irritating. I don't know what God sees in him.

Whoa there, Ray! Watch out for the harp—oh, sorry... didn't mean to...

Ray Charles has accidently bumped into Meredith.

He searches for her hand. 'Hey, li'l one... can you play a song for me?'

Meredith strokes Ray's shoulder. 'Sure... what'll it be?'

Ray runs his hands over the harp. 'Hit the Road Jack, and then I'll get out of your way.'

'You're not in the way. So, what?... God didn't give back your sight?'

'No, no... told him I had my sweet li'l'magination...'

'Oh, good one, Ray... that would have pissed him off.'

Meredith begins playing and Ray sings as he wanders away.

Speaking of imagination...

John Lennon strolls up and they converse as Meredith lightly plays 'Imagine'.

'You know, John... after having been here for a goodly while, I'm really starting to appreciate what you meant by, '... imagine there's no heaven...' I find myself doing that now and again.'

John thrusts forward his head. 'Sure you do, love, but at least you can play an instrument... me an' George are goin' barmy up here.'

Meredith smiles sympathetically and continues playing.

John gives a wave. 'Cheers, love.' He saunters on his way.

Meredith looks over her harp into the distance and spies Slim Dusty. She begins to play, 'When the Rain Tumbles Down in July'.

Did I mention that it never rains in heaven? It did one day. Slim says to God, 'You havin' a drought, mate?' and God goes, '... no...' and Slim says, 'Well, I haven't seen any rain since I been up here... can't ya make it rain?' and God goes, 'Yes... of course I can make it rain...' So Slim says, 'Go on then... give us a good old gully washer,' and God begrudgingly says, '... alright then... I will, if it means that much to you...' and Slim says, '... yeah, well, I'm Australian...'

The next thing you know, it's bucketing down, and everybody is out there with outstretched arms, singing at the top of their voices and you can't tell that the tears are rolling down their faces.

Meredith finishes the tune and looks pensively over her harp.
Suddenly God is there, at her shoulder.
'Oh god! I wish you wouldn't do that… I mean, God, I wish you wouldn't do that.'
God bends down to whisper in Meredith's ear. Her eyes widen with surprise.
'… really! That soon. Oh well, I'd better start practising… this'll be one that we can all relate to—I mean—like.'
God gives Meredith a little pat on the shoulder and walks off.

Meredith adjusts her seat and prepares to play. She establishes a good strong rhythm in her mind. Her head bobs backwards and forwards sharply as she begins to play, 'I Can't Get No Satisfaction'.

Winifred

Winifred Barrett lived in a sprawling lakeside hotel that was being renovated and converted to become a home. Part of the old hotel had been completely refurbished, but there was still a lot of major work to be done on the back half of the structure, which remained dangerously dilapidated.

Winifred's husband, Kane, was a wealthy media magnate who would visit the hotel in his floatplane whenever the mood took him.

The restoration project had begun to expose critical faults in the union between Kane and Winifred—most notably, that he couldn't live away from his work, and she didn't want to leave her new-found home.

They'd met backstage; Winifred was riding the crest of popularity. From utter obscurity, she had made a sensational debut with a scorching dance routine in a mediocre film. Clips of her dancing went viral and she became a media phenomenon in her own right.

Winifred was a bit over six foot, statuesque, unbridled and irrepressibly unconventional. She had no agent, no PR team, not even a Facebook page. Caught up in the media surge, she scoffed at her celebrity status, stared down the cameras and spoke her mind.

She declared that her image on the cover of Vogue would boost sales—a shoot was arranged and an entirely new demographic purchased copies of the magazine.

She said that she wouldn't mind a gig on Broadway—theatre managers vied to be the first to sign her.

That is where Kane came to see her; he of new money, new ventures and unique invention. Immediately, they recognised in each other the providence that they shared; everything they did exhilarated the public—and Kane was all too aware of how that could translate into commercial success.

But Winifred had a desperate secret: she had no ambition. She accepted the faceless adulation with derision and allowed herself to exploit any opportunity that presented itself, but she had no intention of consigning herself to the dubious realm of fame, because she knew that she lacked any particular virtuosity and that the slide out of the public eye would be unbearably demeaning.

And so, she jutted her chin and tempted fate—and whatever she did, the media would hype into a spectacular event. She was the ultimate celebrity because, unlike most, she didn't care about protecting what she had—she just wanted to see what it would take to lose it.

Meeting Winifred in the bustling confines of the dressing rooms backstage gave Kane the biggest rush. He found her quirky insouciance irresistibly attractive; she kept him off-balance in one sense and centred him in another. Winifred was outrageous—and he wanted her ever so much.

He proposed marriage to her. She loved the idea and hugged him needfully.

Kane Barrett paused and collected himself. He had a long and critical think, and decided that marrying Winifred was the right thing to do for many reasons—none of them romantic.

Winifred couldn't believe that someone had managed to

unbalance *her*, and thought that being wedded to Kane was bound to be fun.

Kane *knew* people—that was his particular gift. He'd had a leg up when he inherited his father's business at an early age, but what had made him wealthy was the fact that he was the right man for the age; his understanding of human nature fused with the burgeoning media explosion.

He launched yMe—a social media platform that appealed to the emotionally starved Y generation—that self-indulgent and entitled host that were holding the country to ransom and who took solipsism (the belief in self as the only reality) to extreme levels of narcissism.

Kane Barrett was on a winner.

They married in a cathedral. The images were downloaded by the millions. The photo of Winifred's train, flowing over the flagstones in the mist (from a few strategically placed fog machines), that photo alone made Kane a few hundred thousand. Then the happy couple had flown in Kane's floatplane to honeymoon in a little stone hut on the shore of a lake. A compliant publicity machine made sure the images of the two of them, outside in a hot tub, had gone viral.

Kane was selling an ideal—and millions of urban souls, hunkered in fluorescent lit rooms, imagined what it would be like to have that kind of a life.

Flying over the lake was when Winifred saw the old hotel. Instinctively, she knew that this remnant from a bygone era, positioned on the headland of a bay, was the place that she could retreat to when everything around her vaporised.

Kane didn't know what to think when his bride insisted that they should buy the ramshackle place and make it their home. But

225

the thought of commuting regularly in his floatplane was definitely appealing, and there was something about the enduring majesty of the old hotel that Kane sensed might be a valuable promotional asset.

Renovations began as soon as the sale was finalised, and Winifred made the first of many winding trips from the city along the shores of the lake to her new home.

Standing in the morning sunlight on the huge patio above the flight of stone steps leading down onto the vast lawn, Winifred experienced a peacefulness that she had never known before. The reflections of the mountains on the lake produced a sense of infinity that made her feel glad to be alive.

She didn't want to go back to the city—to be propelled into the hustle of the entertainment industry. She had at last found a place to be—whatever might be in store for her.

She turned and went back inside to the huge kitchen and dropped a couple of logs into the Aga stove.

At first, Kane loved coming home to the hotel on the lake. He would settle the floatplane gently onto the rippled surface and taxi up to the little beach just below the esplanade. Then he would lower the wheels and gun the plane up onto the coarse sand.

Winifred would walk down to meet him and together they would walk arm in arm up the stone stairs to the patio.

He loved the fact that his wife was so tranquil—and so lovely. They would make a hot drink and then snuggle together in one of the window seats overlooking the lake.

Just for a while, Kane would let go of everything on his mind. But then he would become conscious of the isolation, and shortly after that he would worry about whether Winifred was safe, and it wasn't long before he was thinking about his business. Within a day or two, he would be taxiing off the beach, watching Winifred waving to him from the French doors.

Kane's business was notorious. yMe was a platform for adolescents to expose the sullied and demeaning circumstances of their lives. They made money from it.

In the most deplorable irony, individuals would upload images and descriptions of their pitiful surroundings, and other teenagers would subscribe to view the dire state of affairs.

Except that there was nothing mean or shabby about the lifestyles of these young people—they all came from affluent households and they all possessed an abundance of material goods. In some perverted way, entitled youths from wealthy families were inverting their status in order to win attention. And the paradox was that, the better off the individual was, the greater was the gulf between their physical circumstances and their emotional deprivation. This made for compelling viewing.

There were those who claimed that they were being psychologically abused by their parents—cuts in their allowances, denied a motor bike or jet-ski, hated having to eat with the family—petulant bleating like that.

They complained about their teachers, their friends, their enemies, their relatives—they spoke about their binges, the drugs and the alcohol, and they disclosed their thoughts about self-harm and suicide. Everything and anything was discussed, from creepy stalkers to abductions and rapes—from the ordeals of learning to drive to fatal accidents—from bullying to school shootings—from smarmy relatives to... well, anything was fair game at yMe, and it didn't matter if it was all fiction—the objective was to attract curious voyeurs and to make fifty cents per subscription. yMe got the other half of the dollar subscription and there were thousands of members who had more than ten thousand subscribers.

Some kids were making a lot of money.

This was the business model that absorbed Kane Barrett. It was so rapacious that he couldn't afford to spend time away from it, just in case his conscience came to the fore and he began to ask himself the questions that most newspaper editorials had been asking for quite some time. He had to stay ahead of any developments that fiddled with people's freedom to express themselves, no matter how shocking. He had to stay in touch, and a weekend on the lake dulled his edge.

Kane was incapable of reconciling a life at home with his work.

And Winifred resolutely did not want to go back to the city.

They both saw the end of their relationship looming—but Kane would never consider a divorce. Winifred was far too valuable to him.

When she appeared on one occasion at a Barrett-Media promotional, reluctant perhaps, but none the less dynamic, the media interest was off the scale—the gorgeous wife of Kane Barrett who, it was rumoured, lived alone in an abandoned hotel on a lake, re-emerging to take, head-on, the flash and press of the crowds. It was worth millions.

Starry-eyed dreamers the world over, hunched over their devices, vicariously living the glittering life of the Barretts, had more reason than ever to bemoan their own jobless existence—more reason to hash together some newly perceived injustice that they would hurriedly upload on their sordid page.

yMe was a truly paradoxical phenomenon that only someone like Kane Barrett could manage.

Another thing that Kane thought he was managing very well was the estrangement from his wife.

After having indulged his new bride with the purchase of the

228

hotel, it came as a complete surprise to him that she became so devoted to its renovation. He had envisioned that she would add glamour to his public forays, not become a recluse on a remote lake. He was at first confused and frustrated, then angry, then finally, coldly logical.

The refurbishment of the hotel was tremendously costly and Kane liked to keep his eye on things. He also happened to enjoy flying his floatplane along the coast and then veering inland to the lake. So, every couple of weeks, without any notification, he would buzz the hotel and, by the time he was riding up the beach, Winifred would be standing on the grass nearby, ready to help him unload the flowers and chocolates, wines and cheeses and other delicacies that he always brought. She was always happy to see him. He was Kane Barrett... attentive, humorous, exciting—and not someone to be trifled with. That was always there in his eyes.

And she was just as happy to see him take off again, waving to him with her skirt billowing in the prop wash.

Winifred had a lover.

Lloyd Dearborn was a carpenter, and he was the only local tradesman that the Barretts could find. He loved the outdoors, and whenever there was no work on, which was often, he would load up his little skiff and sail to a distant part of the lake where he would fish and explore the mountains and forests. He lived in a tiny hut at the site of the old silver mine which was only a short drive from the hotel.

At the time the Barretts arrived, Lloyd was about ready to move to the coast to find work and maybe build the yacht that he dreamed of. Meeting Winifred and Kane was a stroke of luck for him. He became the project manager of the hotel renovation. It was his job to prepare the way for the teams that came out to do everything from construction and installation, to painting and wallpapering.

The back of the building was in a very bad state. It had been largely dismantled decades before in preparation for a rebuild. But the project had stalled and the frame of the structure had been left exposed to the elements. Some of the guest rooms on the third floor were still intact, and a turret that rose beside a little loft dormer was still original.

This is where Lloyd laid out his bedroll. It was easier than commuting—and he was close at hand.

At first, the site was so busy that Lloyd was totally engrossed in his work. He and Winifred would consult regularly, but the stresses of management were so intense for them both that there was never a thought of the other in a romantic sense.

It was about eighteen months later, when the front of the hotel was completed, that construction began to slow down.

On one of his flying visits, Kane had intimated that rebuilding the back of the hotel was expensive and unnecessary and that it should be completely demolished. The project tapered off, but Lloyd was retained to finish the doorways and walls that separated the two halves of the building.

Mealtimes suddenly became more intimate. Instead of having a rowdy construction crew sitting around on scaffolding planks, Winifred and Lloyd could now enjoy a convivial cup of coffee at the most superb table setting in a freshly wallpapered dining alcove that was light and airy.

Winifred was buoyed by the success of the project. It was due to her competent oversight that the renovations had gone so well. And, she and Lloyd worked well together.

His presence about the place heightened her feelings of solitude, and although she had never been more centred and more at ease with herself, she felt the pang of being lonely each evening as she warmed herself by the stove.

One day in late autumn, after the fog on the still warm lake had begun to thin and the morning breeze had whisked away the lingering tendrils, Lloyd invited Winifred to come for a sail in his little skiff. She packed a hamper of fine food and wine, and together they sailed to a sunny beach where they climbed to a protected hollow in a rock face that captured the sun's weak rays. They spread a thick blanket, and while Winifred composed the edibles, Lloyd hugged her from behind to keep her warm.

On the way back, the clouds suddenly rolled in and the breeze whipped up a chop. Winifred sat huddled against the mast and marvelled at Lloyd's composure as he bobbed the boat through the waves with a gentle hand on the tiller.

It began to rain, and by the time they beached the skiff, even their spray jackets couldn't keep them dry. They rushed, shivering, through the house to the bathroom, and... well, they got to know each other a little better.

Then they tripped up the perilous staircase, up the steep stair-ladder that gave access to the loft and ended up in Lloyd's bed under a pile of eiderdowns.

That night, lying in Lloyd's strong arms Winifred felt a deep exultation; she had fallen in the groove of her destiny, and the old hotel was embracing the both of them.

Months went by.

Kane spent longer and longer away from Winifred and the hotel. Important decisions that needed to be made about the renovation would be put on hold and the ramshackle rear of the building remained a dangerous no-go zone.

Winifred would climb the treacherous staircase to the loft dormer four storeys up and couple with Lloyd on the sunny bed by the window. Without a care in the world, they would lie in each other's arms and tease one another about their dreams and their reality.

One day, Winifred idly remarked, 'You could kidnap me, and then you'd have enough money to buy your boat and go off sailing around the world.' Lloyd gave his typical easy laugh and Winifred added, 'I'd be a very obliging hostage.'

They were lazily playing out a bondage scenario when Winifred suddenly stilled. '... you could keep me here... in this house... no one would know...'

Lloyd stroked her hair. 'Someone would find out sooner or later. The cops would be all over this place.'

But Winifred had a mind to explore this prospect to its fullest. 'If you built a secret room—wouldn't have to be big—I could hide there if anyone came searching. It'd be easy to do. There's so much space, no one would be aware of a hidden compartment.'

'... and then?' Lloyd murmured in Winifred's ear.

'Then... I don't know—you'd collect the ransom.'

'You see, that's the bit that gets tricky—the kidnapper always gets caught.' Lloyd nuzzled into her neck. 'You've really begun to hate him, haven't you?'

Winifred pursed her lips and had a think about this. 'I don't know why exactly, but he makes me angry. He is so conceited—so unreasonably self-assured... and he never gives anyone else a chance to show their ability. He never admits to his mistakes because he has enough money to be able to buy his way out of trouble. Having his wife kidnapped would bring him back to earth.'

A few days passed before the two of them were once again snuggled in the bed, under the eiderdowns. The weather had turned cold and windy and there was no heating in the loft.

'I had a bit more of a think about... you know, a kidnap scenario,'

Winifred said unexpectedly.

Lloyd felt a chill of unease. He decided not to say anything.

'I can carry this thing off myself—kidnap myself.'

Lloyd sighed deeply. 'Why? You've got plenty of money... and I'm okay—I'm not that far off building my boat. Then we can both sail off together. Plus, you'll be able to pay for us to live the high life wherever we visit.'

Winifred went all quiet and Lloyd spent the next half hour in bed gently massaging her feet.

It was many weeks before they rendezvoused again in the double bed by the dormer window. Winifred had had to travel interstate with Kane on a company promotional tour.

She hungrily launched herself at Lloyd and they tumbled about ecstatically in the weak rays of winter sunlight.

Later, while they rested, Winifred said very softly, 'He will never divorce me...'

Lloyd held tightly to her hand and waited patiently.

'... he said that any disruption could trigger a collapse. He says that the stock market is in a fragile state where his type of business is concerned, and that we have to maintain appearances... look confident and buoyant.'

Lloyd allowed Winifred's voice to lull him into sleepiness. As far as he was concerned, nothing had changed—Kane and Winifred were estranged, and she and he enjoyed good times in a secluded niche in her own home. Nothing wrong with that. But her next words instantly filled him with dread.

'I *am* going to kidnap myself... just to create that disturbance that he is so desperate to avoid... just to prick that arrogance.'

Lloyd opened his eyes wide and wondered how he could set about diffusing this notion. 'Don't do it, Winnie... you will get badly hurt and you'll end up with a lot less... a *lot* less than you have now.'

Winifred lifted Lloyd's hand to her lips and kissed his finger-tips. 'I've thought it through—it's easy, and I think I've eliminated the risk.'

She turned to him with excitement in her eyes. 'I can conduct this from here,' she gave a sweep of her arm. 'I leave a ransom note—I don't know... on the dining room table, the little dining next to the kitchen... there's an access to the esplanade from there. The kidnapper could park at the lookout and walk through the trees to the house. I'll knock down that painting that Kane gave me—that awful, melancholy seascape, and I'll kick a bit of a hole in the wall just beneath it as though there was a short struggle... and the door will be left open...'

Lloyd could see the concentration on Winifred's face; she was completely immersed in this fantasy.

'... I'll ring Francine and draw out a bit of a gossip with her, and when there hasn't been anyone at the lookout for a goodly while—and no one's been going to the lookout at this time of the year—I'll just casually say that there is someone coming up to the house and that it might be a lost tradesman or something, and I'll tell her I have to go...'

One part of Lloyd wanted to critique this plan and another part of him wanted to run away from the madness.

Winifred looked directly at him. 'What do you think?'

Lloyd gave a long, contemplative groan. 'I don't know, Winnie. I don't know why you want to do this.'

'I told you,' Winifred said with a hint of irritability, '... to stir him up. *And*,' she looked wickedly at Lloyd from under her brow, '... because it's a good plan.'

Lloyd questioningly spread his hands. 'Is it? You haven't told me how you're going to collect the ransom yet.'

Winifred suddenly writhed into a kneeling position beside Lloyd. 'That's the good bit,' her eyes were wide with excitement, '...

the kidnapper leaves behind a suitcase, and inside is a black, heavy duty garbage bag and black gaffer tape... with instructions to wrap the money in the bag... yeah, and then, to put the whole lot into the suitcase...'

'... ri...ght.' said Lloyd, with a growing sense of disbelief.

'... then,' Winifred continued, '... I swap the suitcase with an identical one, stuffed with the same amount of paper, wrapped in a black plastic bag and taped with black tape. It would be difficult to notice anything different about the contents of the suitcase if the money was in a bag... and the reason for taping it is so that, after the swap, he won't be able to open up the bag to fondle his money... just in case he feels the need to.'

'How much money, incidentally?'

'Two million dollars!' Winifred clasped her hands in front of her face.

Lloyd pouted and frowned. '... two million?... hmmm ... that's a lot and a little all at the same time.'

'What do you mean?'

'Well, two million dollars is a lot of money to get as cash—I would say that nowadays it would be virtually impossible... and two million dollars is peanuts for Kane Barrett to have his loving wife returned to him,' he smirked.

'Oh, I know that!' Winifred gave a dismissive wave of her hand. 'The thing is, I know for a fact that Kane can get his hands on two million. A few months ago I overheard him talking to Roger Buchanan, one of the accountants, and Kane said that he could do, I don't know, some sort of nefarious deal in cash because he had that much at hand for just such a contingency... something along those lines... and I know that he regularly stashes cash somewhere for this building project—you get paid in cash, don't you?'

Lloyd nodded. '... yep, always... and for materials too.'

'There you are, see! He'll have no trouble stumping up two

235

million—especially since he hasn't spent much on the house in the last six months.'

Lloyd breathed a heavy sigh and turned side-on to Winifred. 'Okay... so this becomes a tidy little domestic affair—Kane Barrett comes home to find that someone has kidnapped his wife, and that they will return her unharmed for two million dollars... and because Mr Barrett doesn't want any publicity, and because he's got the money at hand, he takes the suitcase that has been thoughtfully provided, plonks the money in it and waits for the next lot of instructions. Then, one night, you creep inside the house, with an identical suitcase, and you do a swap—assuming of course that you know where he's going to hide the case with two million dollars in cold, foldable—then you sneak out. The next morning, a rock with a note taped to it smashes through the window—that you've thrown from somewhere in the shrubbery—telling him to drive along the peninsula road at a prescribed time and to hurl the suitcase over the bridge or wherever... where it will remain 'til such time that it gets washed out to sea in the next big rain storm. And, if he should get the cops involved, and he won't, they'll just be wasting their time. The next day... hmmm... how were you planning on returning?'

Winifred could hardly restrain herself. 'I was thinking that I could be at home when he returned! You know, driven back home in the back of a van with a blindfold on... lost track of time, never saw anyone or anything... but not mistreated...'

'... hence the designated time for dumping the loot.'

'Exactly.'

Lloyd looked at Winifred with a critical eye. 'It's certainly a kidnap plot that is ideally suited to your particular circumstances.'

'Isn't it, though!' Winifred squealed.

'Just one thing, Winnie... how can you be sure about making the switch?'

Winifred gave a reproving pout and brought her breasts just that little bit nearer to Lloyd's face. '... well,' she began, as she stroked his chest, '... I've thought it through, and I think I've covered every angle...'

Lloyd backed away the tiniest distance. 'No, Winnie... no... I can't get involved... I don't want to get involved—I don't want *you* to get involved... it's crazy.'

'Listen to me, Llover'—which was Winifred's pet name for Lloyd, '... it's very simple... and you're not involved... at all.'

Lloyd looked distinctly worried. He was an uncomplicated soul with very simple needs, and the prospect of a kidnapping appalled him.

Winifred came close to him and whispered in his ear. 'I'm just telling you this so that you can be prepared... so you can have a perfect alibi... but I can do this entirely by myself.' She looked him straight in the eye. 'On the eve of the ransom dump, I will let myself into the house and make myself comfortable in the storage closet in my walk-in-wardrobe that backs onto the bathroom of our bedroom. When I hear Kane showering—and, if he's true to form he'll be in there for at least twenty minutes—he has stress headaches and the hot water soothes it... and, I imagine he'll be experiencing a fair amount of stress just prior to throwing away two million dollars. Anyway, while he's in the shower, I'll leave the closet with the substitute case and just wander in to the bedroom. That's where he'll have the money. It'll be too big to put in the safe—you see, I thought about that—so he'll have it somewhere close by, probably next to the bed, because it won't fit underneath. Then, I do the switch, put the case with the loot in the closet and sneak back out so I can leave the drop details on the doorstep or wherever.' Winifred grinned triumphantly. 'And I've worked out the weight of the money... two million in fifties—because that's what I'll demand, weighs a bit over forty kilograms.'

'Forty kilos! Winnie... you'll never carry it!'

Winifred pulled a superior face. 'I *can* carry forty kilos. I can easily deadlift eighty at the gym.'

Lloyd reached out and stroked Winifred's arm. 'Yeah, but that's in ideal conditions... a suitcase...'

'... has wheels, Llover—you who only ever travels with a day pack.'

Lloyd stopped kneading Winifred's bicep.

'... and, the entire top floor is carpeted, *and*... I'm only going to wheel the suitcase to the closet. When Kane drives out to do the deposit, I'll race back up, grab my stash and leave.' Winifred blinked impishly. 'Have I missed anything?'

Lloyd turned to stare out of the dormer window. From four storeys up, the view out across the bay was uninterrupted. In the distance, low clouds scudded over the tops of the rock-strewn mountain tops. He would go climbing there again when the weather warmed up. He'd sail his little skiff to a bay virtually at the bottom of the range and leave it tied, end for end, to some overhanging branches, and when he returned after three or four days, it would be there, sometimes with a few inches of rainwater in it. He liked the simplicity of communing with nature—and he liked women— who were not always so simple—but he adored their shape, their movements... their needs.

Winifred stroked Lloyd's cheek. 'I have to find out... whether he wants me—or not.'

Lloyd gaped. 'Or not! Okay, okay... and if *not*?'

'... I'll have my answer...'

Lloyd sat up in the bed and knelt in front of Winifred. 'Winnie, this game of... conjecture... has got to stop. He'll *give* you a divorce— soon enough! If you go on like this... this darkness, you'll hurt yourself. Just let it go for the moment—we've got all of this...' he spread his arms wide.

Winifred smiled at Lloyd's concern and took hold of his hands.

'But it's so simple... there is absolutely no risk—and I'm a very capable person, as you know.'

Lloyd gathered Winifred in his arms. 'I don't want to see you get hurt, Winnie... I just don't want to see you get hurt. I care about you, I really do.'

Winifred knew then that, if she was true to him, Lloyd would always be there for her. She made up her mind that this would be her last act of rashness. After this, she would twine herself to Lloyd and find a more rewarding purpose for the hotel.

Winifred was reclusive for the next few days as she went through the plan in her mind. The difficulty... the *only* difficulty was Kane's unpredictability, but as luck would have it, their two-year wedding anniversary was coming up soon, and Winifred knew that Kane would be too observant to miss it. She planned for that time period.

She told Lloyd.

Lloyd looked desolate. He felt powerless to dissuade her, but he didn't want to jinx her so he said, with a sharpness to his eye, 'You know, I believe you can do it—I just can't believe that you *need* to do it. But, it's the old you—audacious and lucky. I'll see you when I get back from the coast.'

That was Winifred's idea—that he should go boat hunting for a week. He was most interested in classic wooden yachts that had been neglected and that he could restore to their former glory. There were a few that he had been meaning to inspect.

They hugged each other. Winifred clung heavily to Lloyd as he massaged her brow with his lips.

Two days before her wedding anniversary, Winifred rang Francine Barker, her former modelling agent, and chatted for a long while about one thing and another, Winifred intimating that her life could do with a little revitalising, and Francine plying none too subtly that there were killer gigs available if Winifred had a mind to strut the catwalk again.

Winifred gave an ambiguous chortle, then suddenly announced that there were two men coming up to the house from the esplanade and that they might be tradesmen and that it was so lovely to talk and that next time she was in the area she would definitely drop in to see her and that they would go out for a coffee. She hung up, slid the phone into her jeans pocket and went to the kitchen and made a cup of tea. Then she wandered into the dining room and stood in front of a large painting—a blue/grey seascape with stormy horizons and with an unloved cottage exposed to the spray. It was nothing like the lake.

She took a sip of her tea, carefully held the cup to her shoulder, then hurled it at the painting. The glass and the cup shattered. Winifred watched the tea as it dripped to the floor. She took hold of the nearest kitchen chair and lunged with it towards the wall, smashing a leg into the wallpapered plasterboard. The chair leg snapped clean off, but there was only a small wedge shaped hole in the wall.

... perfect, thought Winifred, *just a hint of violence—imagination will do the rest.*

The violence of her actions gave her a reassuring thrill; the game was in play.

Winifred walked to the desk that was against the wall next to the French doors that led out onto the patio. This is where she had her laptop—in the warmth of the dining room. She opened it up and switched it on. Then, using her two forefingers, she laboriously typed out a message on a new word document. She wasn't worried about fingerprints.

... they made me type it... I was in shock... in pain... one of them grabbed me...

She went to file and pressed print. The printer whirred at her knee. Shortly, a page fluttered to the floor. Winifred picked it up, inspected it and chuckled. It was the most inoffensive ransom note one could imagine—Calibri font, size twelve, just a few lines.

... perfect...

She walked to the dining table and laid the paper down. Reaching over, she picked up a small vase with its little spray of bluebells and placed it on a corner of the note.

Winifred had a long look at the scene, then went upstairs to her bedroom.

My bedroom... she reflected... *with an immaculately made bed that hasn't been slept in for months.*

She walked straight through the room to the built-in wardrobe. This was actually the middle third of the neighbouring suite. Another third was Kane's wardrobe—which was almost completely bare— and the last third had been converted into a bathroom with floor to ceiling triple insulated windows that gave views across the lake.

Winifred strode directly to a closet with mirrored doors that she pulled open. There was enough room inside for a pile of eiderdowns, laid out one atop the other, to make a very comfortable little nest. She reached in and pulled out a travel suitcase. Winifred closed the doors—slowly—and listened for any squeaks or groans from the hinges. There were none; the hinges had been well oiled.

When she came downstairs with the travel case, she hefted it onto the table then moved to the stove. Once again, she wasn't worried about fingerprints.

... they made me get a suitcase... so I got that travel case that I always take with me when I stay in town...

Winifred pulled a thick log from the wood box and dropped it inside the Aga. She warmed herself and imagined Kane coming into the cold house, putting his hand against the stove door and being able to feel the residual heat.

For her, it was going to be cold for a while.

She took her mobile phone from her jeans. She cupped it firmly then smashed it against the corner of the stove and let the pieces fall to the ground.

... they made me smash my phone... look—there's glass cuts in my palm...

She carefully dabbed the tiny spots of blood onto whiteness of her blouse.

The hotel was far too remote for mobile reception, but Kane had arranged for technicians to put in a dedicated satellite channel that enabled internet and telephone connectivity. It was hideously expensive.

Two days later, just before the sun settled behind the mountains, Winifred heard the floatplane roar over the roof of the hotel. She was lying on Lloyd's bed up in the loft. She put down the book she was reading—one of Lloyd's *Horatio Hornblower* novels.

Her heart began to thump. She picked up the warm eiderdowns that she had been lying amongst and took them to the far wall of the loft where there was a built-in wardrobe. She opened the louvered doors and looked inside at the clutter of Lloyd's camping and fishing gear. She parted the hanging jackets and waders and pushed hard against the back wall. A door opened inwards. One by one, Winifred threw the doonas through the secret door. Then she went back to the bed and remade it from a pile of bedclothes on the floor. She picked up the old sheet and went back into the wardrobe. After pulling the doors closed and swiping the jackets across, she disappeared through the secret door.

Just inside the doorway was a switch that Winifred flicked. A dim, yellow light came on. Next to the door was a mattress. Winifred spread her doonas and let herself sink slowly into them. It was bitterly cold, but she felt too hot to cover herself. She lay there feeling surprisingly exhausted. She hadn't eaten for two days and she hoped that it would show on her face.

... I could smell their cooking... it was horrible... I couldn't eat it...

Winifred sat up, then, stooping to avoid contact with the low ceiling, she moved to the far corner where there was a water container and a cup. She poured some water and sipped it slowly. Then she scuttled back to the makeshift bed and made herself comfortable with her back against the wall.

She heard the plane's engine rev as Kane drove it up the beach, and she imagined his look of consternation as he lifted off his headphones and scanned the porch for her presence. The engine wound down. Winifred knew it wouldn't be long before he came up to the loft in search of Lloyd.

The vibrations of Kane's progress up to the loft preceded the sound of his footfalls on the steps. Winifred felt the faint tremors against her temple as she lay against the wall. Very slowly she reached up and flicked off the light. She could hear the creaking of the stair-ladder as Kane ascended into the room. Suddenly, his voice came to her as he called out to Lloyd. He called again. The only other thing that Winifred could hear was her own irregular breathing. She concentrated on keeping absolutely still. On the other side of the wall it was very quiet.

Lloyd had carpeted the dormer and each floorboard had been screwed in place—not nailed.

'You'll have to be able to move around up here without any give-away creaks,' he'd mumbled to her with a mouth full of screws one day when she'd come up to bring him a coffee.

Later, when the underlay and carpet were laid, it was impossible to hear a person walking around.

Winifred jolted with fright when the coat-hangers in the wardrobe were suddenly swished to one side. Barely breathing, she stared with wide eyes into the blackness of her hidey-hole.

It was quiet again. Winifred's neck was cold with perspiration.

Kane's voice sounded dangerously close by. 'Well, Mr Dearborn... you'd better have a good alibi... better have a good alibi...' Then the wardrobe doors slammed shut.

A few minutes later, Winifred heard the creaking of the stair-ladder. She sighed deeply and let herself sink into the pillows. She knew that she wouldn't be able move until she was certain that Kane was down below. She pressed her head against the wall. The vibrations came to her through the skeletal frame of the old structure. Kane had gone back into the main house.

She had no idea whether Kane had already read the ransom note or not. Did he really think that Lloyd was a potential kidnapper? She'd mentioned in one of her communiques with the office that Lloyd was taking some time off. Hadn't he got that message? It didn't matter—Lloyd would be bum-up in the hull of some old boat checking for rot with a chisel and yarning amiably with the owner.

Yep, that would be a bullet-proof alibi.

... yeah, he was there for, oh... at least three hours... and then we had a fish burger at Danniella's... really nice guy—paid for the meal...

Winifred felt an ache of affection as she imagined Lloyd.

Now that the game had begun in earnest, Winifred suddenly felt the pangs of hunger. Before, she had been too absorbed in the planning to eat. She reached up and switched on the light. Then she delved into a cardboard box filled with groceries. She opened a packet of cracker biscuits and nibbled slowly on one. There were a few uncomfortable realities that she was going to have to face for as long as Kane was there. For one, she couldn't use the toilet on the third floor—it would be too noisy. So she would have to go down four flights to the toilet block at the back of the hotel that the builders had recommissioned whilst the renovations were in progress. That could be problematic—night time was the only safe option.

But she didn't expect Kane to be hanging around. He dealt with matters very efficiently, and the kidnapping of his wife would be no different.

It was very quiet in the secret space. Winifred looked across at the ventilation slot in the wall opposite her. Lloyd had made sure that there was a good airflow into the room. The outside of the vent had been cleverly shrouded so that no light would shine from the room onto other parts of the building.

She sipped at her water and let her head plump into her pillow.

Then, through the mattress, she could feel the unmistakeable tremors of someone ascending the staircase way down below. Her heartrate escalated instantly.

... why is Kane coming back up to the loft?..

She switched off the light and pressed her head against the wall. The unmistakeable vibrations indicated that whoever was about had reached the third floor. Winifred waited for the creaks from the stair-ladder.

Nothing.

Her heart pounded in her chest. She focused totally on the sounds from outside. It was so dark. And so quiet. The sounds in her imagination began to dominate. Was she beginning to hallucinate? Her brain hadn't been nourished over the past two days. She let herself slide into a more comfortable position. She wouldn't be able to go out for a pee. It'd have to be the makeshift potty in the corner.

She fell asleep.

Winifred awoke to the staccato blurting of the floatplane's engine starting up. Even from inside the hide, it was loud. She reached up and flicked on the light and rolled off the mattress. She pulled open the door and looked through the slats of the wardrobe door into the grey light of the loft. It was very early.

The thought of Kane setting off at first light suddenly brought back the memory of the prowler on the steps. She froze. Could she be certain that it had been Kane on the steps? If it *was* someone else, they could still be near. The loft door was closed and there was nowhere for them to hide in the room.

Winifred risked a peek around the doors of the wardrobe. All clear. She scuttled on all fours to the bed and slowly raised her sight out of the dormer window. The floatplane was scudding out into the lake. Moments later, the engines revved higher and the plane skipped over the still surface. Soon it was airborne and veering to the south.

Winifred turned to face the door. She needed to get downstairs. There were important parts of the plan to be organised—after she'd visited the bathroom.

She edged to the door and opened it. The little landing was clear and there was no one on the stair-ladder. Treading as quietly as she could, Winifred made her way down the stairs to the ground floor. Then, after a stop-over in the shabby bathroom, she made her way onto the rear lawn.

It felt wonderful to be out in the open, even though it was cold. She walked by the side of the building to the patio and entered the house through the French doors which was the access that she and Kane had always used and which was never locked. The travel case that she'd left on the dining table was gone. After sauntering through the many living spaces for a look around, she returned to the dining room. The broken chair was where she had left it and the tea stains on the wall seemed to have darkened. It was then that she noticed something odd. In front of the door that gave access to the back half of the hotel, there was an ornamental glass duck with a felt base sitting hard up against the hinge side. Anyone who opened the door from the other side would disturb the position of the duck and not even be aware that it was there.

Hurriedly, she checked the three other doors elsewhere in the house that led to the back of the building. They were marked in a similar fashion.

Winifred felt the tiniest wave of nausea at this confirmation of her husband's cunning. Kane would have noted the exact position of each item either against the door or on the floor.

Winifred spent the day downstairs, cautiously luxuriating in the sunlight of the window seat, nibbling cashews and dried apricots and having cups of hot tea, made on one of Lloyd's gas cookers. She couldn't risk being seen outside, not that there was much of a chance of that.

She went to the bedroom where everything was much as she had expected.

There was no telling when Kane might suddenly return. When he did, she would walk up to her wardrobe in the main bedroom and hunker down amongst the doonas in the closet. It wouldn't be as comfortable as her mattress in the secret hide, but she wasn't going to be there for long.

She went back downstairs and peeped through the windows before settling on the sunny window seat.

Kane's ransom instructions were to wait for more directions on his return. Winifred gave a roguish grin—except that there weren't going to be any more notes on the table. It wasn't necessary. Kane was going to emerge from the bathroom into the bedroom to find that the travel case beside his bed had vanished.

... so much more unsettling—the kidnappers, inside the house!

That would wipe the complacency off his face. It was too difficult to know what to do with the dumped "substitute" case anyway. As Lloyd had said, that was the point where things could get unstuck. If for some reason (and there were plenty) the travel case surfaced, Kane would be more than a little suspicious to hear that it contained nothing more than newspaper.

She had no idea how the disappearance of the case would affect her husband—whether he would storm through the house with a pistol at the ready, or whether he would patiently wait until morning for the return of his wife–a scenario that Winifred was anticipating by "arriving" at the house early enough so that she could "intercept" Kane at the time he decided to walk down to the floatplane.

... they dropped me on the road just before the first bridge... I've been walking for ages... god, I'm glad I got here before you took off... or something to that effect.

Winifred shuffled off the window seat. She'd make a cup of tea. Her gaze panned the back wall. She halted with one hand on the dining table. The little glass duck was sitting some distance away from the back door.

Someone had opened the door.

With a sudden weakness in her knees, Winifred seated herself on a nearby chair.

Had Kane arrived with someone? Someone who stayed behind? She had no way of knowing. Why would he? Who else could be here?

Her face became cold with sweat. Where was this person now? A terrible fear began to settle in her chest. Whoever this person was, they were one step ahead of her and being very secretive about it. But who else knew what she had in mind?

Lloyd!

Lloyd? Surely not! He was... *supposed* to be on the coast. But why would he?... Then again... why not?

Kane didn't want publicity... two million in cash... the wife gets returned, *because she never went missing*, but *she's* not going to say as much... *two million is both a little and a lot all at the same time,* she heard him saying.

... that was Lloyd on the steps last night!

Had he built another secret room somewhere for himself? How

248

was he planning to get hold of the suitcase?

Surely, he's not going to tussle me for it in the bedroom while Kane is having a shower?

She would have to get it first... but then, she herself would become the target.

This deed of betrayal weighed so heavily on Winifred that she slumped to the table, taking in enormous, shuddering breaths.

She was screwing her husband for financial gain, true... but that was different. They didn't love each other and it was no burden for Kane to stump up some cash. But, Lloyd! She had come to believe in *herself* because of him—*he* had almost cried when she'd said goodbye to him less than a week ago. He'd been totally disconsolate as he walked down the grass slope to his pick-up on the esplanade.

But if it *wasn't* Lloyd... then who?

The sound of an aero-engine was upon her before she had time to stand. She could see the floatplane through the window as it curved towards the lake.

Winifred looked down at the table. Her tears glistened on the surface. Hurriedly she wiped them with her sleeve. Then she dashed into the kitchen and put her cup to the back of the cupboard and Lloyd's cooker in the pantry. She threw the teabags into the fire-box.

With a long scan of the room, she made a final check and walked quickly to the stairs.

The duck! My god... Kane! He mustn't know I'm here!

Winifred squatted down. She had incidentally memorised where the beak had been relative to a scuff mark on the door. She repositioned the duck, hoping that it was in the correct place. Then, she quickly walked through the other rooms to check the other markers. They were all undisturbed.

She hastened up the stairs. Through one of the windows she caught a glimpse of the floatplane cutting a frothy ribbon on the water. It headed to the beach and motored up the slight incline.

Winifred shrank back from the window, but stayed there long enough to see Kane alight with the travel case in his grip.

... why is he so early? He's got the money already?...

Winifred closed her eyes and calmed herself. She turned to the walk-in-wardrobe and settled amongst the eiderdowns in the closet. She pulled the door closed.

With all the emotion and the rush of adrenalin, Winifred's breathing only became composed by the time Kane came into the bedroom. She was trying to stay detached from the turmoil in her mind. She sat with her knees up and with her forehead cradled in her arms, focusing on nothing in particular, yet alert to the tiniest sounds.

Kane rummaged around in the bedroom for a while, then left with his habitual slam of the door.

Winifred pondered the likelihood of grabbing the case straight away, but realised that Kane would begin his search in the bedroom and that it would be a bit pathetic to be found by him, squatting in the closet clutching the case. She stretched her legs and made herself as comfortable as possible. She would wait it out.

Outside, a strong wind began to build and the old structure groaned and creaked.

The room was dark when Kane returned. He slammed the door closed and moved straight to the bathroom. Within seconds, the shower was streaming.

Winifred's heart leapt.

Now!

Now the time had come for her to execute the final phase of the plan.

Don't rush it—you've got time—easy...

She pressed her ear to the wall. She could hear the shower gushing. With a pounding heart, Winifred pushed open the closet door. The walk-in-wardrobe was quite dark. Kane had obviously not switched on the bedroom light, but had walked straight through to the bathroom.

Excellent! She would be less conspicuous.

She was actually shaking. The unconscious culmination of an offhand proposition—that she should be kidnapped—made, it seemed, so long ago—was taking over her body. This was all preposterous—but two million dollars lay waiting just a few steps away.

... and Lloyd could be waiting somewhere in the house...

She had to make a decision—deal with one problem at a time. If she *didn't* grab the case, she'd have nothing. She needed to get out of the bedroom and into her hide. And, she would stay there until the opportunity arose to affect her "return".

Winifred took a deep breath and quietly rose. She saw the travel case lying at the end of the bed. She moved to the doorway of the walk-in wardrobe and warily looked around the corner. Clouds of illuminated steam wafted into the bedroom.

Brilliant... no way will he see me through that...

With her eye on the entrance to the bathroom, Winifred strode to the bed and grappled for the handle of the case. Gripping hold of it was a surprising affirmation—everything was going to be okay. She eased out the extension handle and swung the case around for towing.

Still with her eyes on the bathroom entrance, she slid by the bed and headed for the door, holding her hand out for the door knob. Inside the bathroom it was bright and dense with steam. The door was already open.

Good... easy... I'm through...

Winifred turned her head and trod lightly along the short landing to the stairs. The case rolled effortlessly and quietly behind her on the carpet. She stepped down two steps. She was now out of the line of sight of the bathroom. She drew the travel case to her and hefted it to her chest. It was so light that she overbalanced and had to reach out with one hand for the rail.

Her mind became a void. Nothing of the past—nothing of her plans—made sense. She stood motionless against the hand rail.

A footfall at the bottom of the stairs came to her. She slowly turned and looked down. A viscid dread enveloped her.

... the door should have been closed! The case should have been heavy!

Had Lloyd somehow managed to get to the case before her?

Now, there was someone waiting for her at the bottom of the stairs.

Winifred was trapped, yet somehow, being confronted with another person incited that offensive audacity for which she was famous.

'Lloyd!' she said, with an easy derision, '... so good of you to help me out.'

The figure below leant on the rail.

'Well, well,' came Kane's smooth voice, 'I can take it then that he is not *entirely* ignorant of your little scheme.'

Winifred's mind reeled. The travel case fell from her grip and tumbled nosily down the flight of steps, coming to rest on the return landing. For once, nothing sprang to her lips to save her... to dictate terms.

Kane gave a wave in the direction of the dining room. 'I realised that I'd forgotten to check the duck... and I just knew that I wouldn't be able to sleep, being unsure if I was alone here or not.' He commenced climbing the stairs. 'You did a pretty good job of repositioning it... a pretty good job.'

Winifred backed up the stairs a step before she realised that she'd made the wrong response.

... nowhere to go... nowhere to go...

Kane continued his deliberate steps towards her. 'I only realised it was you not two minutes ago. Lloyd is messing around with his boats—I had someone check... yet there is a person mysteriously moving about the house. That wouldn't be a kidnapper... it could only be you.' Kane got to the landing and bent to pick up the case. 'I don't have to tell you how shocked I was,' he said with accentuated reproval, '... but that was quickly followed by considerable relief, and then, by admiration, and now, I have to confess, absolute delight... we're going to have a lot of fun.'

Winifred didn't know what to think—but she knew what she felt. Underneath the revulsion that she had for the man standing below her, she felt a dark fear. It came to her all of a sudden—Lloyd. If she hadn't mentioned his name, then yeah... Kane would think of everything she'd done as some sort of wayward cry for help—his reclusive wife going insane in a gleefully kinky but manageable way. But she'd mentioned Lloyd—disparagingly, true... but it hadn't fooled Kane.

Now, she had provoked the one feature of Kane's personality that she intuitively knew was unpredictable and dangerous—his jealousy.

'I thought it was Lloyd,' she stammered. 'I thought you were in the shower...'

'No, no... it's me... your husband.' Kane hefted the case with one hand. 'Are you disappointed?... with the weight?'

Winifred had to show some deference here if she was going to mollify Kane. 'I guess you win again.. as you always do.'

Kane began to climb the last flight of steps. 'Oh, no... no, no, no... I haven't won anything. Okay, I didn't throw away two million dollars... but I have lost my wife—haven't I?'

Winifred had to do more—go on the offensive—make herself indispensable. 'You're not worried about that are you, Kane? I'll always be available for your promotions.'

Kane was close enough now to the glow from the bedroom door that Winifred could see the emotion in his face. He paused a few steps below her.

'Hard as it may be for you to believe, Winifred… I am actually very hurt that you're treating me this way. Very hurt—because you should be showing me a lot more gratitude… don't you think?'

The sneer in Kane's voice bothered Winifred. This was not the urbane façade that she was used to. He was letting go—he was allowing himself to revert to something corrupt and tainted. She suddenly realised that she had never spoken to him about his childhood.

A billow of steam wafted out of the bedroom door.

Kane slowly rose to the next step. 'Perhaps I should turn off the shower… not that it will run out of hot water—it's a hotel!' he laughed.

With a curt flick of his head, Kane signalled Winifred to go into the bedroom.

There weren't a lot of options for her; resistance was futile and dangerous. She was athletic—he was rangy and well-muscled. She wouldn't stand a chance. She turned and walked slowly towards the bedroom and into the swirling steam. There was nothing that she could use as a weapon and she couldn't jump out of a window. Maybe a degree of submission would placate him.

She sat on the bed and looked up at Kane as he entered the room.

With an exaggerated swagger, he stood before her. 'You know,' he drawled ominously, '… this whole affair has made me feel dirty… used.' He unzipped his jacket. 'Lets you and me have a shower and see if we can't cleanse ourselves of this whole business.' He held out his hand.

To Winifred, it felt like ages since she had felt the reassurance of the travel case handle. Things had deteriorated a lot since then. How much worse was it about to get? She had no options. That was

Kane's modus operandi in every sphere of his life—to be in control.

Winifred took Kane's hand.

He led her into the bathroom which by now was so thick with steam that visibility was not much more than an arm's length.

'Whoa... let me just make a little adjustment here.' He let go of Winifred's hand and disappeared in eddies of steam towards the shower noise.

Winifred's hopes rose. Was this her chance to flee? She needed to reassure Kane. 'I can't see, Kane... I'm going over to the bench to undress.' She knew that if she walked to the full-length windows she would be able to follow them along, back to the bathroom entrance.

'Why is it so steamy in here?' she said, as she groped her way towards the windows.

Kane's voice echoed off the hard surfaces. 'I had the hot on full bore... and it's so cold in here that it's creating all this condensation. Where are you?'

Winifred could see blackness in front of her—she had found the window. She angled her voice at the glass hoping that the reflection would give the impression that she was near the spa. 'I'm trying to find the bench... oh, here it is.'

The sounds of the shower increased.

'Ouch,' came Kane's voice, '... definitely haven't run out of hot water. You can come in now... I've added some cold.'

Winifred felt her way along the glass making sure not to make any squeaky sounds. When she came to the corner of the room, she knew that the entrance was just a few paces away. The cloud of steam was thinning here. She could see the dark shape of the doorway—and the darker shape of someone blocking her way. She froze in her stride.

Kane was too cunning—and cruel. He was tormenting her with false hopes.

Winifred took a step back... and felt her arms being gripped from behind.

Her heart leapt.

Then who...?

Lloyd walked through the entrance, waving his hand at the clearing steam. 'Do this too often, Mr Barrett, and you'll have rot throughout the house.'

Winifred felt Kane's grip tighten on her arms. 'Thank you for your concern, Lloyd. Now, if you don't mind... my wife and I were about to have a shower together, and as far as I'm aware, it's not customary for the hired help to be present on such an occasion.'

Lloyd gave one of his cheery, boyish grins. 'I'm sorry to intrude,' he rubbed deferentially at his forehead, his arm rippling with sinews and strength, '... it's just that I was worried about Winnie, and I felt that I needed to be here—just in case.'

'*Winnie*!... okay...' Kane possessively clinched his arms about his wife's shoulders, '... and what sort of eventuality would we be talking about here, Lloyd?'

Lloyd stood aside. 'Let's talk about this in comfort, shall we?' He moved into the bedroom and switched on the room light. Against one of the walls was a couch that he comfortably settled into.

Winifred emerged from the bathroom with Kane following very closely behind. She studied Lloyd with a stricken look, but he was looking elsewhere. She seated herself on the bed. Kane pulled up a bedside chair, straightened his jacket and crossed his legs.

'Now, Lloyd... I checked on you, and I was told that you were scraping barnacles off the bottom of some boat. I'm curious—do you have a seaplane as well?'

Lloyd gave a deep chuckle. 'That'll be my brother... we're very similar from a distance. I chose a boat at the end of the jetty... told him to look busy for a few days.'

Winifred interrupted. 'So, you've been here... the whole time...'

Lloyd gave a gentle nod. 'Pretty much.'

There was a short silence. Outside, the wind had picked up even more, howling and whistling through the old building.

Kane gave a sudden intake of breath. 'Oh, well... so what have we here? I'm a little confused...'

Lloyd steepled his fingers and put them to his mouth. 'It's like this, Mr Barrett—Winnie contrived a fake kidnapping, and you were supposed to deliver two million dollars for her safe return.'

Kane pursed his lips. 'Oh, dear... but I *didn't* fork out two million and I've got her safe by my side. I guess I got lucky... or, I'm just that much smarter. What do you think, Lloyd?'

Winifred watched as Lloyd crossed his legs and cradled his jaw contemplatively in the palm of his hand. There was something about him that she had never noticed before—a studious calm that unnerved her. He appraised Kane with a cool eye. Not once had he looked at her.

'You're smart, Mr Barrett... and lucky. But you're in trouble—and I think I can help you.'

Kane lifted his chin. 'Can you. Well, I'm eager to hear what my builder has to say about my life.'

Lloyd leaned forward and rested his elbows on his knees. 'I don't know the first thing about your business, Mr Barrett... but I know people that do. They tell me that yMe is suffering from *brand ennui*... their words, not mine. Your clients are becoming bored and weary. Subscriptions are falling and the share market is becoming nervous. Soon the whole platform will implode... your competitors will move in and offer the kids an alternative experience—the same, but different... and you will become another media relic—out of date and irrelevant.'

Kane's eyes narrowed. '... go on...'

Lloyd fixed him with a steely gaze. 'I know what will improve your fortune... but it will cost you.'

Winifred could sense Kane's discomfort—he normally never

allowed anyone to speak uninterrupted.

'How much will it cost me?'

Lloyd spread his hands. '... this hotel...'

Kane snorted loudly. 'Jesus, Lloyd! You're killing me—you're out of your depth. Look, you can't help me... you don't know anything... you're stalling for time—is that it?'

'... and two million dollars in fifty dollar notes,' Lloyd added softly.

Kane swore. He reached into his jacket pocket and pulled out his phone. 'Time is up, Lloyd! Now, you walk out of here and sail off into the sunset... or I'll arrange for the police to come searching for you.'

Lloyd smiled benignly and leant back against the lounge.

Kane prodded at his phone and spoke softly under his breath. 'Lloyd... it will take about forty-five minutes for my helicopter to arrive with a bunch of gnarly security types,' he looked up, '... and they *will* make your life uncomfortable.'

Lloyd spoke just as softly. 'Not as uncomfortable as you will be when you lose everything.'

Kane's phone gave a little squawk. He lifted it to his mouth. 'Ethan! Send the chopper out here pronto, with some serious muscle!'

There were a few small noises of confirmation. Kane put the phone back in his pocket. He looked at Lloyd's complacent little leer and abruptly straightened, his face blank. 'Oh, I get it... silly me— you've just made certain that *Winnie* here, will be safe from harm in approximately forty-five minutes. Well done, Lloyd. But seriously... I wasn't going to hurt her.'

Winifred simultaneously felt both a surge of relief and the grip of fear.

Lloyd gave a little pout. 'Don't be silly, Mr Barrett... I know you wouldn't hurt her.'

Winifred could see Kane's jaw clenching.

Lloyd continued, '... you're focusing on the wrong things. You can't bust me—I haven't done anything *wrong*... apart from walking into the marital shower. *You* haven't done anything wrong. The only one here who has done something wrong is Winnie—faking a kidnap and extorting money. And you want to hang on to her? It doesn't make sense, Mr Barrett.'

Lloyd's ludicrous deference was really starting to annoy Kane.

'Get to the *point*, Mr Dearborn.'

Lloyd gave a little bow of his head. 'I will… when Winnie is seated here, next to me,' and he patted the seat.

Kane did the maths; forty minutes or so and his goons would be here. What did it matter. He looked at Winifred and inclined his head.

Winifred wanted to get up, but the sense of betrayal was overwhelming. She felt utterly inconsequential. The emotion welled in her. She bit her lip and tightly shut her eyes.

Lloyd's gentle voice came to her. 'Winnie… it's okay… come and sit with me. Everything's going to be fine.'

Kane's intimidating voice cut in. 'It had better all be fine, Lloyd.'

Winifred got up and went to the couch. For the first time, Lloyd looked into her eyes.Suddenly, all the easy compassion was there, and she slid next to him and threw her arms around his neck.

He turned his head and kissed her.

Outside, the wind buffeted and shook the building. Squeals and groans from the exposed structure filtered into the insulated bedroom.

Kane's phone chimed. He took it from his jacket and scowled as he listened. '… well, what's the use of having a helicopter on standby if you can't fly out in an emergency! No, forget it… it doesn't matter… I don't need you anyway.'

He jammed the phone back in his pocket and eyed the builder kissing his wife. 'So, Lloyd—I'm waiting for you to save me. What have you got in mind?'

Lloyd took Winifred's hands in his and kissed them. He looked up. 'We're going to kidnap you, Mr Barrett.'

* * *

Winifred wriggled deeper into Lloyd's spray jacket as he leant against the stern rail of the old schooner. She absentmindedly ran her hand over the bump of her belly, and watched the young crew diligently tending to the demands of the boat. Typical summer gusts would ripple across the water and load up the sails, but the crew handled the heeling boat with plenty of enthusiasm and a fair amount of skill.

Lloyd rested his hand atop Winifred's and nuzzled his mouth into her hair.

A young man looked up from the winch that he was tending. 'How am I doing, skipper?'

Lloyd winked encouragingly and gave a thumbs-up against Winifred's belly. He addressed the young woman at the wheel. 'When you're pinching to make a mark, you can use those gusts to your advantage... just bear up a little then ease off as the gust blows out.'

'Gotcha,' came the reply.

In the distance, sunlight glinted from the windows of the hotel. It wouldn't be long before they were anchored. The sails would be covered and the ravenous crew would row to shore in the tender.

In her mind, Winifred checked off the preparations for lunch. Normally she would be there to supervise, but this group had been here for nearly a month, and the catering crew for the day had everything well in control. So, because it was such a gorgeous day, she'd decided to come out with Lloyd.

She thought about the shy carpenter living in a tiny miner's cottage when they'd first met and wondered whether he would ever have achieved what he had if it hadn't been for her reckless impulse to stage her kidnapping. What had she been thinking? She'd been no different from these kids—self-centred and impulsive.

But look at them now! They were working this boat. She looked up at the ridgeline. They'd trekked to the peak and had spent a week in the wild. They helped to run the hotel. They'd come to realise that they were part of something bigger and that their contribution was important. They were no longer the victims and perpetrators of yMe.

It was hoped that when they went home, they would log on and reconnect with the old network and begin to make a change.

It was early days, but the landscape was changing—as it had for yMe.

The kidnapping of Kane Barrett was an appalling perversion that played out over many weeks and was witnessed by tens of millions of subscribers. They happily paid a dollar to see him—a victim in his own wicked website —chained to a mattress and confined to the dimness of a recess with no standing room. What was most shocking, were his desperate exhortations that it was not staged, and that he was truly at the mercy of his abductors. He pleaded with viewers to help raise his ransom, and then raged at the computer camera for the authorities to find him and to bring his captors to justice.

This was real-time media drama. And what were the authorities doing about it?

Nothing, as it turned out. As far as the police were concerned, Kane Barrett was perfectly within his rights to play out a kidnap scenario and to upload it onto his own yMe platform. After all, that was what yMe was all about. 'Bring in the media,' they said, '... they'll sort it out.'

Of course, the media did nothing of the sort—where's the money in that?

They staked out Kane's known haunts, but the focus quickly shifted to his wife's place of residence—the sprawling hotel on the edge of the lake. Why did she hide herself inside? Why didn't she come out in support of her husband? And then, a rumour began— Kane Barrett was a prisoner, high up within the grim, skeletal structure of the derelict back of the hotel.

They parked their rigs on the esplanade, made camp on the lawn, and for once, respected private property laws by not invading the hotel and seeing for themselves. It was much more enthralling for viewers to draw their own conclusions by shuttling back and forth between the grubby sham played out on yMe and the pretentious posturing on mainstream media.

Individuals were engaged in the pursuit of truth in a way that had never been possible before. As a result, cyber traffic was gridlocked, with advertising and media barons making sure it stayed that way for as long as possible.

A few strategic financial inducements had made sure that the authorities remained tight-lipped about the site of the lair and the IP source. 'Investigations are ongoing,' they said.

Kane's whereabouts remained a mystery.

The more speculation there was, the more Kane would snigger as he lounged in his beanbag, sipping at his beer.

For a few hours a day, Kane was not a captive.

Every afternoon, Winifred and Lloyd would ascend to the loft with a meal and beverages. They would softly call out. Inside the secret room, Kane would compose himself as though he'd gone to sleep. Then Lloyd would press a button near the wardrobe that caused the computer to continue to transmit a still shot of the sleeping hostage. Kane would then bundle out of the closet and stretch and moan about how mind-numbingly tedious it was to be online with the lost and confused correspondents who were, in effect, his clients. Then the three of them would sit in the sunlight and eat and talk.

When the light had shifted, Kane would go for a shower, put new sheets on his bed, rub cream onto his wrist where the padded manacle was chafing and complain to Lloyd that he wasn't sure anymore that he needed the money that badly. Then, Winifred would reapply the makeup that gave him his wasted appearance, and he would clamber back into the wardrobe and disappear into the hide.

When Kane was finally "released", amidst a travesty of theatrical news broadcasts, he simply brazened it out and revealed that the very few foolish souls that had actually put forward money for his ransom had been paid back ten times the amount. Result—more traffic on yMe, with credulous teenagers being interviewed about their pledges.

The gulf between the laws of the land and the dictates of social media created a blurred morality that kept innumerable pundits busily debating the culpability of Kane's scurrilous antics. It was a deliberate suspension of the truth amidst the chaos of competing media, and the winners in all of this were, of course, those who dominated the realm.

yMe was in a state of flux, and it was attracting advertising as though the Ys were the last ever generation. Change always produces a degree of insecurity and creates fertile ground for product placement. yMe shares had rebounded on the promise of nothing more than continued speculation. Kane was raking it in.

That was how it was done. This was the proposition that Lloyd put to Kane on that stormy night in the steam filled bedroom—that Kane should establish a certain infamy and profit on the scandal.

Kane couldn't believe that he hadn't thought of it himself. One of his subsidiary companies, Media-Hysteria, was positioned at that very nexus of news and advertising—sensation and promotion—and scandal was grist for the mill.

The young crew had taken the tender back to shore, leaving Winifred and Lloyd on board the *Waimea*. They settled on a bench in the wheel well and looked out to the mountain range in the distance.

Winifred lay down with her head on Lloyd's lap. 'You haven't told me everything about the night you saved me... how did you come up with such a... complicated solution?'

Lloyd stroked Winifred's forehead. 'Pure bluff... desperation—and a sudden flash of insight.'

'Tell me.' She snuggled closer.

Lloyd looked down into Winifred's eyes. 'I'd never intended to leave you alone. I gave Rod my work jacket and told him to finish off a deck caulking job that I got. Then I hitched to the turn-off and walked here... came here in the middle of the night. Kane was already here. I snuck up to the third floor and tucked myself under the tarp that covers the saw bench. I'd put some bedding in there, so I was warm enough. I didn't know how things were going to pan out. When Kane flew out, I thought about seeing you. I went down and opened the door. You were sitting on the window seat. You looked so... in control, that it kind of scared me a bit. I thought that I would only get in your way, so I closed the door and went back under the tarp.'

Winifred looked up into the blue sky. Having Lloyd tell his side of the story brought back all the anxieties that she had felt. She turned her face into his body.

Lloyd massaged her neck. 'When Kane suddenly appeared again, I knew it was game on. I stayed put until it became dark, then I went down to the door... but he lingered in the kitchen, talking on his phone, so I couldn't go in. I hunkered down near the pantry vent. I could hear him wheeling and dealing... being charming one minute then snarling into the phone the next—he was laying out the groundwork to sell the story of his wife's kidnapping.'

Winifred idly stroked Lloyd's chest. 'That's why he didn't even bother with the money.'

'No. He realised that if he paid the ransom, there'd be no story— they get the money, he gets his wife—finished! He had to take it to another level... one that gave him the chance to deploy his media resources.'

'And if things went pear shaped?'

'... he'd still come out on top. It's awful, I know.' Lloyd closed his eyes and kissed Winifred on the nose.

'He was trading my well-being for profit.'

'Well, he had good reason,' Lloyd teased, '... going the other option would have meant losing two million dollars, losing a story and... still losing a wife.'

Winifred could have become angry if she didn't feel such shame— after all, she was the one who kicked off the whole disgraceful episode.

Lloyd read her mind and laughed. 'Some people! Really...'

Winifred squeezed him close.

'Anyway, I suddenly realised that if it was gossip and rumour that he lived on, I could think of something much more sensational.'

With her face pressed into Lloyd's body, Winifred's voice was soft and muffled. 'He really took to it, didn't he—you came up with the perfect solution.'

'Yeah, and I'm glad I did... because I actually had no other plan... and I wouldn't have liked for it to come down to a scrum between the two of us—that could easily have gone either way.'

'You had no other plan!'

'Nuh... nothing—just wanted to be there to make sure you were okay.'

Winifred suddenly sat up with a bewildered look. 'What do you think Kane had in mind... for me?'

Lloyd raised his brow and sighed. 'Well, once he realised it was you, it was like he said... the two of you were going to have a lot of fun. He wasn't going to hurt you... but I'm pretty certain that you were going to be an unwilling participant in some sort of melodrama... images sent to him of you handcuffed to the bed... possibly in my shack near the mine. You'd have had to go along with it—he was just taking advantage of what you'd already set up. Kane had good alibis—he was hardly ever at the hotel. I wouldn't have been implicated—I was caulking a deck. The two of you would have spun out a great story... the cops would be left without a clue, and when the two of you were reunited, he'd have made sure to hog all the media attention.'

The sun was getting lower, but it was still lovely and warm in the wheel well of the schooner.

Winifred nuzzled into Lloyd's neck. 'I wouldn't blame you, Llover, if you despised me.'

Patient as ever, Lloyd said nothing. He turned his head and kissed her brow. They had a lifetime ahead of them.

The wind gusted and turned *Waimea* around on her anchor. The heavy boat lurched and rocked slowly. It was a comforting motion—Winifred liked the idea of being anchored... to the hotel... to the lake... to Lloyd.

Wrong

Stanley Dwyer, financial advisor, was wrong about everything.

Not that he wasn't successful—he was very wealthy and prominent. In his early forties, ostentatious and self-assured, he had found a niche in a disrupted economy. When people's lives were disintegrating and in need of a desperate fix, he was the man they would come to. He made debt look like an asset.

'You are preparing a foundation for future wealth,' he would intone, '... aggressive debt restructuring allows you to deal with a negative investment interval while simultaneously positioning you to exploit any volatility in the marketplace.'

This was typical of the unintelligible and ambiguous advice he would dispense to submissive clients who chose to believe everything he said as though their lives depended on it—which it often did.

So, it came as a bit of a shock to Stan to discover that he was, in fact, wrong about everything. He was wrong about his family—his wife and two sons and a daughter who were always excessively mindful of his needs. He was wrong about his business—he didn't create wealth for people but exposed them to risk. He was wrong about his associates—they didn't like him, because he made them feel confused and inadequate. He was wrong about his politics—

his promotion of *wealth-creation* is a spurious ideology that degrades society. And, worst of all, he was wrong about himself—he wasn't secure in himself, but rather, fearful of failure, for which he compensated with rapacious socialising and networking.

So, how did he discover just how wrong he was about everything, and how did it affect a man whose entire self-image was so vulnerable?

Well, the thing is, that the truth—the undeniable realities in life—were always there in his sub-conscious, but were suspended by his natural hubris, and denied a voice by the unrelenting clamour that came from his mouth.

Then, one day, he got... caught, contracted, whatever... laryngitis. His strident voice, always so ready to impose his version of reality on others, failed. His ability to corrupt a conversation with false logic and overbearing deceit was denied him.

He was mute.

In the highly charged social milieu in which he was obliged to circulate, he was stranded—incapable of asserting himself and directing the course of conversation.

Those around him commiserated and filled the void of silence with chat that, for once, wasn't poisoned by Stan's insidious agendas.

At home, his son, Rory, requested the use of the Range Rover.

'... t-t-to go out... ah, c-c-camping, actually... out in the country... just with Alex... who is n-not my girlfriend ah, as you have supposed, Dad... he's a b-bloke... my lover... I've been meaning to tell you, but the right time just never... hope y-you're not too disappointed... Mum knows... she's c-cool with it.... is it okay if I take the car?... awesome, thanks... g-great talking to you, Dad...'

Stan was stunned, and it must have shown when his second son, Blake, approached him later in the day.

'Dad, you okay?... yeah?... good. You know that investment thing that you backed me for... well, as you know, it's going really, really well—yeah. Ah, but it, ah... I've run into a bit of trouble... of the law, type of trouble, because it wasn't all exactly above board. Dad, I've got to go to court... specifically, narcotics. I don't know what to say—I was stupid. I wanted to be entrepreneurial... big returns... I wanted to be daring. Sorry to lead you on. I thought you sort of knew... sorry...'

Stan was vacantly swirling his third scotch when his daughter rang on the landline.

'Dad?... oh, that's right, you've got laryngitis. I'm just trying to get hold of Mum, but she's not answering her phone. Thought I might get her on the home phone. Um, Dad... you do know, right? About the test results? Mum told you? She said she was. I'm really sorry, but I just knew... I just knew. I didn't do it to hurt you. I accused her, and she admitted. I just had to know for certain... and the paternity results are pretty conclusive. I still love you, Dad. Nothing has changed...'

When Stan's wife, Robbie, came home, she quickly prepared a plate of exotic edibles and set out a spread on the patio overlooking the infinity pool. Stan took his seat, as he habitually did, and listened to her as she poured from the chilled bottle of Bollinger.

'It feels so odd to have you home already, darling. Here you are— cheers. You look a bit wan, sweetheart. Are you sure you're alright? Oh, my appointment was double booked so, I had to wait for ages... and the traffic was ridiculous. I don't know why I bother... but it's the only time I can fit him in—he can fit me in. Sorry, my mind's in a jumble. I forgot my phone—has Geena been home yet? God, she and I are having a crisis of late. The sooner she joins her friends overseas, the better. You haven't even taken a sip, darling...'

Despite the fact that his voice was returning, Stan was very subdued at the office the next day. The staff all smiled encouragingly, but it wasn't until morning tea that his secretary opened up.

'Mr Dwyer... the Ethics Tribunal is close to revealing its findings on the industry. I meant to discuss this earlier, and I know that now is not the best time, with you being unwell, but we don't have much time. Despite what you claim about the individual investor being responsible for their financial pathways, the tribunal will end up pointing the finger directly at us, um... you. I'm just letting you know, in case you have to... you know... protect yourself...'

The decision to clear his mind with a game of tennis didn't improve his humour. His usual doubles partner, Ted, seemed to be of the opinion that laryngitis would preclude him from performing on court and, in the absence of a counter-argument, happily went out with someone far less skįllful and succeeded in winning, due to, as one spectator remarked—*superior communication between the pairing.*

By evening, Stan was pretty much speechless, even though he'd regained the use of his voice. The day had unequivocally placed him in a new paradigm—not his paradigm—other people's paradigms— the paradigms of reality. What he had experienced in just one day, floored him. Why had everyone been keeping secrets from him?

His wife! Unfaithful for eighteen years! Okay, so he hadn't exactly fulfilled the marriage vows either, but hell... where was the trust?

And, Geena! Not his daughter! *What the...?* How was he supposed to act next time she came to him for money? *Yeah!... that'll be an interesting moment—Daddy...*

Ohh... his son... his beautiful son. *When?... why?* Okay, these were different times. Did it matter? Was it *his* fault? Was it a fault? He took another slug, slammed the glass onto the table and groaned.

And when was this court case coming up? *That'll become public! God Almighty... one of my children is looking at goal time! Why didn't*

270

I question the returns? They were way too good to be legal... and I should know. Drugs! Oh, Christ!

And Ted, the creepy bastard—after all my coaching over the past year, he begins a winning streak with a new partner! Haven't I been patient with the gormless twit? Ted has no idea about strategy no matter how forcefully I try to direct him.

Then there was the tribunal—as if the industry needs a conscience! Who were they protecting anyway?—people with more money than sense—gamblers, essentially, who didn't question the unsustainable returns for investment until they lost, and then went whinging to the government's bosom complaining that some shyster had thwarted their rapacious greed. And he only made money if they made money. Okay, he didn't share in their losses, but it's not called speculation for nothing!

Where did all of this leave him?

Stan noticed that his heart was hammering. He suddenly felt very alone. He wanted another drink but resisted the urge because he knew that it would make him even more vulnerable. He had to marshal his resources; his secretary was right about that—he needed to protect himself.

He'd been wrong about everything. Wrong about everything!

Was there anything that he was right about? Anything that would make sense if he... if he...

... if he just shut up and let things unfold without interfering?

The more Stan thought about it, the more he realised that he had no other option but to shut up and take what was coming.

Seriously—there was no way that he could move his wealth offshore and live in some third-world dive with a string of lovely locals at his side. He would end up getting mugged, robbed... killed...

And there was no way that he was going to fake his death—take on a new identity—live with one eye on the rear-view mirror the whole time.

Get a divorce—that was a certain road to ruin—financially, socially... the family...

No—he was curious. What would happen if he continued to remain silent? Would he just be overwhelmed with one unpleasant disaster after another until he... what?... ended up in prison—next to his son! That was an edifying prospect.

Until he... died of some virulent cancer... or worse, lost his mind and spent decades languishing in an armchair with everyone growing richer around him and occasionally harking back to, *Old Stan... is he still alive? Yes? Oh, how awful.*

Stan decided to get another drink after all.

Early the next morning, as he idly stirred his coffee, watching the garden glow to life, Geena came up behind him and hugged him.

'Daddy...' she began in her special way.

Oh, here we go... must be desperate this time—she never gets up before noon.

'... I've got something I want to tell you...'

Whatever it is, you need money.

'... two things, actually...'

Don't tell me you have a girlfriend!

'... first, I want to tell you that I love you... very much. You are my father... you raised me... you were always there for me... long before I came to think that money was the most important thing you could give me. I'm so sorry, Dad. I just want to tell you that you belong to me. I am your daughter and I love you.' She gave her father an extra tight squeeze. 'The other thing that I want to tell you is that I'm going overseas. Not with my friends—I've joined a volunteer group. It's on a remote island in Fiji. They're doing land restoration, and I'm the technical expert that will show them how to use drones to get aerial imagery of the vegetation and the terrain... infra-red, ultra-violet... you know, weed infestations, monitoring biological control methods. I don't know the first thing about that sort of stuff, but I do know how to set up drones, which is what they want help with. You okay, Dad?'

Stan had silently burst into tears. Without moving, he cried until the tears splashed on the bench top.

Geena kissed his neck and stroked away the wetness on his cheeks.

The drive into work had never been so harrowing. Stan's breath came in ragged gasps and sobs. He sighed deeply after he parked the car and composed himself. It didn't matter what the tribunal decided—his daughter loved him.

He entered the office with a soft smile on his face.

His secretary stood poised in the doorway. 'They want you to testify... reveal, well... everything...'

Stan concentrated on reviving his voice. 'That's alright, Rhonda... we'll be the first, shall we?' He gave a cheeky grin. 'They'll cut us some slack... they just want to know how we do what we do... they'll be grateful.'

Around lunchtime, Stan got a call on his mobile.

'Darling, it's me. I'm just ringing to let you know that the Jag has been damaged... well, written off, according to the tow-truck driver.'

'Are you alright, Robbie?'

'Yes, yes... the car was parked, and a removalist's van side-swiped it and pushed it into a power pole.'

'Ouch.' Stan didn't feel up to an involved conversation.

'... yes, ouch. Darling, I was visiting an old friend... don't normally go there... might have parked it a bit wide...'

'Where exactly?'

'Darling… it was an old friend… I saw he lived in the area so I…'

'I want to come and collect you… we'll go and have some lunch.'

'Lunch?'

'Yes. Do you mind?'

'No, darling—Stan… that will be nice. But I can catch a taxi…'

'Don't be silly. Text me the address—I'm on my way.'

As Stan drove, he mentally undressed his wife. It would be fun. She was voluptuous and somewhat beholden to him. Definitely worth the sacrifice of the Jag. It was insured anyway. After lunch and a couple of bottles of her favourite Shiraz, he knew she would be delightfully compliant. Then he would take her home. Okay, so there was another guy in her life—he would turn that into an advantage— women love to be loved. She would feel so wanted. All good!

That evening, as the first cold spell of Autumn, descended into the valley, Stan lit the living-room fireplace and watched as the flickering light played on his wife's face. Her hair was down, her make-up faded, and she was dressed in just a chemise. It had been a great afternoon.

Much later that evening, Rory and Alex returned home in the Range Rover. Their eldest son was visibly surprised to see his parents curled up on the sofa. He stuttered an introduction to Alex.

Stan shook hands and waved them to a seat. He poured the two boys a glass of wine each and waited for them to talk about their adventure. Alex was very forthcoming and recounted how they had overcome various obstacles during their trek. Rory seemed to relax. With the obvious acceptance by his parents of his new friend and the fact that there was so much room in which to contribute to the conversation, the two boys were soon happily regaling the two parents with stories that would normally have remained unmentioned. Even Rory's speech flowed smoothly for longer and longer periods.

Stan said hardly anything—just a few words of amazement and a query or two for more details.

When he was in bed, lying awake, Robbie's foot reached out to him.

'Isn't it wonderful to hear Rory speaking so well,' she said.

Stan just nodded in the dark and stroked her shoulder.

*   *   *

Stanley Dwyer's life didn't disintegrate—in fact, over the year, it improved. They didn't have the house anymore—he'd had to liquify his assets. They'd moved into a small cottage overlooking a park. Its cosiness fostered much better relations between him and his wife.

Rory moved in with Alex. They rented a house with a shop-front and sold bric-a-brac to the influx of trendy homeowners. Their chemistry together made customers feel particularly valued.

Blake got two years. He was over the moon. 'For a while there, I thought they were going to give me a suspended sentence,' he'd confided to his father, '... and that would just have been a nuisance— I've got a conviction either way, but now I've got two years to do my accelerated degree in business.' With nothing to distract him, and a rigid timetable to adhere to, Blake was gaining distinctions in all of his assignments—and was picking up some very interesting extra-curricular information on the side.

Geena's Facebook posts (whenever she was in range of communications) revealed her to be having the time of her young life. Being very musical, she had been adopted by the village children and had arranged for the purchase of ukuleles and guitars to augment their natural singing abilities. She and her troupe had begun performing for visiting tourist boats, and the whole community supported her.

And, Stan found a new tennis partner who was even worse than Ted. The pairing didn't win a single game all year but received a trophy for 'The Most Congenial Doubles Partnership'. Naturally, Stan allowed his partner to make the acceptance speech, and Robbie kept the crowd laughing for about five minutes, because there's a lot more humorous material in losing than there is in winning.

Stanley sometimes wondered whether his new-found quiet was responsible for all the good things in his life. He knew it wasn't. Most of the events were on track to occur anyway; it's just that he would have poisoned the outcomes by interfering.

And his business was growing rapidly. He'd re-employed all the old staff, and his new office was a cosy lounge room. There was no desk—nothing to separate him from those he was advising. His new mantra was ridiculously simple—Invest in Your Home.

He instructed clients to borrow safely and to buy the most expensive house, in the best suburb, they could afford. He eschewed any other form of investment. 'Live in the best home you can manage,' he advised, '... your input will add value, and you will enjoy the benefits of your investment. I can structure your loan so that you can do maintenance and make improvements. It is the most rewarding form of investment, and the most moral. And, it will help to keep you together as a couple.'

Stanley Dwyer had turned around his life—all because he got... caught, contracted, whatever... laryngitis.

THE END

Did you enjoy this book?

I'd love you to leave a review at
www.amazon.com.au/dp/B07DZ51DQB/

Snap a pic of yourself and this book and post it on
Instagram using #petelansbooks

Please consider this book, or one of my other
books, as a gift for someone.

Find more of my books online at
www.amazon.com/pete-lans/e/B07D6FKB4Y/

If you would like to communicate with me
personally, please email
author@petelans.com

Free Short Story!

Email me at author@petelans.com for a FREE copy of
my short story, *Good Morning Sunshine*.

Thrum
~ A Conspiracy to Create Euphoria ~

Thrum is a light-hearted, humorous, respectfully erotic and delicately romantic novel about how little it takes to make people happy.

In a time-worn country town, one woman's accidental, erotic discovery sets in motion a comedy of errors as she and a naïve group of residents conspire to transform their community.

Iris, the angry baker, rediscovers her love of French cuisine and feels bold enough to dress as she pleases. The derisive Ellen, no longer hides her scars and sets about painting the town.

Octogenarian, Moira Gatton, divests herself of all her treasured possessions and gives up smoking. Miranda the dragon, discovers who she really loves. Max, the bikie tattooist, becomes a man as he could never have imagined.

Tiffany fills her life with the things from a shared love. Phoebe's unfettered laugh rings out in her salon ...

... and Ian, for once, knows more about everything than anybody else.

Realm of the Conspirators

A young Australian stockman finds a mysterious briefcase at the site of a plane crash on his family's outback property, unaware that it contains ten thousand-year-old secrets that are at the heart of international power-plays and the global financial-military complex.

Ensnared in the labyrinth world of conspirators, Owen meets Linh, a student-waitress, and together, in some of the most exotic locations on earth, they battle assassins, attack-drones, psychopathic killers, random thugs and a man who lives in a cocoon.

From the simplicity of cooking on an outback campfire, to being smuggled aboard the world's fastest mega-yacht tasked with disarming the dominating elite's ultra-weapon before it annihilates the earth, the young couple utilise every talent in their combined skill-set to evade capture and stay alive, whilst at the same time, coming to grips with a six-hundred-dollar 2010 Lucien Le Moine Chevalier Montrachet and being dressed in vintage haute couture.

As they unravel the mystery of one nation's plan to inhabit the Abyssal Plain and deduce the real purpose of an aid organization's scheme to improve living conditions in a remote corner of the world, Owen and Linh fulfil their love for each other and forge a union that places them dead-center in the sights of the most omniscient conspirator of them all.

Realm of the Conspirators is a New Adult book for all ages that grips readers in a realm of intrigue and action without delving into darkness.